William Bullen Morris

The Life of Saint Patrick, Apostle of Ireland

With a preliminary account of the sources of the saint's history

William Bullen Morris

The Life of Saint Patrick, Apostle of Ireland
With a preliminary account of the sources of the saint's history

ISBN/EAN: 9783337322441

Printed in Europe, USA, Canada, Australia, Japan

Cover: Foto ©Raphael Reischuk / pixelio.de

More available books at **www.hansebooks.com**

THE

LIFE OF SAINT PATRICK

APOSTLE OF IRELAND

WITH A PRELIMINARY ACCOUNT OF THE SOURCES
OF THE SAINT'S HISTORY

BY

WILLIAM BULLEN MORRIS

PRIEST OF THE ORATORY OF ST. PHILIP NERI

Qui s'étonnera que dans une entreprise toute Apostolique. . . . Dieu ait conduit, comme les Prophètes et les Apôtres, un Saint qui paroist leur avoir esté plus semblable qu'aux Saints qui sont venus après eux. . . . En un mot, on y voit beaucoup le caractère de S. Paul.
TILLEMONT, t. xvi. (*Art. S. Patrice*).

FOURTH EDITION

LONDON AND NEW YORK
BURNS & OATES, Limited
M. H. GILL & SON, DUBLIN
1890

TO THE

MEMBERS OF THE CONFRATERNITY OF ST. PATRICK

ESTABLISHED

AT THE LONDON ORATORY,

WHO,

WITH THE CHILDREN OF THE SAINT

IN MANY LANDS,

ARE

THE ENDURING WITNESSES

OF

THE FAITH

WHICH SEETH HIM WHO IS INVISIBLE.

ADVERTISEMENT TO THE FOURTH EDITION.

ON the first appearance of this book in 1878, my critics were encouraging beyond all expectation, but for all that I felt that something was wanting, and that I ought not to be satisfied until it had been subjected to the ordeal of adverse criticism. St. Patrick is still militant and aggressive, and any picture of the Saint which pleases everybody cannot be true to life. The Saints are one with the Church, and inspire the same feelings of loyalty or rebellion. If, therefore, I welcome the fact that my third and enlarged edition has aroused antagonists, I do so, I trust, not under the influence of the combative spirit, but rather because discussion can only serve to enhance the glory of the Apostle of Ireland.

I had made up my mind to introduce a few answers into my Appendix, in reply to my critics. On second thought, however, I have come to the conclusion that it is better to allow the Life of St. Patrick to stand by itself, and speak for itself. I have therefore determined to bring out, in a separate volume, some Essays published on various occasions, in which, either directly or indirectly, I have touched on most of those disputed questions to which my reviewers allude. Everything that has been objected has only served to strengthen my confidence in the security of the foundations on which this Life of St. Patrick has been built. In the present edition, I have contented myself with two short notices in the Appendix of certain theories relative to St. Patrick's Ancestors, and the Roman Mission.

November 21, 1889.

— do not rest on any solid historical foundation, and that it is impossible to make them harmonise with St.

PREFACE

TO THE THIRD AND FOURTH EDITIONS.

THE present edition has been much altered in form and dimensions. It is therefore with some trepidation that the writer awaits another verdict on the part of the benevolent reader. If it turns out that in attempting to improve, he has over-leaped the mark, his excuse must be that in so doing he has acted under strong pressure on the part of those who, on its first appearance, complained of the brevity of the work.

The introduction has been re-written: an inquiry into the state of Ireland at the period of St. Patrick's advent has been introduced into the life, and there are considerable additions, and some omissions, in the body of the work. With something like a pang the writer has been driven to give up the very beautiful legends connected with St. Patrick's infancy, having come to the conclusion that they do not rest on any solid historical foundation, and that it is impossible to make them harmonise with St.

Patrick's autobiography.   When, however, we take
into account that the events which they profess to
record were separated by an interval of more than
half a century from the historic life of the Apostle
of Ireland, and that during that period he was an
exile and a pilgrim, an outcast of fortune—*detesta-
bilis hujus mundi*, as he himself expresses it—there
is nothing wonderful in the fact that the private life
of St. Patrick was not accurately registered in the
very sterile records of the fifth century.   The
imperious requisitions imposed on St. Patrick's
biographer are often very unreasonable, and likely
to become a snare to anxious and over-submissive
investigators.   Surely the biographer of St. Patrick
ought not to forfeit his reputation if he sometimes
says that he is ignorant as regards particular events,
when such large indulgence is granted to the historians of St. Patrick's most famous contemporaries?

St. Patrick's authentic history begins with his
sixteenth year : the period at which he commences
his autobiography.   Outside his own record we have
only vague indications of his early life, by writers
of uncertain dates, the value of whose testimony
depends entirely upon its subordination to the
Saint's own writings.   If any proof is wanted of
this, it is to be found in the perplexities and con-

tradictions of all writers, ancient and modern, who have attempted to build up his life on any other foundation. It is to the neglect of this obvious principle that we must attribute that perpetual piecemeal controversy which has brought so much discredit on St. Patrick's history.

The ephemeral productions of belligerent critics have done more to weaken faith in St. Patrick than all the efforts of the Anglo-Irish Establishment, which for centuries has expended its strength in alternate attempts to capture or to annihilate our national Apostle. Writers who merely make use of his *Acta* to arm themselves with chips and fragments of his history, to be used as missiles and nothing more, have kept alive the impression that there is no animating principle in the record : that it is a body without a soul.

The truth is that few Saints have transmitted to posterity a more perfect revelation of their own lives and character than that which is found in the *Confession, Epistle*, and *Hymn of St. Patrick*, although this will doubtless seem an extravagant assertion to cursory readers, and to those who only use them for literary party-purposes. They are a record, fragmentary indeed in form, but inspired by one inimitable spirit, of the course of a life which was prodigious and unprecedented in every stage. The study of St. Patrick's writings explains how it came to pass that his life was so imperfectly recorded. His simple and awestruck neophytes did not comprehend him : indeed it may be said that St. Patrick is not understood yet; as Cardinal Newman says of St. Joseph, he is a star that is late in rising for the very reason that he is so specially glorious.

The chief additions in the present edition consist of passages from the Saint's autobiography which seem to fit in with the narrative. The effect of such a combination must necessarily be very unfavourable to the Saint's biographers. Nothing that has been written about St. Patrick has ever even approached the exalted level of his own writings ; but if the Saint is glorified by the contrast our object will be attained. Building on the foundations laid by the Saint himself, we can make all other authorities subservient to that ideal which is revealed in his autobiography, which is at once a record of his external actions and a revelation of his interior spirit. At the same time, so far from discrediting the ancient lives of the Saint, this plan invests them with an authority which, standing alone, they have hitherto failed in vindicating for themselves. The *Acta* of St. Patrick, collected and religiously preserved in the *Trias Thauma-turga* of the learned Franciscan Fr. Colgan, are little more than the scattered members of the Saint's extraordinary history. For more than two centuries the literary skill of many learned writers has been brought to bear upon them, but the general impression is that the result has not been satisfactory. We need a guide and an interpreter in studying the mysteries of St. Patrick's life, and that guide and interpreter can be no other than himself. Hypothesis, invention, rhetoric, and that criticism which professes to make a science out of uncertainties have done their best and failed; it is time that they should stand aside and allow the Saint to speak for himself, and if many things in St. Patrick's writings turn out to be beyond our comprehension, it will be both easier and more instructive to endure the mystery than to accept the assumptions of writers who would have us believe that St. Patrick's science never rose to any level higher than their own.

It is only fair to warn the reader that, as far as the following pages are concerned, the mystery of St. · Patrick's birthplace still remains a mystery. Boulogne, Tours, Dumbarton, Kilpatrick, Baunave,

Bristol, Paisley, Cornwall, Glastonbury, Rosnatt
Valley, Perpediaç, Carlisle, Carleon, and Bath still
contend for the distinction, like the seven rival
cities which laid claim to Homer.

These widely distant and distracting national
claims are, indeed, an honourable evidence of the
way in which St. Patrick has taken root, and been
domesticated in many lands ; but for his own part,
the writer confesses that he has never felt any
special inclination to embark in the controversy.
It is clear that the blood of several races ran in our
Saint's veins.   From the well-known classic names
of his father and grandfather, it would seem that
the male parental stem was Roman, and his mother
being a relative of St. Martin of Tours, was probably
an Hungarian.   If, like the Irish St. Columba, or
the Italian St. Francis, St. Patrick's young soul
had developed, and arrived at its supernatural
maturity amidst the associations of his native land,
deriving strength, colour, and beauty from persons
and things around him ; under such circumstances
the identification of the scenes of his childhood
would have a significance and importance which in
his case does not belong to them.   We have his
own words for the fact that it was in a land of
exile that his supernatural life and vocation began ;

for such unquestionably was the meaning of his extraordinary communications with God during his exile in Ireland. Even were St. Patrick's birthplace identified, the lonely summit of Slemish, the birthplace of his spirit, might well dispute its claims to the veneration of St. Patrick's children.

The list would be a long one were the writer to enumerate all the friends, living and dead, and in many lands, who have had a share in the preparation of the present work, extending over a period of more than a quarter of a century. The assistance and restraints afforded by enlightened public discussion in better ventilated subjects, he has had to obtain by correspondence and conversation.

Amongst the many, however, to whom he is indebted he is bound to single out the Deputy Keeper of Irish Records, W. M. Hennessy, Esq., M.R.I.A., and gratefully to acknowledge the priceless hours spent with him in diving amongst the historical treasures of the Libraries of Trinity College, the Irish Academy, and the monuments of Tara, and it is one of his chief aspirations to give the public, in a diluted form, some of the lessons he has learned from this prince of Celtic scholars. Moreover, as will be seen, he has drawn largely from Mr. Hennessy translation of the ancient *Tripartite Life of St.*

Patrick, which is appended to the quarto edition of the *Life of St. Patrick*, by M. F. Cusack, giving the collection an imperishable value. He has chiefly used this simple and unstudied record as a voucher for the fidelity of Jocelyn, the Cistercian biographer of St. Patrick in the twelfth century, whose work, in the text, is always quoted from the Bollandists' *Acta Sanctorum Martii* xvii.

He must also not omit to mention his obligations to his Eminence Cardinal Moran : to his lamented friend J. E. O'Cavanagh, Esq.: to Professor O'Loony, M.R.I.A., for his assistance in collating the text of a passage in the *Book of Armagh :* to Lord Emly, who was the first to put him on the track of the invaluable monuments and traditions of *St. Patrice en Touraine*, and to a writer in the Scottish Review for an ingenious translation of an expression in St. Patrick's *Confession;* and doubtless, there are innumerable similar debts to his predecessors in the fields of Patrician literature which in the course of time he has incurred and forgotten.

It must not be supposed, however, that anyone mentioned above is responsible for the opinions in this work. With one alone the praise or blame of partnership must be shared. At every step he has had to thank his friend Mr. Boardman for the inestimable assistance of enlightened criticism sustained by constant study in lines parallel to those which he was himself pursuing. At the same time he is far indeed from supposing that the work as it now stands is incapable of improvement. A biographer of St. Patrick must ever feel that he is the servant and interpreter of a mysterious master, and therefore it is in all sincerity that the writer borrows the declaration of St. Gregory the Great, as it stands in the preface to Villanueva's edition of the Works of St. Patrick: " *Ab omnibus corripi, emendari ab omnibus paratus sum*".

FEAST OF ST PATRICK, 1887.

CONTENTS.

b

THE LIFE OF ST. PATRICK.

THE SOURCES

OF

ST. PATRICK'S HISTORY.

THE following introduction embraces so many questions that, perhaps, it might more appropriately be
styled a chapter of Patrician evidences.

In the years which have elapsed since the first
appearance of this work, the writer has often reverted to the subject. He has visited the chief
places in Ireland and France whose local monuments
and traditions illustrate the history of the Apostle
of Ireland. He has also personally examined the

I

so-called *Loca Patriciana* of Scotland, and he has
satisfied himself that the North British traditions
are as untrustworthy as those of Ireland and France
are authentic. The results of these studies and investigations have been published at intervals in the
Dublin Review and the *Irish Ecclesiastical Record.*
At the same time he has watched the course of the
current writings of the last few years in the wide
field of Patrician literature, and observed that a
remarkable change has taken place in its tone and
character. Time was when he thought that St.
Patrick's history was for ever doomed to the en-
tanglements of philological criticism and sectarian
conflict, but he thinks so no longer. At length it
is admitted that the life of the Founder of Christianity in Ireland can stand by itself and speak for
itself. St. Patrick was a conqueror, and because
his conquests endure, they are their own evidence.
Moreover, in a way that is almost unparalleled, they
have become the title-deeds of a Church, the succession of whose pastors has never been interrupted.
Hence St. Patrick has always lived in his successors,
and his history has never become the property of the
antiquarian.

While, therefore, the surroundings of the life of a
fifth-century Saint must necessarily suggest many
questions which cannot now be answered, our
ignorance regarding things which have not been

recorded need not weaken our faith in others about which we have satisfactory evidence. We can believe in facts although we do not understand how they came to pass ; and at this stage of the history of Christianity it ought not to be necessary to remind people that Saints have done things which we cannot do, and in ways which are beyond our comprehension, otherwise they would be no more than ourselves.

The flowers and fruits of faith, all springing from one root, are even more varied than those of nature. Hence there are no manifestations of human character and action so diversified as those which are found in the lives of the Saints. Every Catholic country, in every age, has had its own special types of spiritual excellence, and every day new lives of Saints and servants of God appear, which are all original, and objects of interest, even to persons outside the Church, so long as their biographers are in a position to record them with fidelity. On the other hand, we can almost count on our fingers the secular biographies which hold their place in literature, independent of historical or political interest, and the best of them are little appreciated except at home. We can hardly imagine an Italian or a Spaniard growing enthusiastic over Boswell's *Life of Johnson.* The Catholic Saint alone takes root, and is naturalised in every land.

Indeed it often happens, as in the case of St. Martin and St. Patrick, that it is foreigners who have grown most into the hearts of the people, and this devotion is something very different from the evanescent enthusiasm which the young and the ardent feel for the heroes of secular history. The Saints become the spiritual parents of their clients : the life which they impart works out its own image in the souls of their children, and is the same after the lapse of a thousand years as it was in the beginning.

When scepticism, with its irritating assumption of judicial impartiality, attempts to undermine those sacred histories, which are written in hearts as well as in books, it often happens that Catholics are betrayed by their feelings, and set themselves to answer objections which if simply brought face to face, one against the other, would perish in an internecine struggle. Such is the conclusion that the present writer has arrived at from the study of the sceptical Patrician theories of Archbishop Ussher and his successors, Sir William Betham, Dr. Todd, and the Rev. J. F. Shearman. It was hard indeed at first to be altogether indifferent to the opinions of writers whose collective learning made so formidable an appearance. When, however, he found that, while using the same materials, all these writers arrived at different and even contradictory results, he came to the conclusion that, although there was plenty of good matter in their writings, the animating principle, the form of the body, was absent.

The acts of St. Patrick have often been thrown into the cauldron of rationalistic criticism, and the smoke produced by the experiment has led some people to suppose that there was an end of them, until their re-appearance revealed the fact that the exhalations were the product of the new, not of the old, ingredients. In applying this ugly epithet of "rationalistic" to St. Patrick's modern critics, it is necessary to define the sense in which the word is here used. "The rationalist," says Dr. Johnson, "is one who proceeds in his disquisitions and practice wholly upon reason," and he illustrates his meaning by the words of Lord Bacon: "The rationalists are like to spiders, they spin all out of their own bowels". It is true that there are fields of investigation where reason ought to be supreme, where all the subject-matter is on a level with our own minds, and everything can be tested by experience. In such cases it is our true wisdom to imitate the spider. When, however, our minds ascend above this visible world, even though it be no higher than the inferior heaven of philosophy, or imagination, some ruler or guide is essential, if we would escape the Nemesis of Phaeton in the chariot of the sun.

It is plain that the want of guidance is still more urgent in all investigations which lead us into the supernatural world. The rationalist who assumes that, in the mirror of his own intelligence, he can see all that can be seen, and at the same time is certain that he himself is not a saint, is compelled to deny the existence of such beings, after the manner of Dr. Ledwich and his school, who denied that there had ever been such a person as St. Patrick. For such people this is the only logical course, and it is a pity that they cannot adhere to it consistently. History, however, like nature, abhors a vacuum; so when the saint is put out of the way, something else must be forthcoming to fill up the empty space, and the wildest phantasmagoria of distempered fancy are more rational than the caricatures of heroic sanctity which have been presented to us by modern writers of this denomination. In their despairing efforts to escape from all supernatural disturbers of their peace, some have even gone so far as to seek in epilepsy, hysteria, and nightmare for philosophic explanations of the inspiration and energy of the men and women who have converted and civilised the world. There are others, again, whose belief in a supernatural world comes down no further than the Apostolic age; but there is little to choose between such and the unmitigated materialist. Of God's dealings with St. Patrick, the Rev. Dr. Neander writes that there was " nothing wonderful except what may be very easily explained on psychological principles "; and in the same strain Dr. Todd remarks : " He believed, no doubt, that his call was supernatural, and that he had seen visions and dreamt dreams. But other well-meaning and excellent men, in all ages of the Church, have in like manner imagined themselves to have had visions of this kind, and to have been the recipients of immediate revelations." [1]

When writers assume this levelling style in dealing with the inspired records, all believers in Christianity are on their guard. When, however, it is directed against sacred writings, and events whose authenticity is unsupported by inspiration, the attitude even of Catholic minds will vary according to the faith that is in them. Belief in the Saints is a part of the Catholic faith. As soon as we allow them to be pulled down to the vulgar level of ordinary life, they disappear from our sight. In St. Patrick's life there are two elements, the natural and the miraculous, but it is the latter which gives unity and life to the former. The events of his life, taken separately in their mere outward appearance, may be compared with those of Buddha or Mahomet;

[1] Neander, *Church Hist.*, iii. 173. (Bohn's Ed.) Todd, *Apostle of Ireland*, 378.

and those who would have it that one religion is as good as another, which means that they believe in none, will perhaps give the palm to the impostors. It is not for such readers that a Catholic writer composes the biography of a Saint. He writes for those who believe that the Divinity who shapes the deeds even of those who are ignorant of His designs, has made the Saints the conscious agents of His divine and irresponsible authority. To them is given the Word which is never to be unsaid, which is ever as true, and as comprehensive, and as well suited to the needs of men as when it was first uttered by inspired lips. Fourteen hundred years have passed since St. Patrick preached at Tara, and the Word that then gave life to thousands is now the strength and consolation of millions. As fire proves gold, so does time try truth. The endurance and the growth of St. Patrick's power is one evidence that he came from God. His life, his character, and his writings have passed through a very fierce ordeal of criticism ; but, like the religion of which he is the representative, he has outlived all assailants.

Influenced by these considerations, the writer is conscious of a sense of security in his position, which he is obliged to confess was not so strong when he first approached the subject. Looking back along the line of Patrician writers who for a period of more than two centuries have traversed the same field, and seeing that so many had lost their way, he naturally dreaded a similar fate, and more than once he was tempted to follow the example of Montalembert. When this most uncompromising chronicler of the supernatural world fell upon Dr. Lanigan's account of St. Patrick, he threw up the subject in something bordering upon despair, dismissing it with the remark that this learned historian may be consulted " with profit, though not with pleasure ".[1] It would be nearer the mark to say that, as regards the supernatural aspect of the life of the Apostle of Ireland, there is little either of profit or pleasure to be derived from Dr. Lanigan's pages. In common with some other Catholic writers, he has been betrayed into taking a false position. They have allowed St. Patrick's cause to be carried into a court where the judges do not so much as understand the language of the witnesses; and from such a tribunal it is hard to see how, without a miracle, even St. Paul himself could come off victorious.

In dealing with a subject so peculiar, the writer feels that it is his duty to be candid with the reader. Even if it were possible, he does not wish to conceal the fact that he writes in the spirit of an apologist, as well as of an historian. In composing a life of

---

[1] *Moines d'Occident*, ii., p. 13.

St. Patrick, it is vain to attempt to imitate the tranquil style of the biographer whose narrative, drawn from undisputed authorities, flows on in unbroken sequence. St. Patrick is still on his trial before the world in every detail of his wonderful life. It is a battlefield in which the principles of the supernatural life and the claims of Church history are fought out on a gigantic scale ; and this is, and has always been, one chief source of the interest which all questions connected with the Apostle of Ireland arouse in the minds of the enemies, as well as the friends of revealed religion.

It may be said that discussion and argument are out of place in a work like the present. At one time the writer thought so himself. It was his ambition to state facts without any apology, as he himself was persuaded that none was needed; until he reflected that it was too much to expect the same unhesitating faith in those who have been taught to believe that no life of St. Patrick can be written which will satisfy the claims of either ascetical or historical criticism. In the Saint's case, therefore, it is necessary to explain, to defend, and to illustrate by examples, matters which are accepted without difficulty when supported by the authority of biographers of the stamp of St. Athanasius, St. Jerome, or Sulpicius Severus : this must be his

apology for the many argumentative interruptions
which occur in the course of his narrative.

It is now some twenty-five years since he began
the critical study of the original sources of St.
Patrick's history, and at every step he became more
and more impressed with the sense of the organic
unity of the image presented by those simple and
fragmentary records. At that time, unknown to
him, another mind was pursuing the same course in
a more exalted intellectual region, and in 1872
Aubrey de Vere published his *Legends of St.
Patrick.* They are, properly speaking, a connected
life of the Saint in verse ; and it is the verdict of
critics, unaffected by anything like devotion to the
Saint, that this work is almost unapproached in
literature. It is an epic that advances in sustained
majesty from the Saint's youth until his death :
there is the same light from the sunrise to the sun-
set. To one who has studied the Saint's own
writings, and seen their spirit reflected in his
deeds, the *Legends of St. Patrick* have more than
a mere literary interest, when he finds that the
poet has not created the character of St. Patrick
any more than Shakespeare has invented those of
Cæsar, or Catherine of Aragon. Indeed, the poet
is never more than a discoverer—

> " Like some lone watcher of the skies
> When a new planet swims into his ken ".

The life of St. Patrick in its mere outward form—
for none of his ancient biographers have attempted
more—has won the devotion of Catholics for fourteen centuries and in all lands, for the inspirations
of faith gave it life and filled up that which was
wanting. In the pages of Aubrey de Vere it has
stood a further test. It has been tried by the
principles of Catholic art by one who is a master in
that science which discerns the mysterious harmonies of nature and grace in the lives of the
Saints, and the image evoked leaves no sense of
incongruity on the mind of the reader. In the
Legends of St. Patrick we see a contest long drawn
out between the imagination of the poet and the
realities of the Saint's life, in which the latter are
always victorious. St. Patrick is made to measure
his strength with angelic spirits, the powers of evil,
and the gigantic forces of nature, and faith finds
no exaggeration in lines such as these :

> " Tenfold once more the storm burst forth ;
> Once more the ecstatic passion of his prayer
> Met it, and, breasting, overbore, until
> Sudden the Princedoms of the night that rode
> This way and that way through the whirlwind, dashed
> Their vanquished crowns of darkness to the ground
> With one long cry ".[1]

The triumphs of the Apostles of Christ can never
be likened to those of men who have started ideas

---

[1] *Legends of St. Patrick*, p. 40.

of their own, and carried the multitude with them by sheer force of genius or personal influence. The principle that an Apostle is merely the ambassador of God was one to which St. Patrick continually reverted.[1] Now, an ambassador is one who is always dependent on his sovereign, and in the Catholic Church that authority is ever .present and vigilant. Miracles are the credentials of the heavenly messenger, and when they have secured the attention of his hearers their chief work is done. The interest of St. Patrick's history has, to many minds, been diminished by the preponderance of miraculous incidents in the ancient records of his life, although it was natural that these manifestations of supernatural power should have made a predominant impression on the simple minds of newly converted witnesses. There were other and still greater prodigies, the theatre of which was in their own souls, when St. Patrick's words made them one with the Church past and present, and gave them that supernatural life, which was so absolutely their possession that they could infuse it into others, in distant lands, as well as in their own.

While a portion of St. Patrick's history affords a fair field for criticism, the main body of his acts

---

[1] "Behold, I now commend my soul to my most faithful God, for whom, in my lowliness, I am ambassador."—*Confession*, ch. v., § 23 ; *Epistle*, § 3.

belongs to an order of things to which criticism
cannot ascend.   The man who, coming to Ireland
in his old age, turned the current of her national
life, and in the evening of his days converted a
nation of warriors into a nation of Saints,[1] carrying
men with him, not by flattering, but by extinguish-
ing their passions : who, looking back on his work
at the end of his life, saw nothing of his own in it,
so that, dazzled by the light and oppressed by the
mystery, he was fain to cry out, " Who am I, or
what is my prayer, O Lord, who hast laid bare to
me so much of Thy Divinity ? "[2] such an one is the
master, not the subject, of reason.

It is no small reproach to us, the modern children
of the Saint, that it is to a foreigner that we owe
the first, and the boldest vindication of the supernatural majesty of St. Patrick's character in the
face of the animal scepticism with which the revolt
of Luther has impregnated much of the so-called
Christian literature of these latter days.   Tillemont
was certainly no ardent or credulous enthusiast.
Indeed, he has been fairly accused of an excessive
ambition to preserve the golden mean of modera-
tion in all things appertaining to the supernatural

[1] " Terra illa, idolorum antea cultrix, cum mox prædicante
Patricio, fructum dedit, ut Sanctorum insula deinde fuerit appel-
lata."—*Brev. Rom.*, xvii. Mart.

[2] *Confession*, ch. iii., § 14.

world :[1] an impossible aspiration, seeing that we can neither comprehend the *modus operandi*, nor the limits of operations, which have their origin in the mind of One who is infinite. When once they begin we have no rule to tell us when or where they will stop; so that the answer, *Ce n'est que le premier pas qui coûte*, was a reasonable rejoinder to the objector who quarrelled with the narrative of the martyrdom of St. Denis on the score of the great distance which he is said to have walked after his decapitation. We are not surprised, therefore, to find that Tillemont was staggered by some of St. Patrick's miracles : his incredulity on this score only gives additional strength to his testimony in favour of the supernatural majesty of the Saint's character, as revealed in his own writings.

The *Confession of St. Patrick* and his *Epistle to the Christian Subjects of the Tyrant Coroticus*, like so many of the wonders of Christian antiquity, lay like a hidden treasure in the vast storehouse of the Church, until hostile criticism fastened on them, and so aroused the interest and stimulated the investigations of Catholics. The Bollandists published them in 1668, with the life of St. Patrick by Jocelyn, and some twenty years later Tillemont

---

[1] He is severely taken to task by Schüz, for "repudiating the acts of the Saints on the most trifling grounds".—*Nomenclator Literarius*, T. Hurter, S.J., part i., p. 466 (n.).

wrote his abstract of the Saint's life in his *Ecclesiastical Annals.* Having alluded to St. Patrick's " special commission from God," and to the " overflowing plenitude of the Apostolic spirit " with which he was invested, he remarks on the extraordinary number of ancient lives of the Saint, and goes on to say : " We are better pleased to extract his history from documents entitled his *Confession,* which is said to be his own composition, and which is certainly worthy of him. We do not find in it any great number of facts, but I believe that those which are related are a sufficient foundation for the extraordinary veneration paid to him by the Church in Ireland : a better title, perhaps, than the numerous miracles of doubtful probability, not to say more, which are found in the lives.

" There are hardly any in his *Confession.* On the other hand, there are a considerable number of visions ; and the Saint himself tells us that God often directed his actions in an extraordinary manner. But who can wonder, if in an undertaking altogether Apostolic, in which it was necessary to overcome the opposition of men, friends as well as enemies, God should have conducted, after the manner of the Prophets and Apostles, a Saint who appears to have approached nearer in resemblance to them than to the Saints who have appeared in later times. Nevertheless, even amongst these, He

has led St. Cyprian by the same road; and we venture to hope that in the visions which St. Patrick
attributes to himself, we shall find nothing which
is not grave, holy, and worthy of God. . . . .This
writing is full of solid wisdom, as well as of spirit
and fire, and, what is of more importance, it is full
of filial devotion towards God.   In every line we
find evidence of the Saint's extraordinary humility,
while the dignity of his ministry is never abased.
. . .   It also reveals his passionate desire for
martyrdom.   In a word, we see in it much of the
character of St. Paul."

This testimony of Tillemont is worth more than
a volume of ordinary controversy, on the principle
that *cuique in sua arte credendum.*   He belongs to
that race of ancient giants in ecclesiastical history,
who were so great because their energies were concentrated.   He had devoted his life to one subject,
and thus he was able to trace that unity and identity in the history of the Church which is hidden
from the impatient and casual investigator.   "If I
am asked," he observes in his *Avertissement,* "for the
rules by which I presume to distinguish between
true and false documents in the absence of any
knowledge of their authors ; those who have read
the history of the martyrdom of St. Polycarp, and
that of the martyrs of Lyons in Eusebius, with
others which are generally accepted as incontest-

able, will easily perceive that in this study we acquire an instinct in separating that which has the character of antiquity and truth from that which is redolent of fable or popular tradition. Acquaintance with the history, style, and discipline · of the period enables us to judge between writings which are contemporary, and those which probably belong to some later period."

Applying these principles to the writings of St. Patrick, he observes : " His confession is quoted by all the ancient writers of his life, which at least proves its superior antiquity, and it appears to me that it bears upon it that stamp of veracity which would enable it to stand by itself, even if it had never been quoted by anyone ".[1]

Tillemont's profession of faith in St. Patrick is a remarkable instance of the unembarrassed confidence with which acute and critical Catholic minds approach the question of supernatural events.   He desiderates more specific evidence ; but it is plain that he considered that no prodigality of visions or miracles need astonish us in the life of such a Saint as St. Patrick. His language is on the same level as that of Cardinal Newman when he remarks: "Did I read of any great feat of valour, I should believe it if imputed to Alexander, or Cœur de Lion.   Did I hear of any act

---

[1] *Hist. Eccl.*, vol. xvi., pp. 455-464.   He also used the *Epistle,* to which he attributes equal authority—*Ib.*, p. 782.

of baseness, I should disbelieve it if imputed to a
,friend whom I knew and loved.   And so, in like
manner, were a miracle reported to me as wrought
by a member of Parliament, or a bishop of the
Establishment, or a Wesleyan preacher, I should
repudiate the notion.   Were it referred to a Saint,
or the relic of a Saint, or the intercession of a Saint,
I should not be startled at it, though I might not
at first believe it."[1]

Saints are not classed according to the multiplicity
or magnitude of their miracles.   They were very
important to the persons concerned; but to others
they are the least interesting part of their lives.
When grave writers, ancient and modern, compare
St. Patrick to the Prophets, and to St. Paul, it is
the unearthly elevation of his character, rather
than his external actions, which suggests the comparison.   It is certainly very mysterious that such
a parallel can be drawn, and yet leave no sense of
exaggeration or absurdity on the mind of the
reader; even Dr. Todd, with all his jealousy of
supernatural intrusions, finds nothing extraordinary
in this comparison as it stands in the pages of
Tillemont.[2]

The line of this inquiry into the character of
St. Patrick's acts is rather spiritual than literary.

[1] *Present Position of Catholics*, p. 308.
[2] *Apostle of Ireland*, p. 382.

It follows and represents the development of the writer's own reflections during the many years which he has devoted to the study of St. Patrick's life. He is writing for those who believe that while " the Spirit breatheth where He wills," for all that the signs of His inspiration are unmistakable. " Grace," says St. Thomas, " destroys not nature, but perfects it, and supplements its wants." Its gifts are like those of genius, with this difference, they cannot be imitated by any industry of our own. They are always new operations of God's creative power. There have been successful imitations of the greatest writers and artists ; but even the unbelieving world has never been long deceived by spurious Saints. As the least living creature and the lowliest flower are inimitable, so the Saints stand by themselves.

Many strange things are found in books ; but, perhaps, nothing is more extraordinary than the way in which some writers insist on applying the measurement of one time and place to others however distant. By such investigators, the lapse of fourteen centuries and the circumstances of Ireland in St. Patrick's time are ignored, and his biographer is expected to account for omissions, to haggle over every anachronism, and to explain every archaic difficulty in the life of the Saint with the ease and assurance of a minister in Parliament. The three

centuries which intervened between the death of
St. Patrick and coming of the Northmen was the
most glorious period of Irish history. It was a
time of intellectual and spiritual development so
rapid and so universal that the record reads like an
invention of the imagination rather than a sober
statement of facts. Before St. Patrick's time the
Scots were only known as destroyers from the
Grampians to the Alps. Then in the full tide
of their military success, when they seemed on
the point of subjugating Britain, they were drawn
home by a mysterious power, and Ireland was
forgotten until, in the century following St. Patrick,
the torrent of her apostolic armies poured forth
upon Europe : when St. Columba and his disciples
brought stern Caledonia under the sweet yoke of
Christ, and came down from the north upon England,
and St. Columbanus infused new life into the Church
in Gaul, Switzerland, and Italy. It is easy to
understand how Athens enchanted and civilised the
world, and how it was conquered and chained by
the iron hand of Rome. Civilisation was as
attractive and discipline as resistless then as they
are now ; but in the case of Ireland it was self-
instructed barbarians who subdued their fellows,
and came to the assistance of the inheritors of the
wisdom of the world, Christian as well as pagan.
It is high time to set the classic denomination of

barbarian in its rightful place.   If the Irish were
styled barbarians in St. Patrick's time, they were
barbarians of the stamp of Caractacus and Clovis,
and the men who put living blood into the veins of
expiring Europe.   It is their glory that they were
the first of the new born nations of the West who
began the work of the spiritual and intellectual
reorganisation of Europe.   Ireland had already
won the title of " The Island of Saints " at a time
when Clovis and his Franks were still worshippers
of Odin, and the Arian Goths were enemies and
destroyers of Christianity as relentless as the pagan.
Of this period Cardinal Newman writes : " Dreary
and waste was the condition of the Church, and
forlorn her prospects. . . . Her imperial protectors
were failing in power or in faith. . . . In the year
493 in the Pontificate of Gelasias the whole of the
East was in the hands of traitors to Chalcedon,
and the whole of the West under the tyranny of
the open enemies of Nicæa."[1]

This then was the battlefield into which some
fifty years later the sons of St. Patrick flung themselves with all the characteristic fire of their
national character.   The Churches founded, and
the names of Saints enshrined in the grateful
memories of the people of Italy, France, Germany,
and Switzerland, tell of the work which they

---

[1] *Development of Christian Doctrine*, p. 320.

effected. They taught the faith, and the fact that they taught sound Catholic doctrine at a time when heresy was so prevalent is a glory which reverts to their founder. The scholarship of Ireland in those ages when she was honoured as the "Lamp of the West" and the "University of Europe," was not on a level with that of Ambrose, Jerome, and Augustine; it would have been indeed a national miracle had such been the case. Nearly two centuries intervened between the death of Theodosius the Great, with whom the civilisation of Rome may be said to have expired, and the arrival of those fugitives from the Continent who bore with them into Ireland the little that remained of the learning of the dead past. It was the good use which she made of these fragments in an age of almost universal darkness, which, in the sixth century, won for her the first place amongst the saviours of learning and civilisation.[1] When we hold fast to dates, and remember the circumstances of the time, the wonder is, not that Irish scholars wrote Latin and Greek imperfectly, but rather that in those days they were able to write these languages at all.

It is one thing to cultivate letters, and another to use them, and of the two the latter is the more

---

[1] "The storehouse of the past and the birthplace of the future." —Card. Newman, "Isles of the North," *Hist. Essays*, i., p. 124.

difficult and honourable employment. The Irish
monks in the sixth and seventh centuries were
apostles by profession and professors by accident.
If it turned out that they became the pioneers of
learning and civilisation, it was the result of their
exuberant life and energy : a virtue went out from
them of which they were unconscious. The multitude of Irish Saints who, like a torrent, invaded
the continent of Europe,[1] went forth impelled by
gratitude as well as by zeal and charity. Ireland
had already opened her heart to the exiles of that
Roman world in whose name St. Patrick had come to
conquer, not by the sword but by the Cross. " The
pilgrims of the men of Rome and Latium,"[2] invoked
in the Litany of Aengus, were ambassadors, as
well as fugitives. They came in the name of that
great Alma Mater whose children were crying for
the bread of life, and there were none to break it
to them. Faith is ever an inheritance of gratitude,
and the energy with which Ireland set herself to
repay the debt she had contracted with Rome is
an evidence at once of the purity of her faith, and
of the value which she set on that divine gift.

I have no ambition to draw the sword in defence
of the orthodoxy of the ancient Church of St.
Patrick. The wonder is, that with these great facts

---

[1] " Quasi inundatione facta, illa se Sanctorum examina effude-
runt."—St. Bernard, *Vita St. Malachiæ*, cap. vi., § 12.

[2] O'Curry, *MS. Materials of Ancient Irish History*, p. 381.

of history staring them in the face, Catholic writers
can allow themselves to be entrapped and detained
by the objections of those professional critics who
do not take the trouble to learn the difference between a creed and a rubric. The Irish Church, at
home and abroad, was proved to be Roman by her
works, and by the ecclesiastical offices entrusted to
her missionaries, unless, indeed, we suppose that true
faith could have come from an impure fountain, or
that the Catholic Church did not know her own, and
ignorantly accepted the services of aliens and enemies. It sometimes seems as if it were useless to
speak of the divine life of the Church to those who
do not believe in a church : to accept our arguments
is to condemn their own incredulity. Hence our
opponents are always ready with some theory as a
way of escape, and it matters little to them whether
or not that theory has ever been known to fit in with
the ways of men in this world. St. Patrick set up
the Church in Ireland; he fills up its first age; sixty
years of the fifth century, the whole period of the
conversion of the country, belong to him. The
native Saints that followed close upon him in the
next century, such as SS. Brendan, Ciaran, Columbanus, and Columba, or Columcille, found Ireland
already a Christian nation, and when urged by
apostolic zeal, they were obliged to go abroad in
search of work. As there is no stronger proof than

this of the completeness of St. Patrick's work, so the fact that his sons were founders of orthodox churches in other lands is cogent evidence that they were orthodox at home.[1] Montalembert, one of the most learned and dispassionate authorities on the subject, affirms that more than two-thirds of England owed its final conversion to the labours of the Irish monks of the great schools of Iona, Old Melrose, and Lindisfarne.[2] Irish missionaries in Gaul, Germany, and Switzerland fall into the ranks of the clergy as gracefully as their successors in England in our own times, and, even in the parent land of orthodoxy, St. Columbanus'

[1] While this was in the press my attention was drawn to the work of Dr. Loofs, on the ancient British and Irish Churches. He is a Protestant and a German. He has studied the subject with great care, and in our books, and, looking on it as an integral part of the Church history of the time, he weighs the claims of the early British and Irish Churches to be called "evangelical" in his sense of the word. These claims, originated by the centuriators of Magdeburgh, have, he remarks (p. 1), with "fresh temerity" (*nova audacia*) been reproduced by Ebrard. "Truly," he continues (p. 5), "it would be a joy to us evangelicals if it were so, but, alas ! our woe, so unsupported by truth is this view of Ebrard's, that well-nigh everything which he alleges is false." The chief interest of Dr. Loofs' work is found in his common-sense arguments (pp. 72, 97, 104). He finds out, what was always understood by Catholics, that the British and Irish Churches merely differed with Rome on points of discipline : in doctrine, and in the laws of the religious life, they were one with the Church, and its saints all the world over ; therefore they had no claim to be called "evangelical" according to the Protestant sense of the word.—(*Antiquæ Britonum Scotorumque Ecclesiæ.*) Lipsiæ et Londini, 1882.

[2] *Moines d'Occident,* tom. iv., p. 128.

Monastery at Bobbio was the great stronghold of Italy against the Arians. In England, at the Synod of Whitby, A.D. 664, St. Colman and some Irish monks took the wrong side on the Easter question. For some time they held on obstinately to Irish customs against the Roman customs of the day. But those so-called Irish customs were nothing more than old Roman customs which, exactly two hundred and thirty-two years previously, had been imported into Ireland by St. Patrick, the Roman Legate of Pope St. Celestine; their fault being somewhat similar to that of over-ardent admirers of the Mediæval Church in our own times. On the scent of this battle the eagles of controversy have made their appearance, and we fear for many a long day they will continue to hover over the field. Apparently in all simplicity, Mr. Green thus expatiates on the imaginary diversities of "Celtic" and "Latin Christianity": "The science and biblical knowledge which fled from the Continent took refuge in the famous schools which made Durrow and Armagh the universities of the West. The new Christian life soon beat too strongly to brook confinement within the bounds of Ireland itself. Patrick, the first missionary of the island, had not been half a century dead when Irish Christianity flung itself into battle with the mass of heathenism which was rolling in upon the

Christian world. . . . For a time it seemed as if
the course of the world's history was to be changed,
as if the older Celtic race, that Roman and German
had swept before them, had turned to the moral
couquest of their conquerors, as if Celtic and not
Latin Christianity was to mould the destinies of the
Churches of the West. . . . The labours of Aidan,
the victories of Oswald and Oswy, seemed to have
annexed England to the Irish Church," &c., &c.
Then, leaving the seventh, with one swoop Mr.
Green passes over several centuries, and gives
his readers to understand that in the tortures and
miseries of Ireland in conflict with the heathen
Northmen they may read the logical results of
" Celtic Christianity"; but he prudently abstains
from attempting to explain the connection.[1]

The truth is, that from the age of St. Patrick to
our own the Irish Church has been crippled less
than most Churches by the narrowness of nation-
ality. She has never been a State Church, and if she
has suffered in consequence, she has on the other
hand been always free. She has been ever at home
in every Catholic land. In the history of the
Church there are few events more supernatural
than the transfer of allegiance on the part of Irish
monks all over Christendom, when they surrendered
their monasteries, their conquests, and themselves to

[1] *Short History of the English People,* pp. 21-28.

the Roman St. Benedict. Few Saints were better calculated to inspire enthusiasm than those great monastic founders the chivalrous Columbanus, and the mystical Columba, and whosoever understands how strong are the family traditions and legitimate rivalries of religious orders, will find evidence in this pacific revolution that Ireland was one in spirit with Rome. With characteristic generosity the Irish monks kept no account of their donations to St. Benedict. All that we know is that they were everywhere in France, Germany, England, and Scotland,[1] and that everywhere they enlisted under the standard of the Roman patriarch.[2]

In concluding this interlude on the subject of St. Patrick's orthodoxy as revealed in his disciples, it may be observed that the period when the controversies regarding Easter and the Tonsure were hottest in England was precisely the time when the

---

[1] Of Luxeuil, the mother house of the disciples of St. Columbanus, St. Bernard writes that it became a "great nation" (factus in gentem magnam), *Vita St. Malachiæ*, cap. vi. ; and Montalembert says of this monastery, that "During the whole course of the seventh century it was the most celebrated and the most frequented school in Christendom. . . . From the banks of the Lake of Geneva to the shores of the North Sea, each year saw some new monastery founded and peopled by the disciples of Luxeuil, while episcopal cities sued for bishops prepared for the government of souls under the influence of the regenerating spirit of Luxeuil."—*Moines d'Occident*, tom. ii., p. 429.

[2] St. Benedict was born about the year 480, some twelve years before the death of St. Patrick.

very flower of English sanctity and orthodoxy were in Ireland " numerous as bees," in the well-known words of St. Aldhelm. Venerable Bede tells us that " they retired thither, either for the sake of divine studies, or of a more continent life " ; [1] and amongst them we find the glorious name of St. Willibrord, the Apostle of the Frisians, who, at the age of twenty, left his monastery at Ripon, and set off for Ireland, with the approval of his abbot, St. Wilfrid, the special champion of Roman usages, because, says the lections of his Office, " he was all on fire with the longing for a more strict life " (*arctioris vitæ flagrans desiderio*).

The militant spirit of the early Irish Church, and her freedom from internal theological con- flicts, was probably one cause of the paucity and the desultory character of her early ecclesi- astical writings. The monks who stayed at home gave themselves to prayer, and those who went abroad converted the heathen, making no pre- paration for the severe cross-examination which awaited them in our times ; and when, in the age of Charlemagne, three centuries after the death of

---

[1] *Eccl. Hist.*, Bk. iii., c. xxvii. In the preceding chapter he bears testimony to the exalted spirit of self-sacrifice and detachment of the Irish monks, of whom he says: " The whole care of the teachers was to serve God not the world, to feed the soul and not the belly ". See also Henry of Huntingdon, *Chron.*, A.D. 652. This characteristic of Irish apostles did not escape the penetrating glance of Edmund Burke (*Eng. History*, chap. ii.).

St. Patrick, the learning of Europe began to be re-organised, the barbarians of the North came down upon Ireland, and from that day to this the pages of her history have been blotted with tears and blood.

The Canon of St. Patrick, in the *Book of Armagh*, which orders that any case of extreme difficulty (*causa valde difficilis*) should be referred to the Chair of the Apostle Peter (*ad Petri apostoli cathedram*),[1] would long ago have silenced all disputes concerning St. Patrick's connection with Rome, were it not that the Church of St. Patrick so obstinately refused to supply cases for the exercise of the law. The same obscurity rests on the relations of St. Martin and his Church with Rome. In his time " Gaul is said to have been perfectly free from heresies ; at least none are mentioned as belonging to that country in the Theodosian Code".[2] Hence St. Martin, like St. Patrick, imported no

---

[1] *The Canon of St. Patrick* : "Moreover, if any case should arise of extreme difficulty, and beyond the knowledge of all the judges of the nation of the Scots, it is to be duly referred to the chair of the archbishop of the Irish, that is to say, of Patrick, and the jurisdiction of the bishop (of Armagh). But if such a case, as aforesaid, of a matter at issue cannot be easily disposed of (by him) with his coun-sellors in that (investigation), we have decreed that it be sent to the apostolic seat, that is to say, to the Chair of the Apostle Peter, having the authority of the city of Rome. These are the persons who decreed concerning this matter, viz., Auxilius, Patrick, Secun-dinus, and Benignus."—O'Curry, *MS. Materials*, p. 612.

[2] Card. Newman, *Development*, p. 248. Also S. Severus, *Hist. Suc.*, L. ii. cxlv.

difficulties into Roman legislation, and consequently
has left no mark upon it.

The life of St. Patrick must be built up out of
historical ruins ; but when we find that these detached fragments fit in with one another, it is plain
that the sum of the evidence will be multiplied with
quite a peculiar force by the number of the authorities.   This is the argument which more than any
other has satisfied the present writer as to the
authenticity of the lives of St. Patrick in Father
Colgan's collection, included in the *Trias Thauma-*
turga.   The discrepancies in these ancient records
are not more numerous than are commonly found
in our contemporary modern biographies, and they
affect the substance less, owing to the transparent
simplicity and honesty of the ancient writers.   The
image before the minds of all these writers is one
and the same, and it is identical with the revelation
which St. Patrick gives of himself in his autobiography.   This is the more remarkable as it is
plain that the earliest writers of St. Patrick's history
made little use of the Saint's own writings in their
compositions.   Their works are principally made up
from the statements of those who listened to the
Saint's discourses, and witnessed his miracles : the
names of persons and places, and the most trivial
circumstances, being introduced into the narrative
with that minuteness of detail which always dis-

tinguishes the evidence of those who relate their personal experiences. They are chiefly an account of events which occurred before St. Patrick wrote his *Confession;* hence they are independent witnesses. They are very rude in form, but this strengthens rather than weakens their authority, when in these rough outlines we recognise the majestic lineaments of a supernatural character which no mind of man could invent. In the *Confession, Epistle,* and *Hymn* of the Saint, we contemplate the soul of one in whom were fulfilled the words of the Imitation, on the wonderful effects of divine love, " which disputes not about impossibilities, because it judges that it can do and dare all things"; while in the Lives we see the outward effects of that spirit as they appeared to his astonished disciples. The boy who, " before the dawn," on Slemish, " was summoned to prayer by the snow, the ice, and the rain," had already the first fruits of graces which were the pledge and promise of that plenitude of supernatural domination which flashes on our souls in those words of his Hymn at Tara : that sovereign faith and love to which God has linked His omnipotence.

In the name of common sense, as well as of sacred science, we repudiate the usurpation of that " scientific history " which aspires to dissect and secularise a biography so supernatural. In like manner, as far as human understanding can see in

3

the dark, we reject the conclusions of those philosophers who would catalogue St. Patrick amongst the specimens of modern psychological chemistry. Reason is less embarrassed by the prodigies in the pages of the ancient biographers of the Saint, than by the inventions and contradictions of writers who would make the body the interpreter of the soul, as if the mysteries of matter were in any sense less inscrutable than those of mind. As regards the value and authenticity of these ancient records, a glance at the list with which this introduction concludes will suffice for our present purpose. The dates of these works reveal the fact that for more than a thousand years after St. Patrick's death writers were busy with his history in every Christian country, and in spite of interpolations, and of difference of style and language, the character of the Saint and the nature of his work are the same in all their pages.

The miracles of St. Patrick are unquestionably the part which may be fairly disputed without any dishonour to the Saint himself. Unlike his own account of his relations with God, and of his apostolic work, they come to us on the authority of ordinary witnesses. It is quite possible that they were sometimes mistaken, and it is vain to attempt to prove that they were not. All that we can do is to ask those who believe in miracles, why they should withhold from St. Patrick's witnesses the credence which they freely give to others? It cannot be said that miracles were unlikely under the circumstances; and as to their character, they only differ in degree, and not in kind, from those of other Saints; and there is nothing more remarkable in the sacred records, and in hagiology than the different characteristics and dimensions of the *thaumaturgi* who appear in their pages. Miracles are always a tempting subject of controversy. The last word has never yet been said about them. In St. Patrick's case the credibility of his *acta* is inextricably bound up with that of his miracles; and as all his modern biographers have thought it necessary to say something about the characteristics of his miracles, I suppose we cannot avoid the discussion. I do not deny that St. Patrick's history is one whose every page is a trial of faith far greater than that which is commonly met with in Saints' lives; and if the difficulties are enhanced by the fervid language of his Celtic biographers, it may be said, on the other hand, that granting the facts, they are enough to rouse the enthusiasm and colour the style of the most phlegmatic of writers.

It is too commonly assumed that readiness to investigate the subject of miracles is a characteristic of wonder-loving, weak, and illogical minds; whereas

once the possibility of such supernatural inter-
positions is accepted, so far from being an abuse
of reason, it is one of its highest offices to examine
the evidence by which they are supported, and to
determine the extent to which faith is called upon
to go. There are few questions more open to
discussion than that of ecclesiastical miracles. The
miracles recorded in Holy Scripture are alone
matters of divine faith. " In a process of canonisation, for instance, the evidence is not divine. The
facts are in no sense revealed facts, for they are
simply conclusions inferred from the evidence of
human testimony, by which the heroicity of the
virtues, the final perseverance, and the miracles of
the Saints have been proved."[1] If we suppose, as
we have a right to do, that one of the purposes of
God in working miracles is to reveal that He has
uncontrolled dominion over His own creatures,
then we shall not be tempted to deny a miracle
because we cannot see a reason for its performance.
At the same time we find that, as a rule, a great
gift of miracles is only granted for great purposes,
and pre-eminent among these is the conversion of
the heathen. This is admitted even by Protestants.
"Knowledge," says Lord Bacon, " sufficeth to
convince atheism, but not to inform religion, and
therefore there never was miracle wrought to con-

---

[1] T. F. Knox, *When does the Church speak Infallibly ?* p. 64.

vert an atheist, because the light of nature might have led him to confess a God, but miracles have been wrought to convert idolaters, and the superstitious." Edmund Burke, in his account of the conversion of England by St. Augustine, remarks : " It is by no means impossible, that for an end so worthy Providence on some occasions might directly have interposed ". Bacon also, in his *New Atlantis*, in the same strain, observes " that God never works miracles except to a divine and excellent end, for the laws of nature are His own laws, and He exceedeth them not but upon good cause ".[1] Yet what cause could be more worthy than the propagation of that Gospel which He came on earth to establish, and which He commissioned His Apostles to extend and perpetuate.

It is a vain and useless undertaking to attempt to bring home the records of supernatural events to the minds of those who acknowledge no higher tribunal than that of their own opinion. Our real work is with Catholics, amongst whom there are many degrees of faith. If we are asked how much and what parts of St. Patrick's miracles we are bound to believe, I suppose we must answer that so long as we hold that he is a Saint reigning with God, we are at liberty to question each separate detail of his

---

[1] *Advancement of Learning*, Bk. ii., p. 188. *Abridgment of English History*, ch. i., p. 201. *New Atlantis*, p. 205.

history regarding which the Church has made no
decision.   At the same time, however, the further
question arises—Is it consistent with our principles
as Catholics to do so ?   This opens up the question
how far we are responsible to God for the co-operation of our reason in matters of faith, and experience tells us that it is a serious one.   We are bound
to believe that in the Church of God the age of
miracles has never ceased.   This once granted, we
are led to inquire into the consequences of this
belief; and to ask who among Catholics are they
who are most consistent and faithful to the dictates
of reason—those who are ready to believe, or those
who are jealous of such demands upon their faith ?
When we turn to the inspired writings we are plainly
told that not only is readiness to believe accounted
a virtue by God, but that it is actually a source of
miracles so far as the co-operation of man is concerned.   Moreover, reason and natural religion lead
to the same conclusion.   The creature honours God
by belief and trust in His omnipotence and His
goodness; and it is only reasonable to expect that
God will favour those who pay Him the homage of
an unlimited confidence.   " If thou canst believe,
all things are possible to him that believeth," are
the words of the Son of God : this is the divine
promise which the reason of a Catholic, following
the guidance of faith, expects to find fulfilled in the

Saints. It implies an undefined co-operation of God as unlimited as His omnipotence; so that we can never lay down laws as to the lines in which miracles must run. It is, however, one thing to believe that miracles are possible, and another to believe that they have taken place in particular instances; and this leads to that further distinction as to belief in miracles to which allusion has already been made. It is a virtue only so far as it is reasonable; without the restraint of reason it runs into credulity and superstition. At the same time it is certain that the condition of mind implied by these ugly epithets has more of reason in it than the animal apathy of the agnostic: in one case the mind goes astray, in the other it commits spiritual suicide. "There is a superstition," says Lord Bacon, "in avoiding superstition when men think to do best if they go farthest from the superstition formerly received."

The result of the labours of Dr. Todd and others, who have eliminated the supernatural from St. Patrick's life, is a striking proof of the force of this remark. In the acts of the Saint the miraculous element is essential to the narrative; take it away, and at once all reality vanishes, and his history evaporates. Every attempt to strip him of his supernatural character has ended in the fabrication of a drama without a hero, in which a series of effects are produced without a cause. We can hardly conceive a stronger argument in favour of the Saint's thaumaturgic powers. All his biographers unite in stating that at the outset of his apostolate he was brought face to face with extraordinary manifestations of diabolical power, and that his victory was so convincing to the minds of the pagans that from that time all serious opposition to his mission ceased. There is no better established event in history than the fact that when St. Patrick died, A.D. 492, the Scottish, or Irish nation was Christian. It is equally certain that before St. Patrick the warlike Scoti were the terror of the Christian world, and that for the space of nearly a hundred years after his coming they disappeared from the battlefields of Europe, until in the sixth century they returned as apostles of Christianity. Narrowness of the field of action, isolation from foreign influences, rapidity of conversion, continuity and development,—all the elements of certainty are combined in the evidence of the conversion of Ireland ; and when we look for an explanation of the fact, it is impossible to conceive one so rational as that which is given by the writers of the acts of St. Patrick.

It is certainly rather hard on St. Patrick's history that the learned Bollandists should raise doubts about some of the Saint's miracles, on the ground that they are like those recorded in the lives of subsequent Irish Saints. Surely it may be answered that, as the stream of history does not flow upwards, it is the lives of later Saints which must be put on their trial, if there is anything like a charge of plagiarism. The truth is, it is not necessary to suppose it in either case. There is a remarkable sameness in the ordinary miracles of the Saints, which arises from the fact that they are narrowed within the restricted limits of nature, and its necessities, which are the same in all ages. Hunger, disease, blindness, and the pale faces of the dead are ever soliciting the mercy of God through the interposition of His Saints. Nay, the very trick which was played on St. Patrick, when a man who feigned death in mockery of the Saint's power was found to be really dead, is also found before his time in the life of St. Gregory Thaumaturgus, and subsequently in that of St. Anthony of Padua.

It is the question of degree, not of kind, which staggers people in the case of St. Patrick's miracles, and this is especially the case in the narrative of his contests with the powers of darkness. Something more will be said in the body of the work on this subject. Here it is only necessary to observe that no consideration for æsthetic delicacy can justify Christians in temporising in the matter of their confession of belief in the devil. It is true that we have a very imperfect idea of his nature or of the power which God permits him to wield in this world; but no Christian can deny the existence and the power of the evil one. The proofs are found in Holy Scripture, and in the lives of the Saints : in the one case, the evidence is matter of faith ; in the other, it is a development of faith, on testimony which is only second to that of inspiration. At the same time the devil is not a subject of the Church, and she does not define the nature and extent of his operations. There is no study more bewildering and unsatisfactory. The learned Görres has devoted two volumes of his work on Mysticism to the study of devilry in all its manifestations. " Revelation, history, and the study of nature," he observes, " prove that all the provinces of creation, visible as well as invisible, are divided, in the words of an ancient creed, into two kingdoms, one of light, the other of darkness, and that man, placed between the two, is an instance of the same division."[1] This s pretty well all that can be said on the general question. As Satan and his agents come out of the darkness, so into the darkness they return ; hence it is not to be expected that we can know much about them. That which we do learn is principally from contrast with those celestial messengers of God who come in light and depart in light—both are mysterious ; but

[1] *Mystique Diabolique*, Lib. vi., ch. i.

with this difference, that the more we study the nature of evil spirits, the more the darkness thickens, whereas the contemplation of the angels always brings light to our souls, although, like the stars, they are so far above us. Again, diabolical operations are like the passions of man, at one time acting in concert, at another contending and yielding one to the other, according to the idea of the great moralist :

" . . . How came you thus recovered ?
" It hath pleased the devil drunkenness to give place to the devil wrath."

They are like them also in their ungovernable and suicidal fury, and so they serve a great purpose in the designs of God; for like insanity, and the parodies of human degradation which are seen in the brute creation, by contrast they enable men better to understand the beauty of reason and virtue. An inquiry into the extent of diabolical power must, of necessity, be unsatisfactory. Its extent depends on God's permission; we only know what it can do, by ou experience of what it has done. The order of Providence requires that, in this world, it should be inferior to the power of man, as the earth is man's inheritance; so that when the devil is called " the Prince of this World," he is such only so far as men of their own free will submit to him. The explanations of St. Thomas on this point are very clear, and, like all his teaching, they leave the impression that, although he was not infallible, he knew more than any uninspired writer about the relations of the visible and invisible world. It is with the power of the demon to produce extraordinary physical phenomena that we are chiefly concerned in the life of St. Patrick. On this point St. Thomas affirms that demons can produce "all those changes in physical substances of which they are capable, according to their natural qualities," or those which are "produced by the movement of inferior bodies from place to place".[1]

Without pledging ourselves, therefore, to anything like a profession of faith in the record of diabolical interference with the elements which we find in St. Patrick's life, they need not prejudice us against his biographers, seeing that we have such an august authority on the side of the antecedent credibility of such operations; whatever may be thought of the manner in which the acts of St. Patrick are written, the matter is familiar to all readers of Saints' lives.

CHIEF AUTHORITIES FROM WHICH THE FOLLOWING
NARRATIVE HAS BEEN COMPILED.

A complete list of all the ancient sources consulted, if imposing, would be at the same time

[1] I. Q. 114. 4 ad. 2 ; I. 2. Q. 80 c.

misleading. In many, the matter, and sometimes even the words, are the same, and the chief value which attaches to their number is to be attributed to the fact that they are a chain of evidence which carries St. Patrick's history upwards from Jocelyn, in the twelfth century, to the *Book of Armagh*, in the middle of the seventh. From that date to the death of St. Patrick leaves only a hundred and fifty years to be accounted for : a period which might have been bridged over by the memories of two generations. But from the *Book of Armagh*, whose date is certain, we learn that it was itself in great part second-hand, as it refers to previous lives, and tells us that "after the death of Patrick his disciples carefully wrote out his books" (O'Curry, *MS. Materials*, p. 612). The collection known as the *Book of Armagh* includes the *Confession* of St. Patrick, and, however venerable the compilation itself may be, its real authority must be estimated by the place which it holds as a faithful commentary on the Saint's confession or autobiography. In pursuance, therefore, of this principle which has directed him in the composition of his work, the writer ventures to classify the ancient sources of St. Patrick's life in the following order, and at the same time to add a few words of explanation which may be of use to those to whom the subject is new.

1. *The Confession of St. Patrick — Letter to*

the Christian Subjects of the Tyrant Coroticus.
The text of Villanueva (*Sancti Patricii Ibernorum
Apost. Opuscula*, Dublinii, 1835) and that of the
Bollandists (*Acta SS., Mart.* xvii.) have been used
alternately, as it is impossible to prove anything
definite as regards the comparative dates of the
different manuscripts, even including the abstract in
the *Book of Armagh.* Some have supposed that the
latter is the identical copy written by St. Patrick
from the words : " So far the volume which St.
Patrick wrote with his own hand "; but the word
volumen is not in the Saint's style, and the sentence
is incongruous, as well as redundant, following on
the words which immediately precede it : " and this
is my Confession before I die ". As the scribe in
the *Book of Armagh* adds, "On the seventeenth
of March Patrick was translated to heaven," it is
evident, therefore, that the first part of the sentence
is only a voucher of his own fidelity as a copyist.
As to the authenticity and value of St. Patrick's
autobiography, it would be superfluous to add anything to what has been already written.

2. *Triadis Thavmaturgæ sev divorum Patricii
Columbæ et Brigidæ acta, Joannes Colganus,* Lovanii, 1647. This work forms the second volume
of Fr. Colgan's *Acta Sanctorum Veteris et Majoris
Scotiæ seu Hiberniæ*, and contains seven different
lives of St. Patrick, some of which are supposed, on

good grounds, to be the original lives of the Saint, written by his disciples, which Jocelyn used in the twelfth century.

They are classified by Fr. Colgan in the following order, with the names of their authors :

Vita Prima, by St. Fiacc, Bishop of Sletty (in verse).

Vita Secunda, by Patrick Junior.

Vita Tertia, by St. Benignus.

Vita Quarta, by St. Eleran, surnamed the Wise.

Vita Quinta, by Probus.

Vita Sexta, by Jocelyn.

Vita Septima, by St. Evin (The " Tripartite," or " Life in Three Parts ").

Fr. Colgan holds that all these lives, with the exception of the fourth and the sixth, were written either by disciples of the Saint or by authors of the sixth century, to the verge of which St. Patrick's own life was prolonged ; but Mr. O'Curry inclines to the more common opinion that the life by Probus belongs to the tenth century (*MS. M.*, p. 390).

3. *The Book of Armagh.* The manuscript of this work is preserved in the Library of Trinity College, Dublin, and it contains several documents relating to St. Patrick. The Bollandists at Brussels discovered another copy of these writings which has been edited with extraordinary care and ability by Fr. Hogan, S.J. Critics are divided as to the

antiquity of this collection, as compared with the ancient lives in the *Trias Thaumaturga* of Fr. Colgan; but it does not concern us here to discuss the question. It is enough for our purpose that the *Book of Armagh*, the manuscript of which belongs unquestionably to the seventh century, bears testimony to other and earlier lives of the Saint, and that in one and all these ancient lives the picture given of St. Patrick is identical. That it is unsatisfactory cannot be denied. As a rule, the writers confine themselves to the marvellous, for which they are severely corrected in the pages of certain modern writers, and, strangely enough, by some who are Catholics. Advice to our forefathers is something like indignation with circumstances. The old style will always be the old style, and we must make the best of it. Even Jocelyn, who is so roughly handled by Dr. Lanigan and Fr. O'Hanlon for his devotion to the "incredible," is quite as terrestrial as St. Gregory of Tours in his four books *De Miraculis Sti. Martini*. Indeed, the works are so similar in style that we may suppose that Jocelyn modelled his book on that which St. Gregory had written in honour of St. Patrick's great kinsman. It is this life, the *Vita Sexta*, in Fr. Colgan's collection, which is found in the *Acta Sanctorum* of the Bollandists. It is not fair to Jocelyn to say that he was a mere collector of marvels. The Cistercian was a conscientious writer, and many of the most beautiful and characteristic incidents of the Saint's life in the following pages are given almost in his own words. The principal miracles he relates are all found in the older lives, and at the time when he wrote, in the twelfth century, there were other lives of St. Patrick extant, of which there is now no trace. He tells us that he composed his work at the command of the *Heres Patricii*, the Archbishop of Armagh of the day, and of the Bishop of Down, and that he was also urged to undertake the work by John de Courcy, one of the agents of Henry Plantagenet. De Courcy, like the Danes, two centuries before, did homage to St. Patrick, and appears to have been as fully persuaded as the Irish themselves that devotion to the Saint was, even under a political aspect, an important element in Irish affairs.

4. *The Ancient Annals of Ireland.*—For information as to the value and antiquity of these writings, the reader is referred to O'Curry's work on the *MS. Materials of Irish History* (p. 53 *et seq.*). They are a record of the unbroken tradition concerning St. Patrick which was handed down from generation to generation in the Irish monasteries, and it is upon them that we principally depend for the chronology of the Saint's life.

4

Anyone who studies the history of Patrician literature in these countries for the last two centuries will easily understand how it has come to . pass that the history of St. Patrick was so long shrouded in mystery. Much had been written about the Saint; but the vast majority of those writers who had the public ear, from Archbishop Ussher in the seventeenth century, to Dr. Ledwich in the eighteenth, and Sir William Betham in our own, were Protestants. Moreover, none of them attempted to write a life of the Saint; they were content with fragments which were available for controversial purposes, and so St. Patrick in their pages became like the John Doe and Richard Roe of the lawyer — impersonal, shapeless, a mere shadow. At length, in 1829, Dr. Lanigan took the field. He devoted the first volume of his *Ecclesiastical History of Ireland* to St. Patrick; and however much we may differ with him as to the manner in which Saints' lives should be written, no one can deny that in purely historical discussions he prostrated his adversaries of the sectarian school. In 1864 Dr. Todd published his *Apostle of Ireland*, which is one of those productions which represents all opinions except those of its author. The name and position of the writer have sufficed to entrench this work in our public libraries, and to make it a common book of reference, and it will, probably, long be the text-book of those who search for doubt rather than conviction. His object seemed to be to give all parties a share in the Saint, and his book has there-fore that dangerous fascination which inconsistency always exercises over minds to whom anything like certainty in religious questions is an intolerable captivity.

In 1871 appeared the *Life of St. Patrick* by M. F. Cusack. This work is distinguished by its uncompromising defence of the supernatural charac-ter of St. Patrick's history. The present writer has ventured to differ with some of the conclusions in this work, and if it turns out that he is right, he is fully conscious that it must be attributed, not to his own merit, but to the natural development of the subject: an advantage which he hopes will be used at his own expense, by some writer more competent than himself. The value of the above-named work is enhanced by the fact that the large edition also embodies Mr. Hennessy's translation of the ancient manuscripts of the *Tripartite Life of St. Patrick*. The discovery of this venerable treasure was regarded by O'Curry as a most impor-tant vindication of the fidelity of Fr. Colgan, as well in the matter of St. Patrick's history as of the Saint's doctrine.[1]

---

[1] *MS. Materials of Irish History,* p. 345.

The Hymn of St. Patrick's disciple St. Sechnall is interesting as an archæological curiosity, and as an evidence of the doctrine taught by St. Patrick; but, like the Hymn of St. Fiacc, its poetical style takes away from its historical value. St. Patrick's Hymn, or "Breastplate," however, like all the Saint's writings, has a value altogether its own ; but its importance as a revelation of the Saint's interior spirit will be more appropriately considered in the body of the work. The canon of Tillemont, which, as we have seen, he applies to the *Confession* of St. Patrick, may with equal propriety be extended to this extraordinary and inimitable production ; for it also " bears upon it that stamp of veracity which would enable it to stand by itself, even if it had never been quoted by anyone," so that, to borrow the idea of another French writer of a very different stamp, " the inventor would have been more wonderful than the hero". Dr. Petrie gives a Latin version of the Hymn from the Gaelic in his *Essay on Tara* (p. 55), and it has been translated into English by Dr. Todd, Mr. Whitley Stokes, and the Irish poet, Clarence Mangan ; the version given in the Notes of De Vere's *Legends of St. Patrick* (p. 239), with some few alterations, is that which has been followed in the text.

LIFE OF ST. PATRICK.

CHAPTER I.

THE CHURCH IN THE FOURTH CENTURY—BIRTH AND
PARENTAGE OF PATRICK—HIS SIX YEARS' CAPTIVITY
IN IRELAND—*CITO ITURUS AD PATRIAM TUAM*—THE
DESERT—ARRIVAL AT MARMOUTIER.

A GREAT part of the history of the Church may be
found in the Lives of her Saints. In this respect
sacred and secular history resemble each other, for
in both our attention is concentrated on the few
great men who were the representatives as well as
the rulers of their age. The century in which St.
Patrick was born, the fourth after Christ, was one
in which God wonderfully revealed His power, and
as His instruments are ever in proportion to the
work required, the character of our Saint, as one of
God's chief agents at that time, comes before us
invested with all the supernatural grandeur of the

age in which he lived.   It was then that the promise made by God through His prophet seemed on
the eve of its complete and manifest fulfilment :
" The stone that struck the statue became a great
mountain and filled the whole earth ".   The Church
had scarcely come forth from the catacombs, when
the Roman Empire yielded place and retired before
her, surrendering the Imperial city itself to the
Vicar of Christ, while paganism, as it was nothing
more than a religion of the State, was extinguished
by the power that had made it, when Constantine,
in the final exercise of his office of *Pontifex Maxi-*
mus, turned the gods out of the temples, setting
some to stand in the streets, and others in even
more ignoble places.

It is true that heresy, and the usurpations of the
civil power soon chilled the high hopes which had
been enkindled when the lord of the earth became
a Christian ; still it is remarkable that for some
time fidelity to the Church and material prosperity
went together.   It was the first Christian Emperor
who united the empire, and it was Constantine,
and after him the great Theodosius, who upheld
the majesty of the Roman name, and gave it back
some of its old glory ; but the very year that the
latter died (A.D. 395), the barbarians, who in the
century before had shaken the foundations of the
empire, broke once more upon it, and then its long

and terrible agony began. St. Patrick lived through
the years of Alaric, Attila, and Genseric, and saw
the final extinction of the empire of the West, and
it was in the midst of the desolation of those days—
all the more appalling from the contrast with what
had gone before—that God gave him the heart to
undertake the conversion of one of the fiercest of
those races who were then grinding the ancient
world into dust. His life carries us away from the
spectacle of the struggle which was going on around
the great centres of the Roman power, between the
old civilisation and barbarism, and reveals how it
fared with those who lived in countries which
formed the frontiers of the empire. When the
signal was given, and the legions, which for centuries had garrisoned the world, began their retreat
on Rome, many of her colonists, who, under the
shelter of their protection, had gathered together
possessions, and made homes for themselves in the
distant provinces, still clung to the countries
which they had adopted, and, like the stragglers of
a retreating army, it was they who suffered most
from the enemy. To this class our Saint's family
belonged; and his life has a special interest from
the light which it throws on the state of things in
our own part of the world, at a time of which we
have so few records. It tells us how frail was the
tenure of life and liberty for those who were

dwelling upon the shores of Gaul or Britain, when
Scots from Ireland, and Saxons from the banks of
the Elbe or the Rhine scoured the seas, or made
inroads on the mainland at unexpected times, and
in unprotected places. It is hard at the present
day to realise the conditions of life, in that age,
when wars began on land and sea without those
preliminary warnings and declarations which are
now the rule. We know that at the end of the
fourth century through the length and breadth of
Europe there were happy Christian homes wherein
were to be found at once the splendour of Roman
civilisation, and the flowers of Christian purity and
love, and that in the event of an invasion the woes
of the vanquished were wide-spread and terrible in
a way we can now hardly imagine. It was a time
when the fate of those who fell was envied by the
survivors; for then the living death of slavery
was the universal doom. It seemed as if the
dread despotism of brute force was mustering its
forces to extinguish the freedom with which Christ
had begun to make man free; and as it has always
been, the soldiers of Christ went forth to conquer
by sacrifice. Amongst the many victims in this
age of immolation the subject of the following
biography stands pre - eminent. St Patrick's
authentic history begins with his captivity and
slavery; and there is something very mysterious in

the fact that from the first he comes before us as a representative of that crucified life which has so specially distinguished the Church which he founded, and still inspires and governs.

Before we take up the narrative of the Saint's life under the guidance of, and in subordination to, his own autobiography, we must see what can be inferred, with tolerable certainty, regarding his family. His own account is perplexing. In one place he calls his father Calphurnius a *deacon*, and in another a *decurio;* and while the context leaves no doubt as to the correctness of the latter term, the former stands alone. Writing of his vocation and separation from the world, he says : " How came it that I was led to understand, and love the gift of God so mighty and so saving, and abandon my fatherland, and relatives, and the many gifts which with sighs and tears they offered me. Moreover, I then incurred the displeasure of some of my elders. But, God ruling me, I in no way consented or yielded to them ; not I, but the grace of God which conquered in me, and I withstood them all, so that I might come to the Hibernian races (*Ibernas gentes*) to preach the Gospel . . . and give myself and my free-born state for the good of others." And again : " Was it without God (*sine Deo*), or according to the flesh, that I came to Ireland ? Who forced me ? I was bound in the

Spirit that I should never again see anyone of my relations. Do I not love tender mercy, when I thus act towards that nation which of old enslaved me? According to the flesh I am free-born; for I derive my descent from a father, who was a decurio. But I have sold my nobility for the good of others, for which I have neither shame nor sorrow." [1]

This is plainly the language of one whose family held a high place in that Roman society which in many places he contrasts with the barbarian nations amongst whom he was thrown. When, therefore, he mentions that his father and grandfather were in holy orders, we must suppose either that the ancient copyist has made a mistake,[2] or else that the Saint is alluding to what has been permitted in all ages of the Church to married men like St. Gregory of Nyssa and St. Hilary, who have been allowed to take holy orders when separated from their wives by death or mutual consent. The *Confession* was written when St. Patrick's work was finished, concluding with the words: "This is my Confession before I die," and was chiefly ad-dressed to that monastic clergy on whom he had imposed so rigid a law of celibacy.[3]

---

[1] *Confession*, c. iv., § 15 ; *Epistle*, § 5.

[2] See Appendix, p. 284.

[3] Mabillon infers that St. Patrick introduced into Ireland the Monastic Rules which he had learned at St. Martin's Monastery at Marmoutier and at Lerins (*Annal. Bened.* I. viii.). The Rule of St.

On his mother's side St. Patrick was a near
relative of St. Martin of Tours. There is a con-
sensus of ancient authorities on this point, which,
when linked with his subsequent connection with
St. Martin, throws some light upon our Saint's
mysterious origin.' St. Martin, himself a soldier in
his youth, was the son of an Hungarian who held
the rank of tribune in the Roman army, and we
know that St. Martin served in Gaul, as it was at
the gates of Amiens that he divided his cloak with
our Lord under the appearance of a beggar. We are
also told that as soon as he could get free from the
army, he returned to Gaul, and took up his residence with St. Hilary at Poitiers.[1] Gaul had
therefore early become the adopted country of St.
Martin, and in his footsteps had probably come
St. Patrick's mother Conchessa and other members
of her family, seeking their fortunes in that favoured
province of the empire.

St. Patrick begins his autobiography at his
sixteenth year with the account of his exile and

Columbanus, which dates from the century after St. Patrick, imposes
the penance of two days' fast or two hundred strokes of the scourge
on a monk seen speaking alone with a woman (*Reg. S. Columbani*,
Migne, t. lxxx., p. 223) ; and the *Penetential* of St. Cummian, written
in the seventh century, ordains that the priest or deacon who has
broken his vow shall do penance by rigorous fasts and humiliations
for three years, with deprivation of the Holy Eucharist during half
his time of expiation (*Lib. Pœnitentiarum*, Migne, t. lxxxvii., p. 984).

[1] Sulpicius Severus, *Vita B. Martini*, c. iv. and v.

captivity in Ireland. In the beginning of the narrative he says nothing about his own sufferings, but in many places in his writings there are incidental expressions which reveal the agonies of his young soul, when, as he says: "The Lord poured upon us the wrath of His indignation, and dispersed us amongst many nations, even to the end of the earth". In his humility he attributes this calamity to his own sins and those of his fellow-captives; but the sequel shows that, in his case, captivity was to be the beginning of his divinely appointed preparation for the apostolate. He does not tell us who his captors were, or who was their leader. This is always the Saint's way in his writings. He makes no account of the operations of human instruments in the events of his own life; he is always alone amongst men, and seems to be unconscious of any power save that of God. He tells us that "thousands of men" were carried off at the same time by the invaders, who must therefore have come in great force. It was one of those expeditions celebrated by the poet Claudian, who about that time was the Court Poet of the Emperor Honorius, when he describes all Ireland rising at the command of her Scottish rulers, and the ocean foaming beneath their hostile oars:[1]

---

[1] "—— totam cum Scotus Ibernam
Movit, et infesto spumavit remige Tethys".

At this time, A.D. 387, Nial of the Nine Host-ages was Ard-Righ, or chief of the kings of Ireland. He was one of the most adventurous and famous of the Scottish kings, and the Irish annals record his death in the year 405, in Gaul, on the banks of the Loire;[1] where, as we shall see later on, St. Patrick seems again to have fallen into the hands of Nial's soldiers.

In taking up St. Patrick's narrative, we must ever keep before our minds as a guiding principle that his statements can only be understood by setting one against another, so as to measure his language by the exalted standard which was before the Saint's mind. "I was ignorant of the true God," he writes, "and I was carried into Ireland with many thousands of men, as we deserved : because we had turned away from God, neglected His commandments, and been disloyal to our priests, who instructed us for our salvation, and the Lord poured upon us the wrath of His indigna-tion, and scattered us amongst many nations, even to the ends of the earth, where now my littleness is seen among strangers. And there the Lord opened the understanding of my unbelieving heart, so that even thus late I should remember my sins and turn with all my heart to my Lord, who regarded my

[1] O'Curry, *Manners and Customs of the Ancient Irish*, vol. ii., p. 59.

humility and took pity on my youth and ignorance, and watched over me before I knew Him, and before I had understanding, or could distinguish between good and evil, and taught and consoled me as a father with his son.

"Therefore I cannot, and I ought not to be silent concerning the many favours and the grace so extraordinary which the Lord deigned to grant to me in the land of my captivity; for this is our return, that after correction or instruction we should glorify God, and confess all His wonders before every nation under heaven."

If we accepted the Saint's words literally, we might suppose that he was not a Christian at this time; but this would only make the mystery of what follows more incomprehensible; for the Saint continues :

"On coming to Ireland I was daily tending sheep, and many times in the day I prayed, and more and more the love of God, and His fear and faith, grew in me, and the spirit was strengthened. so that in a single day I have said as many as a hundred prayers, and in the night nearly as many ; so that I remained in the woods and upon the mountain, and before the dawn I was summoned to prayer by the snow, the ice, and the rain, and I did not suffer from them, nor was there any sloth in me, as I see now, because then the Spirit was burning within me ".

We must take St. Patrick's apparently contradictory statements as they stand. Whatever view we adopt will not lessen our wonder at the revelation they give of God's dealings with this young soul, which, like that of Moses, amidst the clouds upon the mountain, was brought face to face with God.

So far the narrative of St. Patrick's captivity is complete and unquestionable, and perfect as it stands. We must now see how far it can be supplemented by authentic evidence derived from other sources. It should be borne in mind that after a lapse of thirty-nine years St. Patrick returned to the scene of his captivity. Consequently the events and personages who were connected with it would again group themselves around the Saint, and become known to his disciples. Some ancient writers tell us that St. Patrick's parents were both slain by the invaders, and that two of his sisters were also carried off in the fleet; but as the children were separated in the confusion, they knew nothing of each other's fate. It appears, therefore, that it was only those captives who were young and useful as slaves who made up the thousands of victims of whom St. Patrick speaks.

It is vain to attempt a consecutive narrative of

all the circumstances of this portion of the Saint's
life. It is very remarkable, however, that, thanks
to the absence of cultivation, with its attendant
destructiveness, the scene of St. Patrick's captivity, like so many other places which retain
the mark of his footprints, is probably unchanged in its natural features. No part of the
Saint's history is better established than the
fact that the boy was sold as a slave to Milcho,
a chieftain of Antrim. Father Colgan has discovered in ancient records a notice of a chieftain of
this name in the north of Ulster at the end of the
fourth century,[1] and modern archæological investigations have brought to light the ruins of a rath, or
fortified dwelling, at a distance of three miles from
the modern town of Ballymena, which unquestionably belonged to pagan times, and is supposed to
have been the fortress of Milcho, situated at the
foot of *Sliabh Mis*, or Slemish the mountain,
which was the scene of St. Patrick's lonely novitiate.

St. Patrick's history has suffered so much from
the romantic school of historians, that great caution
is demanded in introducing anything in the way of
speculation into our narrative. At the same time,
as long as a writer holds on to facts, it is not unworthy of history if he tries to impart to his readers
the impressions which they have made upon him.

[1] *Acta SS. Hib.*, p. 741.

The pilgrim who has studied St. Patrick's acts in
that Catholic, and therefore truly critical spirit
which takes in the whole instead of halting at every
interruption, will find at Slemish a commentary on
the Saint's history written on the face of Nature.
Standing on the ruins of the fortress of Milcho,
the past returns with all its mysterious revelations.
The mountains, the elements, and probably most of
the surroundings of the scene are unchanged, and
tell their tale with a clearness and eloquence sur-
passing the writings and the monuments of man.
The boy who, without help from man, alone amidst
pagans, made that rugged mountain a ladder by
which to ascend to heaven, had already attained to
heights of sanctity which we cannot measure. He
had received an infusion of that spirit of austere
self-sacrifice which heaven so honours that its
inhabitants descend to commune with its posses-
sor. So we do not wonder when Probus tells
us that at this time " an angel visited the boy every
seventh day, and spoke to him as man is wont to
speak to man ".[1] This, we may suppose, was one of
those extraordinary favours which the Saint tells
us that the Lord deigned to grant to him at this
time.

Milcho, whose name will appear again in our
narrative, was not allowed to remain in ignorance

---

[1] *Trias Thaumaturga,* p. 49.

of the spiritual gifts of his mysterious slave, and
his obduracy at this time must not be forgotten in
his subsequent history.   Jocelyn relates that Milcho
had a dream in which the Saint appeared to his
master in the night, as it were all on fire, coming
so close that the burning hair of the boy seemed
to suffocate him.   Milcho pushed him away; whereupon the flames turned aside and seemed to envelop
and consume his two little daughters, who lay asleep
in the same bed, and finally the wind dispersed
their ashes over many parts of Ireland.   When
Milcho questioned the Saint as to the meaning of
his dream, he told him that the fire which he saw
was the faith of the Holy Trinity, which to him
would be announced in vain; but that his daughters
at his preaching should believe in the true God, and
that, dying the death of the just, their relics would
be honoured in many parts of Ireland.

From this it would seem that St. Patrick had
at that time received a revelation of the work for
which he was destined; and this the Saint himself
seems to imply when in his *Confession* he attributes
his triumph over those who opposed his laborious
episcopate to "the gift of God which had been
granted to him in the land of his captivity".[1]

St. Patrick's captivity, as he tells us, lasted for
six years.   During this period he had time to learn

---

[1] *Confession*, ch. iii., §§ 11, 13.

the language of the country, and to acquire a knowledge of the manners and spirit of the people. This
was a preparation for his work which has seldom
been granted to the missioner. At the end of this
period he received a revelation that his time of
servitude was at an end; and the fact that the
duration of his captivity was determined by God
implies that his life at this time was altogether
under a special divine guidance. The Saint himself
was impressed with this conviction, as we learn from
one of those abrupt sentences of his *Confession*
which say so little and suggest so much. It follows
without any break after his account of his austerities
and prayers on Slemish : " And there indeed," he
continues, " on a certain night I heard a voice that
said to me, ' You have fasted to good purpose, you
shall soon return to your fatherland ' (*cito iturus
ad patriam tuam*). And again after a little time
I heard the answer telling me, ' Behold, your ship
is ready '. And it was not near, but at the distance
of some two hundred miles, and I had never been in
the place, neither had I any acquaintance with the
people who lived there."

The reader by this time will have perceived that
St. Patrick's writings are of such a character that
they require a running commentary in order to
make them fit in with the narrative. We observe
that he speaks of the answer which he received

(*responsum audivi*) : a form of expression which recalls the statement of Probus concerning the angel with whom he had familiar intercourse.

It is this part of his life, more than any other, which is almost unexampled, save in the pages of Holy Writ, and yet the facts come to us on authority which somehow carries with it its own credentials. Since the Apostles, the Saints in their vocations and dealings with God have been led in the way of obedience to higher powers in the Church, and as a rule they have depended in some way on others ; whereas in St. Patrick's case it is impossible to resist the conviction that at this time he was absolutely the pupil of the Spirit of God ; so that we may venture to apply to him the words of the Apostle St. Paul : " For neither did I receive it of man, nor did I learn ; but by the revelation of Jesus Christ ". The Saint continues : " After this, leaving the man with whom I had passed six years, I fled, and in the strength of God, who directed my way, I reached Benum,[1] and I had no fear on the way until I gained the ship ". Our chief interest in the course of this mysterious journey arises from the fact that it enables us to explain St. Patrick's connection with the dwellers in the forest of Focluth, by whom

---

[1] The reader must be patient with obscurities in this narrative, and the identification of Benum is one ; it was probably a port, the name of which has not survived.

later on he was summoned to return to Ireland ;. and the arguments for this opinion form an important part of the chain which connects St. Patrick with St. Martin.

All that need be here observed is that it is clear that the whole term of St. Patrick's captivity was passed with one master and in one place, and therefore when, hereafter, we shall find that he was acquainted with people on the other side of the island, it is only reasonable to suppose that this knowledge was acquired on the occasion of his flight from the East to the West coast of Ireland.[1] When St. Patrick came in sight of the ship, he found that it had already put off from its moorings, and when he asked to be taken on board, the captain refused him in an angry manner. Then, says the Saint, "When I received this answer I turned away from him to go back to the cottage where I had stopped ; and on my way I began to pray, and before I had finished the prayer I heard one of them shouting to me, ' Come quickly, for these men call for thee ' ; and at once I returned to them, and they began to say, ' Because in faith we have understood thee, come and make friends with us in any way you please '. And on that day I had to mount into their ship for God's sake.

[1] From Slemish on the east coast to his place of embarkation on the Western Sea : about 200 Roman miles, as stated in the *Confession*, ii., § 6.

Yet I had [not] hoped that they would say to me,
Come in the faith of Christ, for they were pagans.
However, this I obtained from them, and at once
we set sail."

It appears from this passage that the Saint
had made some profession of faith which at first
had irritated the unbelievers ; but how their hearts
were changed he does not tell us, for it is one of
the characteristics of his style that he gives us no
explanation of mysteries, as if he always assumed
that the faith of the reader would be similar to his
own.

"After three days," says the Saint, "we reached
the land, and for twenty-eight days we made our
way through a desert. Food and drink failed us,
and hunger pressed us sorely. And one day the
captain said to me : ' How is it, O Christian ? You
say that your God is mighty and can do all things.
How is it that you cannot intercede for us ? Pray
for us, for we are nigh to death with hunger, and
it will go hard with us ever to see the face of man
again.' Then I said to them plainly : ' Turn with
your whole heart to the Lord my God, to whom
nothing is impossible, that this very day He may
send us abundant food for our journey, for His
storehouses are always full '. And, by the help of
God, so it came to pass. For, behold, a herd of
swine appeared in the way before our eyes, and the

men killed a great number, and they were refreshed with their flesh, for many of them had fainted and been left half dead upon the way. And after this they gave supreme thanks to God, and I was honoured in their eyes.

"From that time forward they had an abundance of food. They also found wild honey, some of which they offered to me, and then one of them said : 'Give thanks to God ; this is part of the sacrifice,' whereupon I tasted no more of it. But in that same night, while I slept, Satan tempted me fiercely (which I shall remember as long as body and soul hold together). As it were, a great stone fell upon me, and all my limbs were paralysed. Then in some way that I do not understand it came into my mind to call upon Elias. And while these things went on, I saw the sun rise in the heavens ; and as I cried 'Elias, Elias,' with all my strength, lo ! the splendour of that sun fell upon me, and all at once shook off the weight. And I believe that my Christ came to my assistance, and that His Spirit then cried out for me, and so I hope that it will be in the day of my distress, as the Lord testifies in the Gospel. 'In that day,' He says, 'it is not you that speak, but the Spirit of your Father that speaketh in you.' On our journey He gave us food and fire, and dryness every day, until on the fourteenth day we arrived amongst human beings. As I have said above, for twenty-eight days we wandered in the desert, and on the night of our arrival we had come to the end of our provisions."

So far we have a narrative which, in spite of the imperfections of the Latin text and of our translation, is full of mysterious beauty. Every line vibrates and tells of one who was the organ and the instrument of some power which was as incomprehensible in its operations as it was certain in its results. At this point, however, there is a gap of several years in the Saint's autobiography, so we must seek elsewhere for evidence as to the locality of that fatherland or *Patria* to which the Saint was miraculously directed. It is plain that we must either accept the history as supernatural or reject it altogether. It is assumed, therefore, that the reader who has followed the narrative thus far believes that God fulfilled His promise when He told the Saint that he should return to his own country.

It should be observed that the Saint gives us no dates, and that, with the exception of the names of his father and grandfather, and of a prince whom he excommunicates, there is not a single proper name to be found in St. Patrick's writings, although it is certain that he was in relations with some of the greatest Saints of his age. From this time

forward, therefore, we shall get little help from the
Saint himself in our investigation of the order and
sequence of his life. Now and then passages in his
mysterious writings will throw light upon our way,
but this is all.

As regards the term of St. Patrick's journey,
the conclusion of the present writer is that it led
him to his kinsman St. Martin at Marmoutier, in
Gaul : his arguments for this opinion will be
found elsewhere.[1]

One mysterious witness, one abiding landmark
on the line of our Saint's journey, however, deserves
special notice, for its own sake as well as an evidence
of the immemorial tradition which unites St. Martin
and St. Patrick. In the course of the Saint's
journey from Bordeaux by Trajectus to Tours,
he was obliged to cross the Loire, and after the
lapse of fifteen centuries the spot is still marked as
sacred by the inhabitants of Touraine. There we
find a memorial of the Saint which tradition
declares to be coeval with his flight from Ireland
and his passage of the Loire on his way to St.
Martin. I allude to the tree which unfailingly
every year at Christmas time is seen covered with
what are called the "Flowers of St. Patrick".[2]
The neighbouring village and commune bear the

---

[1] "St. Martin and St. Patrick," *Dublin Review*, Jan., 1883.
[2] *Vide* Appendix.

name of the Saint, while documents relating to the adjacent church of *St. Patrice* prove that the devotion to the Saint was already established at *St. Patrice* some nine hundred years ago.[1]

[1] *Cartulaire de l'Abbaye de Noyers*, pp. 11, 69.

CHAPTER II.

As soon as the biographer of St. Patrick is deprived
of the Saint's own guidance, he feels that he is
expected to make good his ground at every step,
and that it is not enough to give his facts unless at
the same time he can defend them. When this has
been done by merely multiplying quotations from
ancient authors, without any attempt at estimating
their relative value, very little advance has been
made. Certain modern writers have tried to
explain away the statements of St. Patrick's biographers, who tell us that our Saint was the companion of St. Martin at Marmoutier, suggesting
that this means nothing more than that he was

for a time a resident at the Monastery of St.
Martin. In order, therefore, to avoid the imputa-
tion of writing romance rather than history, in the
following chapter something must be said as to the
origin and value of this theory. We trace the
objection to certain controversial necessities which
demand the reduction or division of the age as
well as the personality of the Apostle of Ireland.
St. Martin died A.D. 397. St. Patrick, as we have
learned from himself, was twenty-one years of age
at the time of his escape from captivity, and, as we
shall see, he spent four years with St. Martin. Thus
twenty-five years of St. Patrick's life are accounted
for, starting from his birth in the year 372, and St.
Patrick survived St. Martin for a period of ninety-
five years, as he did not go to heaven until the year
492. If we believe the annals of ancient Ireland
and St. Patrick's biographers—and we may well ask
who else are we to believe?—we thus obtain from the
records of another country a most triumphant historical confirmation of the world-wide tradition that
St. Patrick attained the age of six-score years.[1]

It is necessary thus to anticipate in order to
make good our foundations. Outside his own writ-

---

[1] The writer has treated the subject of St. Patrick's longevity
at greater length, in two articles in the *Dublin Review* (July, 1880,
and January, 1883), entitled "The Apostle of Ireland and his
Modern Critics" (republished, Burns & Oates), and "St. Martin and

ings there is no part of St. Patrick's early history so solid as that which is bound up with the great St. Martin, and the traditions of Marmoutier, which even before St. Patrick's time was the citadel of learning as well as of devotion in Gaul. Unlike the less favoured sanctuaries of Great Britain and Ireland, over which the destroyer has passed again and again, Marmoutier has had an unbroken history; from St. Martin to the age of Clovis and the Francs, and thence through the period of its peaceful Benedictine occupation down to the French Revolution and our fathers' time. Its annals tell us of "many Irish Saints, who came thither following the example of their Apostle St. Patrick". Amongst these Marmoutier claims to have been the

St. Patrick". The ancient authorities on his side are overwhelming, viz.:

1. *The Tripartite Life.*	10. *The Book of Howth.*
2. *The Book of Armagh.*	11. *Annals of IV. Masters.*
3. *The Vita Secunda.* } Colgan.	12. *The Chronicum Scotorum.*
4. *The Vita Quarta.* }	13. *Marianus Scottus.*
5. *The Lebher Brecc.*	14. *Nennius.*
6. *The Annals of Tighernach.*	15. *Giraldus Cambrensis.*
7. *The Annals of Ulster.*	16. *Florence of Worcester.*
8. *The Annals of Boyle.*	17. *Roger of Wendover.*
9. *The Annals of Innisfail.*	

For the sake of those who are staggered by the mere idea of so long a span of life, he produced the evidence of the famous Dr. Harvey, to the effect that Thomas Parr reached the age of one hundred and fifty-two years and nine months, and that of another medical writer who gives us a list of 2003 centenarians, of various nations, 17 of whom are said to have lived to the age of 150.

instructor of the glorious St. Finian,[1] who is said to
have founded his famous school at Clonard as early
as the year 520, so that it is not improbable that
he went to Marmoutier in the lifetime of St. Patrick:
thus the historical connection of Marmoutier with the
Apostle of Ireland was perpetuated in his disciples.

In resuming the thread of our narrative, it should
be observed that amongst those ancient biographers
of our Saint who bring St. Patrick to St. Martin,
Probus is the only one who seems to have made any
attempt to harmonise his narrative with that of the
Saint.   He is also the only one who gives us geogra-
phical information, which is obviously an essential
element in a description of a journey.

He tells us that in company with the Gauls, St.
Patrick travelled from *Brotgalum* to *Trajectus*,
which is found in the ancient map of Gaul on the
river Dordogne, about sixty miles to the east of
Burdigala, or *Burdegala*, the modern Bordeaux.
Whatever doubt may have existed as to the accuracy of the writers who identified *Brotgalum* with
Burdigala is set at rest by the identification of
Trajectus.   From *Trajectus* to Tours, a distance of
about a hundred and sixty miles, St. Patrick's way
lay through an immense wilderness of some five
thousand square miles, where even at the present

---

[1] Martène, *Hist. de l'Abbaye de Marmoutier*, t. i., p. 372 ; and
Mabillon, *Annals Benedict.*, t. i., p. 208.

day the inhabitants find it hard to defend themselves against the devastating floods of the Loire,
the dread monarch of French rivers, with its count-
less tributaries. That this desert of which St.
Patrick speaks was the result of floods, explains
the Saint's expression already quoted, when he says
that God "gave us food, and fire, and *dryness* every
day" (*siccitatem quotidie*). Thus Probus leads St.
Patrick northward through the desert until he
brings him to the banks of the Loire, and obviously
to the very spot commemorated by the faithful
traditions of *St. Patrice.* It is the generally-
received opinion that Probus wrote his *Life of St.
Patrick* in the tenth century ; and Father Colgan's
arguments, grounded on intrinsic evidence in the
text,[1] leaves no doubt in our minds that Probus was
a foreigner. In all questions, therefore, concerning
St. Patrick's life in Ireland, this writer must take a
secondary place as compared with those authors
who have preserved the home-made history of the
Apostle of Ireland. In another point of view, however, his writings have a value which is altogether
their own. They establish the fact that nearly a
thousand years ago—that is, some four hundred
years after the death of St. Patrick—the footprints
of the Saint on his way to St. Martin were still
marked and reverently venerated, and thus the

---

[1] *Trias Thaumat.*, p. 61 (n.).

itinerary of St. Patrick in Probus must be regarded as one of the title-deeds of that venerable *Églisè de St. Patrice* and those mysterious *Fleurs de St. Patrice,* which, according to the immemorial traditions of Touraine, mark the spot at which St. Patrick crossed the Loire when he emerged from the desert. Probus goes on to say that " the Blessed Patrick arrived at Tours and joined Martin the Bishop, with whom he remained for four years, receiving the tonsure and admission into the clerical state, and he held fast to the doctrine and learning which he received from him ".[1]

When St. Patrick arrived at Marmoutier there was little in the external aspect of the place to reveal the work which was going on. St. Martin had chosen it on account of its seclusion and separation from the world, and with his disciples he observed a rule of life very similar to that of the Eastern anchorites. Some lived in cells made of wood, and others in the caverns which may still be seen at Marmoutier, and the casual observer passing by would probably have seen nothing in the settlement to distinguish it from any other colony of poor squatters on the banks of the Loire. Yet never in succeeding ages, in the days of its

---

[1] *Trias Thaumat.,* p. 48. Two ancient Breviaries of Rheims also give four years as the period of St. Patrick's stay with St. Martin. —Lanigan, *Eccl. Hist.,* p. 157 (n.).

greatest celebrity, was Marmoutier so glorious as at that time. From its huts and caves missionaries went forth to become the founders and princes of that spiritual empire which was to take the place and enlarge the boundaries of the Roman empire; for " where then was there a church or city which did not aspire to possess priests from the Monastery of Martin ? " These are the words of his biographer, Sulpicius Severus,[1] who was as careful and conscientious a writer as he was a learned and spiritual man. He was the intimate friend of St. Martin, while his knowledge of the state of the Church at the time enabled him to form a comparative estimate of St. Martin's influence on his age. It seems clear that he regarded St. Martin as the foremost figure in that apostolic army whose conquests were then advancing from the rising to the setting of the sun; and from the extraordinary and widespread devotion to St. Martin in the Western Church, we gather that this was the general impression of his contemporaries.[2]

The life of St. Martin, like that of St. Patrick, is one continued challenge to unbelief. He was an unlearned man;[3] he wrote nothing; he

---

[1] Cap. x., § 9.

[2] In France alone, there are 3,560 parishes dedicated to St. Martin. —*Vie de St. Martin*, La Marche, p. 670.

[3] *Homo illiteratus*, Sulpicius Severus, cap. xxv., § 8.

does not appear to have given any special rules
or laws to his disciples, and yet he founded an
empire.   The fact remains, although reason cannot
explain it.   If it was able to do so, it might perhaps
produce the same results, whereas, as a candid
infidel writer acknowledges, no philosopher has ever
yet succeeded in correcting the morals of a single
village.   We know that St. Martin did an immeasurable work.   If we are asked what was the secret of his
success, the supernatural character of the man is our
only answer.   Born in Hungary of heathen parents,
about the year 315, at the age of ten we find him,
as it were, forcing his way into the Church, carrying
heaven by storm, and at twelve he was a hermit in
desire.   We see him as a young soldier, fearless
and tranquil in the presence of the apostate Julian,
or dividing his cloak with his hidden Lord at the
gates of Amiens.   We follow him into solitude, or
again, when by a stratagem he was enticed from it,
captured, and set upon the episcopal throne of
Tours.   We see the Bishop in the long hours of the
night prostrate at the door of Avitian, until an
angel roused the tyrant with the words, "Can you
sleep while the servant of God lies at your
threshold?" or healing the leper by his kiss in the
presence of the multitude at the gates of Paris.
Such as these are the facts related of St. Martin's
life before men.   Of that other life with God, from

which he drew his strength, little is known, save that he held continual and familiar intercourse with the inhabitants of heaven. This we learn from the following narrative in the *Dialogues* of Sulpicius Severus, in which the disciple Gallus is introduced as spokesman :

"One day as I and Sulpicius were keeping watch at his (Martin's) door, for some hours we had sat in silence, and with great fear and trembling, much as if we were the sentinels of an angel's tabernacle ; for the door being closed, he knew not that we were outside. Meanwhile from within we heard the murmur of voices, and at once there stole over us a sort of horror and amazement, and we were overcome by the feeling of some divine manifestation. After the lapse of about two hours Martin joined us, and then the same Sulpicius (for no one was more familiar with him) implored him to explain the reason of that religious fear which we both acknowledged that we had felt, and also to tell us who had been speaking. with him in his cell . . . then after a long pause (for there was nothing which he could refuse to Sulpicius ; perhaps what I am going to say may seem in- credible, but I call Christ to witness that I speak the truth, unless there be anyone so sacrilegious as suppose that Martin was a liar), 'I will tell you,' he said ; 'but I beseech that you reveal it to no

one ; Agnes, Thecla, and Mary were with me,' and
he described the countenances and dress of each.
And he confessed that they, as well as the
Apostles Peter and Paul, were his frequent
visitors." [1]

St. Martin's miracles and his conflicts with
infernal spirits were continual, and perhaps as
prodigious as anything which is found in the lives
of the Saints. We observe, however, that Probus
makes no reference to their influence on the mind
of St. Patrick; he alludes only to the "doctrine
and learning" which the disciple received from his
master. St. Martin was St. Patrick's first spiritual
master, and therefore the one most likely to make
an impression and leave his mark on our Saint's
soul, who was then in his twenty-second year;
whereas his relations with St. Germanus of Auxerre
could not have commenced before the year 418.
Up to this period St. Germanus was a courtier, and
not at all a pious one; [2] and, moreover, he was six
years younger than St. Patrick, who when he joined
St. Germanus would have completed his forty-sixth
year.

When, however, we seek to discover the nature

[1] *Dial.*, ii., cap. xiii.
[2] St. Germanus, like St. Ambrose, was called to the episcopate
miraculously, and by an intervention of God even more wonderful,
as St. Ambrose was a Saint from his youth.

of the influence which St. Martin exercised over his young disciple, we feel that we are on sacred ground, which it becomes us to tread reverently. As we advance in our subject we shall see that in their external characteristics the apostles of Gaul and Ireland were very like each other. The circumstances under which they were placed were similar, and the same faith within them worked in the same way and produced similar results. That which in a very special way distinguishes these Saints is the fact that they were missionaries under circumstances analogous to those of the Apostles. They were in great measure their own witnesses. Those to whom they came were acquainted with no others, and, like the Apostles, they received individually that diversity of supernatural powers which in later ages has been divided amongst many. The authority of the Church was their strength and security; but that authority was for the time apparently altogether vested in themselves. Miracles were the credentials of their embassy from Christ; but they were less wonderful than that power which went forth with their words, and evoked an organised and enduring Church from the simple words of the *Credo*.

If, then, we were to say that St. Martin had power to impart such gifts to his disciples, we should seem to be attributing to him the prerogatives of that Divinity who works in the souls of His Saints after the manner of that primæval ordinance imposed upon "the tree that beareth fruit, having seed each one according to its kind". It is the independence and originality of St. Patrick's supernatural character which arouse our admiration, and this is what we have a right to expect from what we have already learned. In all external things—in monastic discipline and ecclesiastical studies—he was a novice, but internally he had already had dealings with God as intimate as those of St. Martin himself. The veil had already been drawn aside, and he had become familiar with the supernatural world; hence we are not surprised that he has left no record of the wonders that he witnessed at Marmoutier: to him such things had ceased to be extraordinary.

The four years of St. Patrick's sojourn with St. Martin bring us to the year 397, the year in which St. Martin died; and although we have no positive statement of the fact, it seems clear that St. Patrick left Marmoutier immediately after this event, and that it was at this time, when he had reached his twenty-fifth year,[1] that he began that life of per-

[1] The chronology of St. Patrick's life up to this point, as it is rigorously deduced from the Saint's *Confession* and from Probus, in a very remarkable manner supports the arguments of the Bollandists, Tillemont, and Mgr. Chevallier in their triumphant vindication of the year 397, as the date of St. Martin's death.

petual pilgrimage which was to fill up the years until his election to the apostolate. In so doing he would probably have the approval of the successor of St. Martin, even supposing that he was a subject of the community, which is not likely. Long pilgrimages appear to have been the fashion at Marmoutier in those days when monks could carry their rule with them, finding cloisters in the forest and on the mountain side wherever they went throughout the length and breadth of Europe. St. Patrick did but follow the example of those seven brothers, Les Sept-Dormants, who, in the lifetime of St. Martin, and with his sanction, left Marmoutier and spent five years in visiting *les grands pèlerinages du monde.*[1]

If, therefore, it is well-nigh certain that St. Patrick remained at Marmoutier until the death of St. Martin, we may number his young kinsman amongst the disciples that wept and prayed around the deathbed of the Apostle of Gaul, in that memorable scene when, with the gates of heaven already open, the Saint consented to prolong his

[1] The history of *Les Sept-Dormants* of Marmoutier must be distinguished from that of *Les Sept-Dormants* of Ephesus in St. Gregory of Tours (*De Gloria Martyr.*, L. i., c. cxcv.). The seven brothers of Marmoutier, according to Dom. Martène, were nephews of St. Martin, and consequently cousins of St. Patrick. It is interesting to note that the chapel of the Saints, at its restoration in 1881, was blessed by Mgr. Colet, Archbishop of Tours, on the Feast of St. Patrick (*Notre-Dame des Sept-Dormants,* pp. 19, 81. L'Abbé Püan. Tours, 1881).

exile if he were still necessary to his people. At
the burial of St. Martin, St. Patrick must have met
St. Ambrose, who at one and the same time was
present and visible to his flock in the Cathedral of
Milan, while he performed the obsequies of his
friend St. Martin at Tours ; and thus St. Patrick
had the privilege of catching inspiration from the
face of the man who had converted Augustine,
and brought Theodosius to repentance, and whose
memory lives in the Church as the representative
of her majesty in resisting and reproving the sins
of princes.

St. Gregory of Tours, writing in the century
after the death of St. Patrick, gives the following
account of this memorable instance of bilocation :

"It came to pass on this day of the Lord, after
the lection of the Prophet, when the reader,
standing before the altar, was about to begin that
of St. Paul, that the most blessed Bishop Ambrose
slept at the altar. Many observed it, but no one
presumed to awaken him, while two or three hours
passed in this way. Then they aroused him, saying,
'The hour is past, let our Lord command the reader
to proceed, for the wearied people are waiting'.
Then Bishop Ambrose replied, 'Be not troubled,
for this sleep has been of great profit to me, to
whom God has manifested so great a miracle. For
you must know that the soul of my brother Martin

the priest has departed, and that I have paid the last offices to him in the usual manner ; the little chapter *(Capitellum)* alone, I have not finished, because of your interruption.' In astonishment and wonder, they noted the day, and having made careful inquiries, they found that the Saint had passed away on the same day, and at the same time when the Blessed Confessor declared that he had assisted at his obsequies." [1]

From the death of St. Martin until the mission to Ireland embraces a period of thirty-five years of St. Patrick's life, and few indeed are the indications we can obtain as to the order of events. One thing, however, is certain, from the Saint's own words. During all this period he was pressing onwards to the apostolate of Ireland in the face, not merely of coldness, but of positive opposition, and this as well from his ecclesiastical superiors as from his relations. As far as our Saint himself is concerned, this one thought of his undaunted and

---

[1] *De Miraculis S[ti] Martini* (Migne), vol. lxxi., p. 919. This tradition has been questioned by those who held that St. Ambrose's death preceded that of St. Martin ; but the Bollandists defend it in a dissertation on the year and day of the death of St. Ambrose, prefixed to the Acta SS. April, tom. i., using it as one of their arguments for fixing the death of St. Ambrose in 398 ; and to his connection with St. Ambrose, they attribute the great honours paid to St. Martin in the Church of Milan. M. de la Marche, *Vie de St. Martin,* says that St. Paulinus of Nola, St. Martin's contemporary, celebrated this event in verse ; but I have not succeeded in discovering the poem.

persevering energy is by itself enough to give
unity and interest to this period of his life; but
if we would understand how it came to pass that
St. Patrick's aspirations after the conversion of
Ireland met with so little sympathy, we must take
a glance at the state of the Church during those
years in which our Saint waited for his commission
while the pent-up fires of apostolic zeal burned in
his bosom, annealing, not consuming, the energies
of his soul.

St. Patrick lived in what is truly called the age
of the Doctors of the Church. He was the contemporary of St. Jerome, St. John Chrysostom, St.
Ambrose, and St. Augustine. In those days the
chief field of the Church's work lay within the
limits of the Roman empire, which had been handed
over to her on the conversion of Constantine, just
fifty years before the birth of St. Patrick. In the
fourth century we hear little of missions outside
the empire; even St. Martin's work was carried on
in countries nominally subject to Rome. Then,
while St. Martin was still living in the year 395,
the death of the great Theodosius laid the empire
prostrate at the feet of the barbarians. The year
408 saw Alaric at the gates of Rome, and in the
footsteps of Alaric came horde after horde of
barbarians, involving the cities of the empire and
the sanctuaries of the Church in a common destruc-

tion. At such a time and under such circumstances defence rather than aggression must to many have seemed the only rational aspiration of the ministers of the Gospel; and that such was the opinion of St. Patrick's friends appears from the following passage in his *Confession*, in which, as far as we can follow him, he seems to take up the narrative of his life at the time of his departure from Marmoutier on the death of St. Martin:

"And again, after some years, I was once more taken captive, and on the first night I remained with them. But I heard the divine response telling me, 'You shall be with them for two months'; and so it came to pass. On the sixtieth night the Lord delivered me from their hands.[1] Again, after a few

---

[1] The Saint does not tell us who his captors were on this occasion. The words, "I remained with them," convey the impression that they were the Scots, his old familiar persecutors, and that his second captivity was a continuation of, and similar to the first; for it is certainly very remarkable that, as has been already observed, we find Nial of the Nine Hostages and his Scots again in St. Patrick's *patria* on the Loire, in the year 405, just eight years after the death of St. Martin. The fact that the banks of the Loire were one of Nial's favourite hunting-grounds must be borne in mind in weighing the evidence for the opinion that Gaul was the country from which St. Patrick was carried off in his youth. The south bank of the river was held by the *Pictones* or *Pictavi*, whose name suggests the idea of relationship with the Irish Picts, and others of the same race in Caledonia: the fact that the *Pictones* took the side of Cæsar against the Gauls supports the view that they were comparatively recent intruders in Gaul.—H. Martin, *Hist. de France*, i., pp. 153, 167.

years, I was with my relatious in Brittany, who
received me as a son, and in the language of faith
implored me that now, at least, after all my tribu-
lations I should never again leave them ; and there
in a vision of the night I saw a man named Vic-
tricius, coming as it were from Ireland, with
innumerable letters, one of which he gave to me,
and in the first line I read, ' *The voice of the Irish*';
and as I repeated the first words of the letter I
seemed at the same moment to hear the voices of
those who dwelt near the forest of Focluth, which
borders the Western Sea, and they cried as it
were with one voice, ' We beseech thee, holy youth,
to return, and still walk amongst us '.   And my
heart was melted within me, and I could read no
more, and I awoke.   Thanks be to God, seeing that
after many years the Lord has granted them that
for which they supplicated."

We see, therefore, that the Saint never faltered
in his purpose, and that heavenly encouragements
were not wanting.   On the other hand, there is
nothing to show that at this time his apostolic
vocation received any human acknowledgment or
sympathy.   On the contrary, we gather from his
writings that our Saint had his full measure of that
chalice of scorn and humiliation which is the
ordinary divine preparation for all great spiritual
exaltation.

No apology need be made for irregular quotations from the Saint's *Confession*, as he himself continually inverts the order. He writes as one already entering into that higher world in which there are no boundaries of space and time. In the following passage, which occurs in the beginning of the *Confession*, the Saint is evidently exulting over the confusion of those who at one time despised him, and yet there is no savour of self in his language : the glory is altogether made over to God. "Husbandry was created by the Most High,[1] as has been declared by the same Spirit of the living God. Wherefore I was at first a husbandman, an exile, and unlearned, not knowing how to provide for the morrow. But this I know for certain, that verily at first I was humbled, and I was as a stone lying in deep mire ; and He who is powerful came, and in His mercy He lifted me up, nay, raised me on high, and placed me on the height of the enclosure. Therefore, most earnestly I am bound to lift my voice in making some return to the Lord for all His gifts, so great in time and in eternity, which the mind of man cannot estimate. What then ? Wonder, all ye who fear the Lord, great and little, and you, ignorant lords of rhetoric, listen, therefore, and scrutinise. Who is He who

[1] *Eccl.* vii. 16. See also 1 *Cor.* iii. 9, where St. Paul seems to express the same idea.

has raised me up, fool that I am, from amongst
those who appeared to be wise, and learned in the
law, and powerful in word, and all other things;
who has breathed upon me, one abominable in the
eyes of the world beyond all others (even though I
be such), so long as with fear, and reverence, and
without complaint, I should faithfully serve this
nation to which the charity of Christ has transferred
me, and made me over for my life, if I shall be
worthy, so that I may serve Him in all humility
and truth."

The state of Gaul in those years which immediately followed the death of St. Martin gives a
special significance to this passage. At that time
Gaul was one of the most favoured of the provinces
of the Roman empire. The Alps lay between it, and
protected it from the barbarians who in the year
400 had entered Italy, and for a time the semi-pagan
literature and arts of Rome seem to have found a
shelter in the schools of Gaul, with no small damage
to the austere Christian simplicity of the Church of
St. Hilary and St. Martin. In such a state of
things St. Patrick, "a husbandman, an exile, and
unlearned," as he styles himself, was not likely to
meet with much encouragement in his efforts to
prepare himself for the apostolate, and in the above
extract we read the history of more than thirty
years of hope deferred and faith that never failed.

The ancient lives of the Saint help us very little as regards this part of his history. They merely tell us that he went from place to place as a pilgrim, and that he passed some time at Lerins, the *Insula Tamarensis* or *Insula Beata* of the ancients, which at that time was one of the most famous sanctuaries of piety and learning in the world.

In pursuing this commentary on the autobiography of St. Patrick, the writer wishes to be quite candid with the reader. He is fully alive to the fact that the road he is traversing is at the present point an obscure one, and that his views may be disputed. All that he can say in their favour is that they are the result of long and patient study. He has compared St. Patrick's statements with those of his ancient biographers, and tried to read both in light borrowed from the lives of the Saints of the fourth and fifth centuries of the Church; and he has come to the conclusion that the chief cause of the obscurity which surrounds the character of St. Patrick is to be found in the impatience of those narrow-minded critics whose way is to fasten on some one difficulty and worry it to death, refusing to believe anything where they cannot comprehend everything.

We now come to consider how St. Patrick was prepared for his apostolate, and how it came to pass that one so destitute of ordinary qualifications obtained so high an office in the Church as that of an apostolic bishop; and it must be borne in mind · that we ground our opinion of his apparent incompetence, not on his own expressions of humility, but on the unmistakable evidence which is found in the simple-hearted and eloquent irony of his triumph over his learned opponents and critics.

In the following passage St. Patrick goes further and reveals that his episcopal consecration was the result of the direct interposition of God:

"And on another night, whether in me, or near me, I know not, God knows, I heard sublime language, as of some who in spirit sang within me, and I knew not who they were whom I heard, neither could I understand until the end of the discourse, when He spoke to me thus: 'He who gave His life for thee, He it is that speaks in thee'. And so I awoke. And again I heard One praying within me, and I was as it were within my body, and I heard Him above me, that is, above the interior man, and there He prayed fervently with groanings. And while this went on I was amazed and wondered, considering who it was that prayed within me. But at the end of the prayer He said that He was the Spirit; and I remembered the words of the Apostle, saying, 'The Spirit helps the weakness of our prayer; for we know not what we should pray for, but the Spirit Himself asketh for us with unspeakable groanings,' which things I cannot express in words. And again : 'The Lord is our advocate, and He Himself pleads for us '. And when I was tried by some of my elders, who because of my sins came to oppose my laborious episcopate, truly in that day I was sometimes fiercely pressed, and might have fallen in time, and for eternity. But for the honour of His Name, the Lord spared a convert and pilgrim, and very mercifully came to my assistance when under this oppression, because I was not altogether worthy of this stain and reproach. I pray to God that their act may not be accounted a sin. . . . Therefore on the day when I was cast off by those mentioned above, on the same night, in a vision of the night, I saw a writing 'without honour' before my face. And then I heard the divine reply saying, ' We have seen with displeasure the face of My chosen one stript of his name '. It did not say, ' You have seen with displeasure'; but ' We have seen with displeasure '; as if He then made Himself one with me, even as He has said, ' He that toucheth you toucheth the apple of my eye '."

From these extracts we gather that St. Patrick's election to the episcopate was altogether supernatural, so that, as far as we can make out from his writings, he met with hardly anything but hostility and opposition from men. It should also be observed that in no other way can we explain the absence of all acknowledgment of personal obligations in one with whom humility and self-abasement amounted to a passion. It is this extraordinary blank in his autobiography which has opened the way for the theory that St. Patrick started for Ireland on his own account, and set up a Church for himself—a view which has great attractions for some minds. It is natural that it should recommend itself to those who have no conception of the operations of the Divinity in the shaping of the Church. Those, however, who believe in the divine origin, life, and unity of the Catholic Church will hardly consider the theory to be worthy of serious refutation. St. Patrick's account of his election to the apostolate is certainly the most mysterious part of his life. At the same time it is not altogether without a parallel. Direct divine vocations did not cease at the Ascension, as we learn from the call of Saul and Barnabas; and although in later times God seems to work more and more by the divinely appointed *magisterium* of the Church, for all that He is still the irresponsible dispenser of His gifts, and supernatural endowments are as real and as clearly recognised now as in the age of the Prophets and Apostles. The fact that St. Patrick founded a Church whose faith has never failed is one of those proofs of union with the See of Rome which in the mind of a Catholic dispenses with all need of other evidence. Stability, and that growth which unites one generation with another, is the undisputed appanage of Catholic faith. Fourteen centuries of perseverance have canonised the Church of St. Patrick, and proved that he communicated to Ireland the faith which he received from St. Celestine, of whom the author of the *Tripartite* says : " To the comarb (successor) of Peter belongs the instruction of Europe ".[1]

St. Patrick's writings give us very little indication of the extent to which he prosecuted ecclesiastical studies at Marmoutier, Lerins, and the other monasteries and sanctuaries at which he resided. It is certain that he studied under St. Germanus, Bishop of Auxerre, who, as we learn from the *Book of Armagh*, introduced St. Patrick to the notice of the Pope.[2] The same authority tells us that this was the second visit of our Saint to Rome, whither he had turned his steps in the first instance some thirty years previously. There is a concensus of ancient writers to the effect that in the years preceding his consecration St. Patrick led the life of a pilgrim. As we have seen, this is one of the titles which he gives himself, and

[1] *Tripartite Life*, p. 377.
[2] *Documenta de St. Patricio*, E. Hogan, S.J., pp. 24, 25.

in the "Sayings of Patrick," in the *Book of Armagh*, we read: "I had with me the fear of God, as the guide of my path through Gaul and Italy, as well as in the islands of the Mediterranean Sea".[1] With the exception, however, of the narrative of the journey to Marmoutier in Probus, there is nothing consecutive in this part of St. Patrick's history: the ancient writers had plainly only general information imported from a distance, out of which it is now impossible to construct a chronological narrative. We must be content with the help which they afford in our efforts to interpret and illustrate the Saint's own statements.

For nearly forty years St. Patrick was pressing on to the goal of his vocation; his eyes ever following the sun as it set over the Western Sea, and those forests of Ireland from whence came the cry of the little ones who asked for the bread of life, and there were none to break it to them. Youth passed away, and maturity, and, if we take as our measure the duration of an ordinary life, old age had begun to creep upon him, and as yet his work was not even commenced. When we ask what sort of preparation for the apostolate were these wanderings "through Gaul and Italy and the islands of the Mediterranean," we find ourselves in that "bright

---

[1] *Documenta de St. Patricio*, E. Hogan, S.J., p. 57.

darkness" of the mystical life which rests on
every page of the life of the Apostle of Ireland,
and our sense of God's special operations is in
proportion to the depth of the mystery. Surely
at this stage of our study of the Saint's life
we can have no hesitation in classing him amongst
those servants of God whose mission it was to
humble the mind of man by confounding all its
rules and calculations. Seven hundred years after
St. Patrick another man appeared in this world,
whose words and character exercise a fascination
over men's minds very similar to that of St. Patrick
St. Francis of Assisi, in his way, was as incomprehensible as the Apostle of Ireland, and when Bossuet
attempts to give an explanation of the mystery of
his life, he is driven to fall back on those words of
Tertullian : " ' Truly it is credible because it is
foolish . . . it is certain because it is impossible '.
Thus, the consolation of our faith is to silence
human reason by those bold propositions which it
is utterly incapable of comprehending." [1] This is
the wisdom of St. Paul in other words : the only
interpretation of St. Patrick's history, and the event
has proved that what in another would have been
pride and delusion, in our Saint was a special
inspiration of God.

That St. Patrick had a profound knowledge of

Panégyrique de S. François d'Assise.

the text and mysteries of Holy Scripture is evident from his writings ; but of other learning there are no signs. " I doubt much," says Tillemont, " that there are any satisfactory proofs of his having ever given himself to the study of human learning . . . having, without doubt, set himself less to science than to piety, for which God had already given him a great love." [1]

It is certain that St. Patrick was in relations with St. Germanus of Auxerre, and that under the guidance of this Saint he was prepared for his episcopal consecration. As we shall see, the date and circumstances of this event have been recorded, but we are in the dark as to the period of his life at which he was ordained priest. The life by Probus, and the Scholiast, or Commentator, on St. Fiacc's metrical life, are the most precise in their statements regarding this part of the Saint's history. Of his life with St. Germanus, Probus writes : " He passed the time in utter submission, in patience, obedience, charity, and chastity, remaining a virgin in the fear of the Lord, and walking, all the days of his life, in holiness and simplicity of heart". The Scholiast tells us that he studied the " Canons and all other ecclesiastical learning under Germanus," and then goes on to say that he told St. Germanus that he often heard in heavenly visions

[1] *Hist. Eccl.,* xvi. 783.

(cælestibus visionibus) the voices of infants sum-
moning him to Ireland ; and St. Germanus, he adds,
sent him to Pope St. Celestine, who, having already
sent St. Palladius to Ireland, "paid no regard to
him" *(nec ei honorem dedit).*

The writer then tells us that while St. Palladius
was engaged in his unsuccessful enterprise, St.
Patrick retired to the islands of the Mediterranean.[1]
All this fits in with St. Patrick's account. It is on
a supernatural invitation rather than on his natural
or acquired qualifications that he depends, and the
contradictions and disappointments which he endured are the ordinary lot of those who, like the
Prophets and Apostles, are raised up by God in
solitary majesty, with credentials which are derived
direct from heaven.

One of the most remarkable characteristics of
our Saint's vocation is the tenacity with which he
held on to his purpose of obtaining episcopal consecration. The holy ambition of other missionaries
has gone no further than the desire of individual
sacrifice. St. Patrick anticipated and demanded a
spiritual empire, and the revelation he has left us
of his intimate knowledge of the mind of God,
which was so marvellously corroborated by the
results of his apostolate, are convincing proofs that
in this he acted under a special divine inspiration.

[1] *Trias Thaumaturga*, pp. 5, 48.

It is not to be wondered at that such an unusual vocation had to make its own way. It is no dishonour even to Saints to suppose that they do not always understand each other, and certainly the impression left on us by St. Patrick's writings is, that all his consolations, and all help, came direct from God, and that he owed nothing to man.

This seems to be the meaning of the following words, which are found at the conclusion of the Saint's account of the opposition made to his consecration :

" Therefore I speak boldly : my conscience does not accuse me. God is my witness that I have not lied in the things that I have related. . . . The Lord is He who is greater than all. I say enough. Yet I ought not to hide the gift of God which was imparted to me in the land of my captivity. Because I then earnestly sought for Him, and there I found Him, and He preserved me from all iniquity, because of the indwelling of His Spirit, who has worked in me even to this day. But the Lord knows how, if I had heard these things from man, peradventure I should be silent, for the sake of the charity of Christ.

" Therefore I faint not in giving thanks to Him who has preserved my fidelity in the day of my temptation, so that to-day I can confidently offer to Him the Sacrifice, and consecrate my soul as a living victim to my Lord, who has saved me in all my difficulties ; so that I may say, Who am I, or what is my prayer, O Lord, who hast thus laid bare before me so much of Thy divinity ? So that this day I should exalt and magnify Thy name in every place, as well in adversity as in prosperity, rightfully receiving with an untroubled mind whatsoever may come, whether good or evil, ever giving thanks to God, who has taught me to believe in Him without doubting unto the end; who has lent His ear to me, so that in those latter days I had the heart to face a work so holy and so wonderful, and to imitate those of whom it was of old predicted by the Lord that they should announce His Gospel as a testimony to all nations before the end of the world. As we have seen, so it has been completed. Behold we are witnesses that the Gospel has been preached to the limits of human habitations."

With this extract we may conclude the account of St. Patrick's preparation for his mission ; and if the line of argument pursued leaves many details undetermined, it is to be hoped, on the other hand, that it will help to reveal what is still more important ;—to lay bare the interior spirit and supernatural gifts of the Apostle of Ireland. They belong to an order of things which overrides all mere historical criticism, in the minds of those who believe that the Saints are the visible agents of that unseen God whose operations are never on a level with our thoughts. The Saints are subjects of history in that which is seen, and so far reason and faith keep company; but beyond that there are things which have not entered into the heart of man—another world into which unaided reason cannot enter. When reason stops and can go no farther, faith takes wings, and unless reason is content to borrow them, it must remain for ever in its exterior darkness.

With the elevation of St. Patrick to the episcopate begins his public life. As a simple ecclesiastic there was little to give "a local habitation and a name" to the events of his life. But as soon as he became a prince of the Church, the central figure around whom subordinate agents, and the interests of a multitude ranged themselves, then, as might be expected, dates, and places, and the persons with whom he was connected assume a more fixed and determinate character. It is certain that St. Palladius was sent to Ireland by Pope St. Celestine A.D. 431,[1] and that within a year from that time St. Patrick followed him.[2] In this year, therefore, we must place the elevation of our Saint to the episcopate. The following is the account of the mission of St. Palladius, which was written when

[1] *St. Prosper Chron.* (Migne), t. li., p. 595.

[2] Dr. Petrie, *Antiq. Tara,* p. 75, declares that "A.D. 432 is the year in which, according to all authorities, St. Patrick came to Ireland," and if the word "authority" is restricted to its legitimate sense, his language cannot be accused of exaggeration.

the event was still fresh in the memories of the people of Ireland : " Palladius, Archdeacon of Pope Celestine, Bishop of Rome, and forty-fifth successor of St. Peter in the Apostolic See, was ordained and sent to convert this island, lying under wintry cold. But he was unsuccessful, for no one can receive anything from earth unless it be given to him from heaven; and neither did these fierce barbarians receive his doctrine readily, nor did he himself wish to remain long (*transigere tempus*) in a land not his own ; wherefore he returned to him who sent him. On his way, however, after passing the first sea, having begun his land journey, he died in the territory of the Britons." [1]

St. Patrick does not tell us what was the impression made on his mind by the failure of St. Palladius. When we call to mind the many intimations which he had received that God had chosen him for the apostolate of Ireland, it is not too much to suppose, that to him the retreat of St. Palladius from her shores was a revelation that his own time was come, rather than a cause of discouragement, and that the undaunted intrepidity of the man who, at such a time, offered to renew the conflict, must have made itself felt at Rome : the recognition of supernatural heroism is a gift which belongs by divine right to the Apostolic See.

[1] *Book of Armagh*, fol. ii., ap. Petrie, *Antiq. Tara*, p. 108.

Probus, who, as has been remarked, above all the ancient biographers of our Saint, impresses us with the conviction that he had authentic information regarding many of the events of St. Patrick's career on the Continent anterior to his consecration, tells us that before setting out for Ireland the Saint took a journey to Rome to obtain the apostolic benediction of Pope St. Celestine. "But first," says this writer, "he thus prayed to God: 'O Lord Jesus Christ . . . lead me, I beseech Thee, to the Chair of the holy Roman Church, that receiving authority there to preach with confidence Thy sacred truths, the Irish nation, by my ministry, may be gathered to the fold of Christ'; and soon after the man of God, Patrick, being about to proceed to Ireland, went, as he had desired, to Rome, the head of all the Churches, and having asked and received the apostolic benediction, he returned, pursuing the same road by which he had journeyed thither." [1]

It is certain that St. Patrick was consecrated bishop in the year that followed the failure of the mission of St. Palladius, but there is considerable controversy regarding the name of his consecrator, and the place at which the ceremony was performed. Unfortunately for the record of this event, it is one of the cardinal points in the strange discussion which has been started in modern times regarding

[1] Probus, *Trias Thaumat.*, p. 48.

the Roman mission of St. Patrick. An overwhelming array of ancient Irish writers are witnesses to the fact that St. Patrick received his commission from Pope St. Celestine : there is not a dissentient voice amongst them. When, however, we try to trace the steps of the transaction in the pages of his ancient biographers, we are embarrassed by a number of details relating to St. Patrick's pilgrimages, without dates or sequence, which appear to have been inserted on the principle that no fragments should be allowed to perish. On these the antagonists of the Roman mission have fastened, with the intent apparently of increasing rather than of diminishing the confusion. On this point it will be enough to say that, if not exalted criticism, it is something like common sense to hold that St. Patrick's clergy and converts knew very well how he came to be appointed supreme head of the Church in Ireland, and that they were certain to transmit the information correctly, and if the narrative of his consecration, in the words of Dr. Todd, is in some places "curiously lame," a proper allowance for what he styles "forgotten geography,"[1] and, we may add, forgotten forms of ancient names, will teach us more respect than this writer shows for such venerable relics of ancient literature.

[1] *Apostle of Ireland*, pp. 327, 335.

The following is the account of the event by an author whose arguments and conclusions hold together, because the study of the ecclesiastical records of his country is to him as simple as an investigation of a family history.   Cardinal Moran[1] agrees with the Bollandists in fixing the spot of St. Patrick's episcopal consecration at the modern Ivrea, styled *Eboria* by Fr. Colgan, *Ebmoria* in the *Book of Armagh*, and *Euboria* by Probus.

"John of Tinmouth writes that St. Patrick 'turned aside on his journey to a certain famous man named Amator, a chief bishop and Saint, and obtained the rank of bishop from him'.   Probus says he was 'a man of wondrous sanctity,' and 'a chief bishop'; and Maccuthenus, in the *Book of Armagh*, also styles him 'a wonderful man, a chief bishop'.

"Now, it is difficult to conceive a bishop so remarkable amongst his contemporaries, and so famed for his sanctity, and yet uncommemorated in the many records of the French Church about the year 430.   Neither in the synod then held in France, nor in the lives of St. Germanus and of the other great ornaments of France at that time, is there found any mention of his name.

"But if in Gaul, neither a town can be found to correspond with *Eboria*, as all acknowledge, nor a bishop who might answer for St. Amator, can such

[1] *Irish Ecclesiastical Record*, Oct., 1866.

a town and such a bishop be found in Italy? We unhesitatingly answer that they can. Indeed, as to the town in which St. Patrick received the intelligence of the death of Palladius, we precisely find at the foot of the Alps an *Eboria*, or *Eporia*, also styled *Iporia* and *Eporedia*, lying on the route from Ravenna (where probably St. Germanus then lived) to Gaul and Ireland. This is the modern town of Ivrea. Formerly travellers passed through it in journeying from Italy to Gaul. It was the route pursued by the army of Hannibal in olden times, as by the first Napoleon in the beginning of this century. What is more striking, it was the road hallowed by the relics of St. Germanus when they were translated with solemn pomp from Ravenna to Auxerre. We learn that from Ravenna they were first conducted to Vercelli, and there the presence of the angelic choir around the Saint's relics was said to have dedicated the newly-built cathedral. From Vercelli to Ivrea, and thence along the Alps, the triumphal route is marked by the many churches dedicated to St. Germanus, each of which was erected on the spot where his precious relics were deposited for a little while. Thus in the town and small diocese of Ivrea there are at present seven chapels bearing the name of St. Germanus, and marking the route taken in this sacred procession.

"It is, perhaps, no small confirmation of the

opinion that *Eporia*, or Ivrea, was the town thus
referred to by our ancient writers, that it brings
together, in one harmonious whole, all the elements
of their at first sight discordant narrative. We
understand at once how our Apostle is said to be
on his way from Pope Celestine when he received
in Eboria the news of the death of St. Palladius;
we understand how it is that St. Patrick's consecration is so emphatically described as having been
performed in a neighbouring town, *in conspectu
Theodosii, in conspectu Celestini*, and again *in
conspectu Germani*. There is nothing, indeed, to
prevent these accounts from being literally true.
The history of St. Germanus justifies the conjecture
that he was then actually at the Court of the
Emperor, who often journeyed to and fro from
Ravenna to the imperial city Turin, the *Augusta
Taurinorum* of those times. The Popes, too, are
often met with, even in the scanty records of that
age that have come down to us, visiting Ravenna,
the headquarters of the Western Empire, and other
cities of North Italy. . . .

Some one will, perhaps, say that there was no
Saint at that time in the north of Italy whose name
corresponds with Amator, or Amatheorex, remarkable for his learning and sanctity. We reply that
there was at this time the great St. Maximus ruling
the See of Turin, which city, in a straight course, is

not more distant than a few miles from Ivrea. The
name Maximus in the old Celtic form would be
precisely Amahor, and the transition from that to
the various Latinised names given above is easily
explained.

"From all this we may conclude that St. Patrick,
when he received intelligence of the death of St.
Palladius, was still in close relation with Pope Celestine, as also with the Emperor and St. Germanus;
that the town of Eboria, at which he had arrived
when the intelligence was brought to him, is no
other than the modern town of Ivrea, hallowed by
the memory of the other ornaments of the Church—
St. Malachy and the blessed Thaddeus; and, in
fine, that it was from the great Doctor of Turin, the
illustrious St. Maximus, that our Apostle received
his episcopal consecration."

The chronology of the life of St. Maximus is like
that of St. Patrick : it has to be put together with
the help of events, rather than of dates. His
famous Homilies, of which more than two hundred
have been collected by Migne, prove that he was at
Turin in 423, in the reign of the Emperor Honorius,
who in 404 had transferred the seat of the empire
from Rome to Ravenna, and that he was still on
the episcopal throne of Turin when Attila came
down upon Italy in 452. His exhortations to
his people on this occasion are impregnated with

that same spirit of immeasurable faith which distinguishes the writings of St. Patrick.

In St. Maximus, therefore, our Saint would find a kindred spirit : one who like himself was, so to speak, intolerant and jealous of human interference in the work of God. His advice to his terrified flock, when Attila was approaching, reads like a page from the Confession of St. Patrick : "We see you," he says, "fortifying the gates of the city ; but it is the primary duty of strengthening the gates of justice which presses on you . . . for it avails nothing to defend the walls with bulwarks, and at the same time to provoke God by sin ". The event justified the strategy of St. Maximus : Attila turned aside, and Turin was one of the few cities of Italy which escaped the ravages of the Hun who adopted the mysterious title of " the scourge of God ".

The episcopate of St. Maximus embraced many of those years which were spent by St. Patrick in his Italian pilgrimages. It is therefore probable that the two Saints were known to each other long before the date of St. Patrick's consecration.

As regards St. Patrick's consecration in Italy, it is absurd to suppose that the records of the Irish Church can be at fault. Objections grounded on obsolete and perplexing forms of the names of persons and places in old Irish manuscripts may be dismissed as instances of mere pedantic combativeness. In like

manner the supposition that his admirers were
driven to decorate St. Patrick with the character of
a Roman legate in order to support his authority
is utterly opposed to the whole tenor of St. Patrick's
acts. Ancient Irish writers are content to mention
the fact; for it never appears that they supposed
that the orthodoxy, or the mission of their miraculous apostle, could be called in question : people
do not inquire minutely into the credentials of
those spiritual ambassadors who raise the dead.
Whatever may be the difficulties of St. Patrick's
life, his Roman mission is not certainly one of them.
Without attempting to enlist that high-sounding
expression "unanimous" on our side, we may say
that ancient Irish writers who allude to the subject,
and the traditions of the Irish Church, undisputed for
ten centuries, all declare that St. Patrick received
his mission from Pope St. Celestine. We have no
reason to suppose that the decision of the Pontiff
was preceded by all those official forms which
attend the appointment of a metropolitan in our
own times. The episcopate was the only difficulty,
as we see from St. Patrick's writings : for the rest
his mission merely meant the apostolic blessing on
one who was about to go in search of martyrdom.

CHAPTER III.

THE public or missionary life of St. Patrick, on
which we are about to enter, introduces us to a
world whose characteristics are, in some respects,
even stranger than those supernatural events which
have been related in the first part of his life. We
can illustrate St. Patrick's personal relations with
God by examples drawn from the lives of other
Saints, even when we are compelled to look for
those prototypes amongst the Prophets and Apostles.
On the other hand, the rapidity, completeness, and
bloodless triumphs of his apostolate may be truly
said to have had no parallel in ecclesiastical history.

It will therefore be worth our while to inquire whether we can discover anything in the state of Ireland at the time which may be regarded as a providential preparation for a work which was altogether so divine.

If the object of all history is to get at the truth rather than to exalt individual heroes, the obligation is imposed with special strictness on the ecclesiastical historian. It is his duty, as well as his privilege, to summon witnesses from the past, who in their own day were unconscious of the importance of the evidence which they possessed. This assumption of judicial authority is doubtless beset with many snares; but from the worst of these, an insolent and domineering treatment of his authorities, the writer will do his best to keep clear.

The proposition with which he starts will surprise some of his readers. He believes, and hopes to demonstrate, that in the fifth century, amongst all the nations outside the sphere of Greek and Roman arts and legislation, pagan Ireland was one of the most favoured as regards laws, literature, and the arts of life. The common impression is certainly opposed to this view; but the subject is one in which common impressions are absolutely worthless, seeing that all authorities from the days of Petrie and O'Curry are on the other side;

and although it is a truism to say that the opinion
of one man who has mastered his subject ought to
go farther than that of thousands who know nothing
about it, in the peculiar circumstances of Ireland
it is well, here, vigorously and emphatically, to
insist upon the principle.

For many centuries, as regards her history, Ireland has occupied the place of the lion in the famous
moral legend of "The Lion painted by the Man".
Hence the revelations of her actual and authentic
history, as they emerge into the light, are so many
successive surprises to the literary world. Irrespec-
tive of its own intrinsic importance, Irish history is
interesting as an example of the judicial and avenging power of time. From the day of Henry Plantagenet—that is, for seven hundred years—England
has been before the world as spokesman for Ireland.
During that time middle-age literature has passed
into modern literature, and all the while Ireland has
had none of her own. In the great parliament of
letters she has not been represented, and it is
therefore not wonderful that her case has not
been fairly stated. Moreover, from the days of
Giraldus Cambrensis and Mathew Paris, the so-
called history of Ireland, as it went forth to the
world, was, in great part, written for diplomatic
purposes, and each falsehood became the parent of
a brood. Take, for instance, the "Spurious Bull of

Adrian IV.".[1] Without name of sender or receiver, unsigned, unsealed, and undelivered, it was worthless as an ecclesiastical or political instrument. Its venom, and that of other kindred forgeries, lay in the motives which were supposed to influence the Popes. Those epistles, well worthy of the title of *False Decretals*, that condemned the Church and nation of SS. Celsus, Malachy, and Laurence, once entrenched in the pages of the court historians of Henry II., became the text of honest, as well as dishonest, writers in subsequent centuries.

---

[1] Such is the judgment of his Eminence Cardinal Moran. To this great writer belongs the glory of being the first clearly to see, and to unveil, the absurdity of this fabrication. Before the Cardinal many had wondered, doubted, and too patiently endured the darkness. We have now a growing literature on the negative side. *Vide* Card. Moran, *Irish Eccl. Record* (Nov., 1871) ; *Analecta Juris Pontificii* (May, 1882) ; and three articles in the *Irish Eccl. Record* (Aug., 1885), by the present writer. In a notice of Jungmann's *Dissertationes Selectæ in Historiam Ecclesiasticum*, in the *Dublin Review* for January, 1886, p. 207, Canon Bellesheim of Aachen remarks : "Of still greater interest, perhaps, is the dissertation, occupying pp. 209-228, which discusses Henry II.'s claim to Ireland, and the Papal documents it was founded upon. Here we have the important question, Is Hadrian's Bull to be considered authentic ? German critics appear not to be at all favourable either to the Bull, or to the document in which Alexander III. is said to mention it (I refer to an able Article in the *Katholik* in 1864). Professor Jungmann's arguments produce the same effect on the reader's mind. He, however, refrains from giving an express decision against it. . . . I may, however, point out that the latter, taken in connection with the able articles from the pen of Father Morris in last year's *Irish Ecclesiastical Record*, Aug., 1885, seem to give a final negative answer to the long-agitated question whether or not Hadrian's Bull is genuine."

Now it is a reasonable inquiry to ask what the Irish monks, once the instructors of England herself and of a great part of Europe, were about all this time : was Ireland not fairly judged by default ? The answer to this question must be sought for in the history of the times, and the peculiar circumstances of the country give special importance to the explanation. Christianity had taken possession of Ireland as if it were a natural growth in the hearts of her people. There was none of that violence which in other countries turned the swords of the persecutors upon themselves, and subverted their national institutions. St. Patrick, and successive generations of Christian legislators following in his footsteps, built up society in Ireland on old foundations : clans, laws, literature, everything except religion remained as it was. When, therefore, her clannish or patriarchal system was stigmatised as barbarous, merely on the ground that it was unlike the military despotism of the Normans, Irish writers, supposing that they thought it worth while to answer the objection at all, could only reply that it was useless to dispute about a matter of taste ; while, as regarded results, it was plain that if the new Cæsarism had the best of it in the art of destruction on the battle-field, Christian civility had found a more congenial home and more docile instruments amongst the clans.

For nearly four centuries, from her conversion in the fifth until the first irruption of the Northmen in the ninth, Ireland presented a spectacle of spiritual and intellectual glory which without exaggeration may be styled unparalleled, if we confine the word to its literal and restricted meaning. If her history had had a counterpart, it would have obtained a much readier credence from an external and unbelieving public. As regards this period of Irish history, there is perfect unanimity amongst all historical writers who measure and value men and things by a Christian. standard. From Tillemont to Montalembert, Döllinger, and Cardinal Newman, all such witnesses agree, and draw a picture of the period in language coloured by an enthusiasm which would certainly discredit their testimony, were these writers open to the amiable suspicion of the colour-blindness of domestic prejudice.

In the ninth century came the Northmen. They came not from one point; not across one frontier: the ocean was theirs, and like a serpent their fleets folded the little island in their deadly embrace. Never was there such resistance against such odds; and, while the Northmen conquered Sicily, and Normandy, and England, Ireland kept up the struggle, and remained victor of the field, with a diminution, as it is computed, of five-sixths of her population. Churches, monasteries, and

learning were gone : all was lost save faith and
honour, and even these were seriously imperilled by
the presence of heathen foreigners, who, as a consequence of mixed marriages and other fatal alliances,
had been allowed to settle in the country.   Such was
the gulf of fire and blood which separated Ireland
from her former glories when the Northmen, in
another form, appeared again upon the shores of
Ireland, headed by Henry Plantagenet, the master
of the best part of the chivalry of France, as well
as that of England.

When, therefore, Giraldus Cambrensis, and
similar brilliant and accomplished political novel-
ists on the other side of the Channel, began their
so-called historical work, they had it all their own
way as regarded the past and present history of
Ireland, and, for the reasons already given, they
found it necessary to blacken the past in order more
successfully to defile the present.   Irish men of letters
did not answer, for very obvious reasons.   Few
remained to write, and fewer still in England were
ready to read any story save that which suited
their own purposes ; and thus, like the story of
Mary Stuart in her prison of Fotheringay, false
histories of Ireland went forth over the civilised
world, awaiting the slow but inexorable verdict—

" . . . Of time,
The old justice, who tries such offenders ".

The exuberance of the sources from which the history of ancient Ireland is yet to be drawn may be estimated from the fact that the two libraries of Trinity College, Dublin, and that of the Royal Irish Academy, contain 600 manuscript Gaelic works, which, if printed, would fill 30,000 large quarto pages,[1] and to these must be added similar almost unexplored literary treasures in the British Museum, the Bodleian, the Roman, the Burgundian, and other libraries at home and abroad. These works, so far as they bear on the early history of Ireland, may be divided into two classes—the Annals and the Historic Tales ; and, although they differ widely in their character, they are almost equally valuable in building up the early history of Ireland. No country can produce more sober records than those ancient annals of Ireland, whereas the Historic Tales are not unlike those modern sketches of St. Patrick and other Saints, in which facts are merely used as fuel for the writer's imagination, with this advantage on the side of the Tales, that they do not pretend to be history. The laconic simplicity of the monks who collected the ancient traditions of Ireland has laid a heavy burthen on those who set themselves to the task of completing their unfinished pictures, and

---

[1] O'Curry, *MS. Materials of Ancient Irish History*, p. 200.

this is true of Christian as well as of pagan times. When, for instance, we turn to the monastic *Annals of Ulster,* the following are the only entries, between 432 and 492 : the era of St. Patrick, in which the name of our Apostle appears :

" 432. Patrick arrived in Ireland in the ninth year of Theodosius the younger, and the first of the episcopate of Sixtus, the forty-second bishop of the Roman Church (as they are numbered in the chronicles of Bede, Marcellinus, and Isidore), and in the twelfth year of Laeghaire, the son of Niall.

" 439. Secundinus, Auxilius, and Iserninus, being bishops, were sent to Ireland to assist Patrick.

" 441. Leo being ordained the forty-second bishop of the Roman Church, the Catholic Faith of Patrick the Bishop was approved.

" 443. Patrick the Bishop, shining in our Ireland, amidst the fires of the faith, and doctrine of Christ.

" 492. Patrick, Archbishop and Apostle of the Scoti, went to his rest on the 17th of March, in the 120th year of his age, sixty years after his coming to Ireland to baptise the Scoti."

As has been observed, it must not be supposed

that such dry historic bones as these are all that we
possess of ancient Irish history. From the historic
Tales and Poems of the bards we obtain abundant
materials wherewith to clothe them with flesh and
blood.

The object of this chapter is to present the
reader with a very brief sketch of the state of
Ireland at the time of St. Patrick's advent, and this
by the combined evidence of annalists, bards, and
St. Patrick's own writings. It must be borne in
mind that the bards wrote in Gaelic, and St. Patrick
and the annalists chiefly in Latin, and that it was
only within the last thirty years that anything like
an exploration was possible in the interminable
catacombs of our ancient Gaelic literature. The
Franciscan Four Masters, and Father Keating, in
the middle of the seventeenth century, collected and
collated manuscripts while lying hid amongst the
mountains of Donegal and Tipperary, with soldiers
and blood-hounds on their trail. They did a
superhuman work ; but it is needless to say that
the treasures of Celtic antiquity laid up in the
strongholds of the dominant religion were not put
at their disposal. The time at length came when
the greatest scholars of the Catholic and Protestant
party found a neutral ground and combined, and
the world was electrified by the historical and
archæological discoveries of Petrie, O'Curry, and

O'Donovan, and if Dr. Todd had not written his *Life of St. Patrick*, he would have a still better claim to be numbered as one of the lesser stars amongst this band of scholars. It is the work by which he is best known ; indeed it is to some almost a popular text-book of Irish ecclesiastical history. It certainly contains a great deal of valuable detached historical matter ; but no one who knows anything about the subject can fail to observe that the book was written for controversial purposes during the excitement of the agitation on the question of the Disestablishment of the Irish Church, and that the dignitary of the Establishment fell into the snare of using a grave historic question in the interests of his party.

As history is based on authority, and as the most important part of this chapter is drawn from the writings of Professor O'Curry ; for the sake of the many who are strangers in the fields of Irish literature, it is necessary to show cause why we should accept his testimony. Although it would be presumptuous to give an opinion as to the comparative eminence of modern Celtic investigators, there is certainly one characteristic in which O'Curry stands pre-eminent. If the term philosophic historian may be applied to one who makes unadulterated historical facts coalesce and take life by their own inherent affinities, then O'Curry

certainly deserves the name. Other writers cultivated special fields of Irish Gaelic literature, but
O'Curry took in the whole. "He belongs," says
Mr. Matthew Arnold, "to the race of giants in
literary research and industry—a race now almost
extinct." Of his *Manuscript Materials of Ancient
Irish History*, Mr. Skene remarks: "For the
masterly and complete survey taken of the subject, as well as for accurate and minute details,
they are almost unexampled in the annals of
literature"; and in the same strain Dr. O'Donovan says of O'Curry that there were various Irish
manuscript authorities "unexplored by any but
himself".[1]

The personal character of a writer is of special
importance whenever he is dealing with subjects
in which he is supreme. In such cases he is a
judge; whereas, when they are already the common
property of many, authors are commonly little more
than commentators. The cordial admiration which
O'Curry obtained, from contemporary writers opposed to him on points which were very fiercely
contested, is a triumph which few men attain in
their own day. O'Curry occupied the chair of Irish
History and Archæology in the Catholic University

---

[1] *On the Study of Celtic Literature*, p. 28. Introd. Dean of
Lismore's book, p. lxxxvi. *Annals of Four Masters*, Introduction,
p. liii.

of Ireland at the time when Cardinal Newman was president.   In the preface to the *MS. Materials of Ancient Irish History* we have an account of the relations of those great men, which reveals the fact that the Cardinal was the first who accurately measured the gigantic intelligence of the humble Irish scholar.   The touching simplicity of the following passage, in which O'Curry dwells on his own deficiencies, proves that he was truly one of those who looked on himself as the servant, not the master, of truth, and that nature had taught him the lesson, now too often forgotten, that—

> "Study is like the heaven's glorious sun,
> That will not be deep-searched with saucy looks".

"The course of my studies in Irish history and antiquities had always been of a silent kind.   I was engaged, if I may so speak, only in underground work ; and the labours in which I had spent my life were such that their results were never intended to be brought separately before the public on my own individual responsibility.   No person knows my bitterly felt deficiencies better than myself."   He adds : "There was, however, among my varying audience one constant attendant, whose presence was both embarrassing and encouraging" ; and he describes his astonishment when this auditor, his illustrious president, informed him that not only had he found time to attend the lectures, but that in addition they were to be published at the expense of the University.[1]

Cardinal Newman was not a Gaelic scholar; still it must be borne in mind that the Lectures were delivered in English, and that critics who like the Cardinal possess the practised faculty of detecting historical and literary assumption and inconsequence can almost instantly take the measure of a writer or speaker from his style. It is not true to say that O'Curry's matter was strange to one who, perhaps, above all living men, knows how it is that the dead past speaks again to the dispassionate and patient listener. Armagh, and Durrow, and Clonmacnois, silent for centuries, were eloquent once more. Voices were heard which told as well of pagan as of Christian times, and the harmonies of nature and grace, and the triumphs of faith in Ireland were discovered to be identical with those which Pontus and Gaul witnessed, when Gregory and Martin were sent to those countries as the plenipotentiaries of a Divine Master. O'Curry was the representative of ancient Ireland at that memorable time when Christian Oxford, risen from the dead, went over to Ireland to be united, in the person of her greatest representative, with the sister on whom the tomb had never closed, and his commentaries on Irish history have for ever ex-

[1] *MS. Materials of Ancient Irish History*, Pref., p. viii.

9

ploded the grotesque historical inventions of Trinity College—an institution which never has had any Catholic traditions, and therefore seems incapable of comprehending them.

O'Curry believed that the Irish ecclesiastical chroniclers told the truth within the limits of human fallibility, just as Cardinal Newman and his school believed in St. Athanasius and St. Jerome ; and such writers have all that conscious strength which is derived from confidence in their foundations.

In all those departments of history wherein ecclesiastical writers are either witnesses for their own times, or a link with the past, Catholic students have a manifest advantage over their antagonists, arising from the fact that they believe in their authorities. Time was when this was deemed to be an essential condition in the composition of history. Although it is so no longer, in the case of many writers, it is evident that they are half-conscious of the insecurity of their position. Historians who, with Gibbon, include the monks and bards of Ireland in a common category as "the two orders of men who equally abused the privilege of fiction," can make little use of either ; so, by the help of probabilities, analogies, and suppositions, they set to work to produce something original of their own.

When the scholars of the revival at Oxford drew Church history from the writings of the Fathers, they allowed their readers to judge for themselves as to the probability of Saints and Fathers being either deluded or dishonest. In a similar manner, O'Curry deals with the writings of his own spiritual ancestors. He does not pretend to know facts better than they were known by eye-witnesses, and, therefore, his writings are free from that assumption of oracular infallibility which gives so strong a tinge of the ludicrous to the writings of many of his contemporaries.

O'Curry does not profess to do more than prepare the way for future historians, and it is probable that he himself had very little idea of the way in which his labours would light up the Christian history of his country. He found that for centuries innumerable works on ancient Ireland had been published which were worse than useless. Writing in 1862, he declares that, in order to get a correct idea of that history, "students must first cast behind them almost all that has yet been printed on the subject," by authors "who never took the trouble to learn to read the ancient MSS. . . . the flesh and blood of all the true history of Ireland ".[1]

---

[1] *MS. Materials*, Pref., p. vii., and p. 436. At p. 154 he gives an amusing account of a visit paid him, in 1839, by Moore, accompanied by Dr. Petrie. O'Curry had before him a number of dark and time-

Such being the state of modern Irish literature, it is easy to understand how St. Patrick's history was submerged in that universal deluge of historical inventions, and, as the waters have not yet quite subsided, the most serious difficulty in the way of his biographer is to know what his readers will allow him to take for granted. Hence the importance of getting hold of some well-established authority. No dispassionate reader who has gone through the three great volumes of O'Curry's works, with Dr. Sullivan's learned introduction, can resist the conviction that it is not the want, but the exuberance of ancient and authentic records which has oppressed and confused inferior investigators, and driven them to take refuge from study in the less laborious territories of theory and speculation.

The main facts of Irish history, as given by O'Curry from secular sources, in no way differ from the records of the ancient Irish ecclesiastical annalists. His greatest triumph is to be found in the way in which he makes the Ossianic Historic Tales and Poems fit in with these austere histories. As might be expected, chronology is the greatest difficulty in the history of a nation which had few permanent relations with neighbouring countries.

worn Gaelic MSS., which, when Moore had scanned, he turned to Petrie and said : "I never knew anything about these before, and I had no right to have undertaken the history of Ireland".

This, however, in no way weakens the evidence which he gives regarding the triple colonisation of Ireland by the Firbolgs, Tuatha dé Danaann, and the Milesians or Scots, the dominant race at the period of St. Patrick's advent. There is little doubt that, like the Irish, the Highlanders, the Welsh, and the Bretons of to-day, all three were of the same race and with a similar language, although differing in character and manners. This accounts for the ease with which they amalgamated and formed one nation. St. Patrick in his writings always calls Ireland *Iberio*, and alludes to the Scots as a race distinct from the Hibernians, or Irish proper. He wrote as one familiar with the domestic life of the people, while St. Jerome and foreign writers were only acquainted with the country as *Scotia*, and the people under the title of Scots, who were the latest colonists, and the race which, as we shall see, was always foremost in all foreign military enterprises. Some knowledge of the character of this regal and dominant race is therefore necessary if we would understand St. Patrick's work.

In entering on this question, the investigator on O'Curry's principle, must "cast behind him" almost all that has been written, even by venerable ancient authors, who had never seen the Scots at home. It must be remembered that Ireland was outside the Roman world until she was spiritually annexed by St. Patrick, and that neither Tacitus nor St. Jerome had more than the very vaguest idea of her internal state. The Scots were well known in Britain and Gaul, and as far as the Alps, but chiefly as desperate adventurers, the Raleighs and Drakes of the third and fourth centuries. Nial of the Nine Hostages (379 to 405), the king in whose reign St. Patrick was carried prisoner into Ireland, was slain on the banks of the Loire, and his nephew Dathi, who succeeded to the throne, was killed by lightning in the Alps (428) on his way to Italy; and this appears to have been the last historic outburst of the belligerent Scots.[1]

It is remarkable that the army of Dathi is said to have been composed of Scots from Caledonia, or Alba, as well as from Ireland. Celtic historians are now pretty well agreed that up to the period of St. Patrick's advent and the conversion of Ireland, the north-western provinces of Caledonia were practi-

[1] The account of Dathi's adventures is found in the tract entitled "Sluaghid Dathi co Sliabh n-Ealpa, or the Expedition of Dathi to the Alps" (O'Curry's *MS. Materials*, p. 284; *Manners and Customs*, ii., p. 59). The Abbé MacGeoghegan, chaplain to the Irish Brigade under Louis XIV., in his *History of Ireland* (p. 94), tells us: "The relation of this expedition of Dathy, mentioned in all the Irish writings, agrees with the Piedmontese tradition, and a very ancient registry in the house of Sales, in which it is said that the King of Ireland remained some time in the Castle of Sales". The officer who related the tradition assured MacGeoghegan that it was told to him by the Marquis of Sales at the table of Lord Mont-Cashel, who had taken the marquis prisoner at the battle of Marsaille.

cally annexed to the mother country. The separation, and even hostility, manifested in St. Patrick's writings between the Christian Scots of Ireland and their pagan kindred in Caledonia, is an extraordinary evidence of the revolution effected by the Saint's mission, which began just four years after the death of Dathi.

According to the same authorities, nearly a century anterior to this date, the first settlement of the Scots had taken place in Argyleshire,[1] under the leadership of Cairbre Riada, of whom Venerable Bede writes : "The Scots who, migrating from Ireland under their leader Reuda, either by fair means or by force of arms, secured to themselves those settlements among the Picts which they still possess". It is certain that it was the support of military contingents from Scotia Major which made the periodical invasions of the Scots so serious a trouble to the Romans in Britain. The Picts, as is evident from the *Life of St. Columba*, the best record we possess of their condition, were an inferior race, with apparently little organisation, and without national traditions, thinly scattered through the country ; whereas in Ireland there was an overflowing and very martial population. Venerable Bede says of ancient Ireland that, "for wholesome-

---

[1] Airer-Gaeidhil, the district or region of the Gaeidhil (O'Donovan).

ness and serenity of climate, Ireland far surpasses Britain. . . . The island abounds in milk and honey, is not without vines, and is famous for the chase of fish, fowl, stags, and roes."[1] At the same time all the ancient literature of the country bears testimony to her stores of wealth in gold and precious stones ; and strange as it reads now-a-days, it was the plenty and treasures of Ireland which attracted the hungry and avaricious Danes, three centuries after St. Patrick.

The study of the military organisation of the Scots gives us a curious and most valuable insight into the state of the nation at the period of St. Patrick's mission. No people have ever been perseveringly great on the battle-field who have not been at the same time distinguished by great national virtues : mere savage ferocity is self-destructive. Aubrey de Vere, with his exquisite and unrivalled perception of the ancient Irish spirit, observes : "The military rules of the Feinè included provisions which the chivalry of later ages might have been proud of".[2] We shall revert to this subject in noticing the Ossianic poems, and content ourselves here with quoting the four primary rules of the Fienè, or standing army of Ireland in the third century :

[1] *Eccl. Hist.*, Bk. i., c. 1.
[2] *Legends of St. Patrick*, Pref., p. xvii.

"There are four conditions which every man who was received into the Fianns was obliged to fulfil :

"The first condition was, that he should not accept any fortune with a wife, but select her for moral conduct and her accomplishments.

"The second was, that he should not insult any woman.

"The third was, that he should not refuse any person for trinkets or food.

"The fourth was, that he should not turn his back on (that is, fly from) nine champions."[1]

It was in Caledonia that the Romans first made the acquaintance of the Scots from Ireland; and the fact that they were there brought under the notice of Roman historians supplies us with some standards of measurement and comparison which are of great value in illustrating Irish records.

For more than four hundred years the Romans had held possession of Britain. Many of the emperors had visited the country, or commanded the armies which defended this important province of their empire; but during this period they had suffered Ireland to remain unmolested. It is strange that the Romans, so insatiable in their

---

[1] Keating ap. O'Curry, *Manners and Customs of Ancient Irish*, ii. 381.

thirst for conquest, should never have made an attempt to subdue that island whose mountains rose so near them in the west, especially when we consider how grievous and persevering a thorn it was in the side of the imperial Colossus. Tacitus tells us that Agricola, who governed Britain A.D. 78, had contemplated the invasion of Ireland, and that under an appearance of friendship he retained with him an Irish prince who had been exiled, in the hope of using him for his own purposes. Agricola's reason, says Tacitus, for urging the Romans to invade Ireland was that by its conquest they would strengthen their hold on Britain—when Roman armies were everywhere triumphant, and the dangerous example of liberty was taken away : *Si velut e conspectu libertas tolleretur*.[1] The event justified the foresight of the great Consul, and the trouble that Irish warriors gave to the conquerors of the world is not the least of their military distinctions.

Eight years subsequently we find Agricola face to face with a disciplined army of Highlanders in the Grampians, and in 207 the Emperor Severus followed the same foe into their fastnesses at the loss of 50,000 of his soldiers, leaving a permanent garrison of 10,000 men to guard the wall or line of fortresses which he erected on the northern frontier

---

[1] *Vita Agricolæ*, § 24.

of Britain.[1] At one time it seemed as if the Scots, with their allies the Picts, were in a fair way to get possession of the South as well as the North of Britain. In 368 they advanced as far as London.[2] The Roman legions, whose leaders were slain, gave way before them, and they were only driven back on the arrival of Theodosius with reinforcements from Gaul. But in 446 they returned, and then it was that the Britons appealed to the Romans for help in the well-known letter which begins : " To Ætius, thrice consul, the groans of the Britons "— going on to say : "The barbarians drive us to the sea, the sea drives us back to the barbarians ; between them we are exposed to two sorts of death— we are either slain or drowned ".[3] The Romans at this time were unable to defend their own capital, much less their provinces, so the Britons turned to the Germans. for help, and opened their gates to those Saxon allies, who soon proved worse enemies even than the Scots.

For nearly four hundred years Ireland kept up an intermitting contest with Rome ; and although the expeditions of one small island which borrowed nothing from other quarters cannot be compared to those barbarian deluges from the North, when one

---

[1] Lingard, *Hist. England,* vol. i., p. 46.
[2] Knight's *Hist. of England,* vol. i., p. 54.
[3] Ven. Bede, *Ecclesiastical History,* Bk. i., c. 13 ; ed. Giles.

horde pushed on another, they are an evidence of
the existence of that permanent and powerful military organisation which is recorded in Irish annals.
During these centuries Ireland possessed a numerous and well-disciplined national militia, whose
duty it was to hold themselves in readiness to assist
their countrymen in Caledonia (Alba) in any great
emergency. Their number throughout the country
may be estimated from the fact that in the reign of
Cormac Mac Airt as many as 7500 were stationed
at Tara.[1] In the *Annals of the Four Masters* we
find the following entry : " The Age of Christ 240
. . . the fleet of Cormac (sailed) across Magh-
Rein (*i.e.*, the sea) this year, so that it was on this
occasion that he obtained the sovereignty of Alba ".

It is strange that so little use has been made
of St. Patrick's writings as a means of giving
life to the pagan records of his time. It will
always be difficult to understand the history and
the manners and customs of a people who, in
a spiritual sense, have left no lineal successors.
If Christianity makes us strangers in the midst
of the Mahommedans and Buddhists of our own
time, much more is this the fact in the case of
nations of which the skeletons alone remain in
their dead records. In St. Patrick's time, and for
many subsequent centuries, there was very little

[1] O'Curry, *Manners and Customs of Ancient Irish*, vol. ii. 377.

comparative, or philosophical history written. Men described what they saw, or related facts as they were handed down from their forefathers, omitting the links which bound them together, which were manifest to themselves, but which we find it very hard to supply: facts which were well known being taken for granted.[1] Hence the importance of the testimony of a writer who looked on these things with eyes like our own, and made use of our modes of expression. St. Patrick was already old when he returned to Ireland. For more than thirty years he had been familiar with the features of Roman civilisation in Italy as well as Gaul, and therefore the incidental judgments on Irish life which are found in his writings are of immense importance in supplying us with something like comparative standards. He speaks of the people as made up of distinct

[1] Something like this is still found in remote districts of Ireland. The Irish peasant will take it for granted that the historical personages and events of his country, long before the Christian era, are known to everyone. Some years ago, as the present writer was walking amidst the glens of Sliabh Mis, near Tralee, he came upon a party of woodcutters, and an old man in the company remarked : " If you go up to the top of the glen, your reverence, you will see the marks of her heels on the flagstone ". " Whose heels ? " " Why, Scota's, to be sure," said he, evidently very much surprised at the question. Now we learn from the Book of Drom Sneachta, written before St. Patrick's time, that it was on this spot that, long before the Christian era, Eber Finn and Amergin, the sons of Milesius, defeated the Tuatha dé Danaann, and that their mother Scota, from whom the Scots derived their name, was killed in the battle.—O'Curry, *MS. Materials*, p. 448.

races (*Ibernas gentes*), and in two different places
of the "sons of the Scots" and the "daughters of
princes," in the same category, which evidently
implies that the Scots were a distinct class, and that
they were regarded as the nobility of the country.
He describes one Scottish lady whom he had baptised as *una Scotta benedicta nobilis, pulcherrima.*
Now it is plain from several passages in his writings
that he attached a very definite meaning to the
word "noble," and that by its application in this
instance St. Patrick meant to convey the idea that
this Irish lady possessed those graces of mind and
manner which are the characteristics of nobility.
Again, when he tells us of the gifts and ornaments
which the Irish women tried to force upon him,
even flinging them upon the altar (*super altare jac-
tabant*), he confirms the testimony of Irish writers
regarding their wealth and independent possession
of property.[1]

The value of these glimpses of Irish life in our
Saint's writings can only be appreciated by those
who have made some progress in the study of the
history of the times. His evidence is similar to
that of Cæsar in the case of Gaul. The Saint had
even better opportunities of observation than the
conqueror, and we find that intimate knowledge in
both cases was accompanied by respect and admi-

---

[1] *Confess.*, iv., §§ 15, 18 ; v., § 21 ; *Ep.*, § 6.

ration for the so-called barbarian nations. In the mouth of a Roman citizen the word "barbaric" often implied nothing more than that simplicity of manners which distinguished the young and hardy races of the North, as contrasted with the luxurious inhabitants of Greece and Rome. The immeasurable separation between Christian and pagan civilisation effected by monogamy, and the abolition of slavery, has given a meaning to the term very different from that which was attached to it in St. Patrick's time.

The comparative variety of the institutions of any country is a fair test of its intellectual growth, and tried by this standard Ireland in the fifth century held a high position amongst pagan nations. If the sword was the chief institution it was so everywhere; for in those days time was measured by battles, and history was written in blood. People who ran their eyes down the entries of the ancient annals of Ireland, after the manner of the investigator who, with the help of a card, slipped over the pages of the Bollandists, and found nothing in them, have come away with the impression that from the days of Cimboeth[1] to those of Lae-

---

[1] In *Irish Annals,* he is synchronised with Ptolomey Lagus, B.C. 289, and Tighernach fixes the reign of this monarch as the period at which Irish authentic history begins. *Usque Cimboeth omnia monumenta Scotorum incerta sunt.* "All the monuments of the Scots to the time of Cimboeth were uncertain."—O'Curry, *MS. M.,* p. 63.

ghaire and St. Patrick, the history of Ireland is little
more than a catalogue of wars, domestic and foreign.
We shall see that there is much more to be told,
and that what Edmund Burke, speaking of a later
period, calls the " interior history of Ireland," is to
be learned from the study of the writings of her
bards and legislators.

As we have seen, the Venerable Bede tells us
that in his time Ireland was more fertile than
Britain.   O'Curry and Dr. Sullivan supply us with
convincing evidence of her great agricultural wealth,
and of the existence of those treasures of gold and
precious stones which attracted the Northmen.   On
the evidence of a document of the fifth or sixth century, which gives the number of landholders at that
period in Ireland, Dr. Sullivan calculates that the
population was at least three millions.[1]   The number
is certainly large as compared with other countries
at that time, and explains the continual overflow of
population which took place from heathen as well
as Christian Ireland.   At the same time it is certain
that the country did not depend entirely on her
own resources for the support of her inhabitants.
Tacitus, writing in the reign of Trajan, some three
centuries before St. Patrick, tells us that in his
time Ireland was already known as a theatre of

---

[1] O'Curry, *Manners and Customs of Ancient Irish*, Introd., pp.
xvii. and xcvi.

commercial enterprise,[1] and we have every reason
to believe that the prosperity of the country
continued until St. Patrick's time, and that the
merchants from Gaul, with whom the Saint escaped
from captivity, were representatives of those numerous traders who in those days frequented the ports
of Ireland.

The intellectual development of Christianity in
Ireland was almost as wonderful as her rapid conversion. St. Patrick was hardly laid in the tomb
before legions of Irish religious teachers began to
spread themselves over Europe. St. Columba and
St. Columbanus both belonged to the first half-
century after St. Patrick's death. It is quite
possible to suppose a nation of rude savages
suddenly subjugated by supernatural powers such
as St. Patrick possessed, but that he should have
been able all at once to fit such a people to be
the instructors of Europe is more difficult to comprehend. This is the dilemma in which short-
sighted jealousy has involved those writers who,
for sectarian and political purposes, have devoted
their energies to the work of defiling the Irish
character at its fountainhead, and there is something like malice in the vengeance which outraged
history has taken on them.

[1] " Aditus portusque per commercia et negotiatores cogniti."—
Agricola, ch. xxiv.

If it were possible, it would be safer altogether to avoid the fascinating but slippery ground on which stands the cradle of the Scottish race. Ethnology is so complex a science, and shifts its ground so easily, that he must be a bold man who ventures positively to lay down its laws. The charm of O'Curry's writings, which bear upon this difficult subject, is found in the way in which he gives us documents and facts which speak for themselves. From these Dr. Sullivan proves that in pagan times there were in Ireland " two distinct types of people —one a high-statured, golden-coloured, or red-haired, fair-skinned, and blue, or grey-blue-eyed race; the other a dark-haired, dark-eyed, pale-skinned, small or medium-statured, lithe-limbed race ".

The celebrated Queen Meave, or Mab, whose glories have been sung by Aubrey de Vere, is described in the *Tain Bo Chuailgne* as "a beautiful, pale, long-faced woman, with long, flowing, golden yellow hair; upon her a crimson cloak, fastened with a brooch of gold over her breast". Again, the king, Conaire Mor, is depicted as " a tall, illustrious chief, with cheeks dazzling white, with a tinge like that of the dawn upon stainless snow, sparkling black pupils in blue eyes glancing, and curling, yellow hair," while his swineherds are " *Dub, Dond,* and *Dorcha,* 'black,' 'brown,' and 'dark'. Judging from the ancient tales, the ruling classes in ancient Erin appear to have had the same prejudice against black hair as the Norsemen had. All who claimed to be of noble birth should have fair, or rather golden-coloured, or at least brown hair, blue eyes, and a fair skin—three characteristics which are especially dwelt on in describing a warrior or king."[1] In our times, therefore, O'Connell, in his physical character-istics, might have stood for a representative of the dominant Scot of ancient Ireland, and Curran for one of the subject race. Already in those days race rivalry aspired to be scientific, and our ancestors, who ostracised dark men, were the worthy predeces-sors of those modern political ethnologists who are content to study the moral characteristics of the nations of to-day, by means of observations made amongst the bones of their forefathers. Those ancient Irish records read us some very wholesome lessons. When we find that the Irish Celts, the Greeks, Persians, Slavs, Britons, Gauls, Germans, and Scandinavians, were all originally one race, with a common language, ethnology is led back to its fountain in Genesis, and we are taught that national glories, whatever they may be, are to be attributed, not to the inherent superiority of any race, but rather to the very impersonal influence of circumstances.

Quietly, but irresistibly, the wandering science

[1] *Manners and Customs of the Ancient Irish*, vol. i., p. lxxii., &c.

of our origin is being led back to its fountainhead
in Paradise. Every day the evidence becomes
more convincing as regards the common origin
of those conquering Asiatic tribes who peopled
Germany, Gaul, and the neighbouring islands of
the Atlantic, and infused new life into the decrepit
Greek and Roman world. The ancient Irish
annalists describe one tribe, or rather family, the
Milesians, advancing westward, following the sun,
like their descendants in our own day, until they
reached Ireland. They tell us that they were
Scythians, a generic term used in the Book of
Machabees, and by St. Paul, to designate the people
of Northern Asia and Europe, and that on their
arrival in Ireland they found it already peopled by
the Tuatha Dé Danann, whom they conquered, the
latter having in their day subjugated the Firbolgs,
whom they found already in possession. At the
same time, it is very remarkable that the Milesians,
or Scoti, acknowledged that the Tuatha Dé Danann
were not only predecessors at Tara, but also their
superiors in learning, and the arts of peace.
M'Firbis gives an extract from an ancient Irish
work, composed before the introduction of Christianity, which not only confirms this fact, but also
seems to imply that it was from the conquered
race that the ministers of the national religion were
chiefly drawn. If this view be correct, it may

serve to explain the fact of the rapid conversion of the warlike chiefs, and the long continued opposition of the Priests and Druids. It also throws light on the remarkable fact, which will be referred to later on, that no representatives from amongst the Druids were present at the council assembled to assist St. Patrick in the revision of the Brehon laws.

In the *Book of Genealogies* above mentioned, which has been brought to light by M'Firbis, a comparison is drawn between the soldier and the professor of Druidism, which is anything but flattering to the latter. It is an example of that which is not uncommon in false religions, whose ministers are allowed by their followers to take a lower level in morals than that which they themselves adopt. The Scoti, or sons of Milesius, are described as " bold, honourable, daring, bountiful," while the Tuatha Dé Danann " are vengeful, plunderers, and adepts in all Druidical and magical arts ".[1] What Druidism and its arts were will probably always remain undetermined. There is only one religion which has a reasonable history, and knows the secret of its origin. Mr. O'Curry styles Druidism, or magic, " the very imperfectly investigated, religion, or philosophy, of the more ancient nations of the East," and he quotes the words of Pliny,

[1] O'Curry, *MS. Materials*, p. 223.

that " in Britain the magic arts are cultivated with
such astonishing success, and so many ceremonies,
at this day,[1] that the Britons seem to be capable of
instructing even the Persians themselves in these
arts ". At the same time, O'Curry concludes his
interesting chapter on Irish Druidism with the
remark that " there is no ground whatever for
believing the Druids to have been the priests of
any special positive worship" ; and he adds : " I
cannot satisfactorily specify the forms and doctrines
of our ancient system of paganism. . . . There
are some curious allusions to an educational connection with Asiatic Magi, in some of the stories of
the very early Gaedhelic champions, some of whom
seem to have travelled by the north of Europe to
the Black Sea, and across into Asia."[2]

Beside this gloomy current of primeval necromancy flowed another and a purer stream of heroic
human song. The spirit of Ossian, who represents
the chivalry of nature, was more akin to the souls
of the warlike Scoti, and, as it came to pass with
Clovis and his Francs, at the end of the same
century, the chivalry of nature in Ireland did
homage to sacrifice, and found its ideal of perfection
in the Crucifix. As we shall now see, it was
amongst the Bards that St. Patrick found his most

---

[1] *Circa* A.D. 60.
[2] *Manners and Customs*, vol. ii., pp. 179-228.

influential auxiliary. In the year 443, eleven years after his landing in Ireland, St. Patrick took his place in the great council which assembled for the purpose of remodelling the laws of Ireland on a Christian basis. Three volumes of these laws, from the MSS. of O'Curry and O'Donovan, have been published,[1] and they are one of the most remarkable evidences which we possess of the complete Christian conquest of Ireland by St. Patrick. From that time the *Senchus Mor*, or "Great Book" of the Brehon statutes, was known as the *Cain Patraic*, or " Law of Patrick ". If any proof were needed of its great antiquity at the time of its revision by St. Patrick, it would be found in the extraordinary minuteness and subtlety of its provisions. Indeed, in St. Patrick's time it is evident that the ingenuity of the lawyers had in course of time invented so many complications, that, like our own old Chancery law, it had expanded almost beyond the limits of human comprehension. It embodies a code of minute legislation, embracing offences as well against the reputation as the bodies of men ; taking account of injuries done by dogs and by the incursions of bees. At the same time we discern in this complex web of enactments an elevated spirit of natural justice, from which modern legislators might learn many useful lessons.

[1] *Ancient Laws of Ireland.* Dublin, 1865.

The weak are protected against the strong; the rights of women to their own property, even after marriage, are carefully defined; and homes are provided for the orphan, under the most minute and tender regulations.

The *Cain,* or " Law of Fosterage " (vol. ii. of the modern translation, pp. 147 to 193) provides for such things as the dress and food of children, according to their rank, and for their punishments, in the following words : " It is safe to strike or libel them, but so as no blemish or nickname has been given or a wound inflicted on the body ". Then it presides over their amusements and occupa tions. " Chess-playing, riding, swimming, are to be taught the sons, and sewing, cutting-out, and embroidering to the daughters." As examples of the *Cain Lanamhna,* or "Law of Social Connexions" (pp. 344 to 421), we may cite the following: " In the connexion of a woman on the property of a man, the contract of the man is good without *the consent* of the woman ; except *as regards* the sale of clothes and food and the sale of cows and sheep ". Again : " The woman may entertain half the number of the company of the man, according to the dignity of the husband of the woman ".[1]

The following is the account given by the Four

---

[1] *Ancient Laws of Ireland,* vol. ii., introd., p. lvi.

Masters of St. Patrick's share in the revision of this code :

" The Age of Christ 438. The tenth year of Laeghaire. The Senchus and Fienchus of Ireland were purified and written, the writings and old books of Ireland having been collected [and brought] to one place at the request of Saint Patrick. These were the nine supporting props by whom this was done: Laeghaire, *i.e.* king of Ireland, Corc and Daire, the three kings ; Patrick, Benen, and Cairneach, the three Saints ; Ross, Dubhthach, and Fearghus, the three antiquaries."[1] No mention, as has been already observed, is made of any minister of paganism, and this is the more remarkable as it seems quite certain that Laeghaire was not a Christian. The foremost spokesman on the Irish side was Dubhthach, the chief Bard. He was already a Christian, and in a curious poem prefixed to the *Senchus* he says : " I follow Patrick since my baptism ". The conversion of this extraordinary man was one of the most important events in St. Patrick's apostolate, and the ancient author of the introduction to the *Senchus* gives us the following account of the part which the poet played in the councils of the nation : " St. Patrick, after the death of his charioteer Odran, and the judgment

[1] O'Donovan's translation. O'Curry gives 443 as the date of this event.

which was pronounced on the case by Dubhthach
Macua Lugair, chief of the royal poets, and chief
Brehon of Erin, requested the men of Erin to come
to one place, and hold a conference with him.
When they came to the conference, the Gospel of
Christ was preached to them all; and when the men
of Erin heard . . . all the power of Patrick since
his arrival in Erin, and when they saw Laeghaire
with his Druids overcome by the great signs and
miracles wrought in the presence of the men of
Erin, they bowed down in obedience to the Word
of God and Patrick.

"It was then that all the professors of the
sciences in Erin were assembled, and each of them
exhibited his art before Patrick, and in the presence of every chief in Erin.

"It was then that Dubhthach was advised to
exhibit the judgments, and all the poetry of Erin,
and every law which prevailed amongst the men of
Erin, through the law of nature and the law of the
seers, and in the judgments of the island of Erin,
and in the poets.

"Now the judgments of true nature, which the
Holy Ghost had spoken through the mouths
of the Brehons, and just poets of the men
of Erin, from the first occupation of this island,
down to the reception of the Faith, were all exhibited by Dubhthach to Patrick. What did not

clash with the Word of God in the written law, and
in the New Testament, and in the consciences of
the believers, was confirmed in the law of the
Brehons by Patrick, and by the ecclesiastics, and
by the chieftains of Erin ; for the law of nature had
been quite right, except the faith, and its obligations, and the harmony of the Church, and the
people. And this is the *Senchus.* "[1]

In the concise and simple language of the antique
world this extract sums up the whole of our previous
argument. It tells of a nation which, up to the time
when Christianity was presented to it, retained
much of the simplicity of that law of nature, which,
while it " enlighteneth every man that cometh into
this world," is dependent on circumstances for its
development. The Brehon laws and the Ossianic
poems prove that the people to whom St. Patrick
preached were remarkable for their intellectual
activity, and for their adherence to fixed principles
of justice. Such endowments and virtues are gifts
from God, and must be regarded as providential
preparations for higher things. God has chosen the
weak as His agents in the propagation of the Gospel;
but it is also true that these agents have ever sought
out the strong in the intellectual and moral order, as
their most worthy antagonists. As the subjugated
philosophy and poetry of Greece and Rome became

[1] *Ancient Laws of Ireland,* vol. i., pp. 1, 9.

servants of the Gospel, so we need have no hesitation in attributing a similar office to the heroic literature of Ireland, which, in its native purity, approached nearer to the standard of original justice. The influence of national ballads is proverbial, and no nation was ever more swayed by poetry than ancient Ireland. The scope of its teaching may have been narrow, but it was none the less powerful in consequence. If it did no more than inspire chivalrous sentiments, and elevate the condition of woman, its work would be immeasurable. Now both these characteristics are found in ancient Irish poetry. The following lament of Chuchulaind over Ferdiad, his former companion in arms, whom he had slain in the foray of Queen Meave, is worthy of the best days of Christian chivalry :

> " O Ferdiad, treachery has defeated thee !
> Unhappy was thy last fate ;
> Thou to die, I to remain :
> Sorrowful for ever, is our perpetual separation.

> " When we were far away, beyond
> With Scathach, the gifted Buanand,
> We then resolved that till the end of time
> We should not be hostile to each other.

> " Sorrowful the morning—a Tuesday morning—
> That the son of Daman was bereft of strength.
> Alas ! I loved the friend
> To whom I have served a drink of red blood.

" Until Ferdiad came into the ford,
  Dear to me the beloved Ferdiad :
  It shall hang over me for ever.
  Yesterday he was larger than a mountain ;
  To-day there remains of him but his shadow."[1]

We are not concerned now with the artistic
and literary excellence of the Ossianic poems, but
with something more important. They are a
revelation of the ideas, the social relations, and
ruling principles of the time. In the fifth century they were the voice of the people's heart, like
the songs of the Troubadours, or Jacobite ballads.
Moreover, they had a sort of legal authority, as
the Bard, and the Brehon, or Judge, belonged to
the same order and worked together; and thus the
poet and the lawgiver in Ireland were often one
and the same.

Great, however, as was the power of the Bards, the
reader will hardly feel inclined to go so far as those
modern writers who have started the theory that
St. Patrick himself and Irish Christianity were
nothing more than evolutions of native poetic

[1] O'Curry, *Manners and Customs*, vol. iii., p. 445. Compare
Prince Henry's lament over his antagonist Hotspur :

" For worms, brave Percy ; fare thee well, great heart !
  Ill-weaved ambition, how much art thou shrunk !
  When that this body did contain a spirit—
  A kingdom—for it was too small a bound ;
  But now two paces of the vilest earth
  Is room enough."
                              —*Henry IV.,* v. 4.

genius. In the words of an eloquent representative of this school : "Patrick was but one of many prehistoric figures floating in the imagination of the people, and deriving life, colour, and movement from the Bards, the ever-ready exponents of the dumb wishes and desires of the people".[1] The ardour of this advocate of Christianity by evolution outstrips our present argument. The "dumb wishes and desires" of the people of Ireland for heroic ideals were evidently very strong, but the supposition that they were distinct and energetic enough to give "life, colour, and movement" to an archbishop of Armagh and an unbroken line of successors is certainly an exaggerated compliment to the poetic muse.

The fact is that poetry in Ireland, like poetry everywhere, was a very inconstant and inconsequent auxiliary of religion. It had more affinity to the Gospel in theory than in practice, and the Bards were as unwilling as other men to surrender power. So far, therefore, from St. Patrick being a hero of the Bards, it is evident from their writings that ere long they became jealous of his influence, and their struggle to preserve their dominion over the minds of the people supplies us with a very interesting incidental evidence of the authenticity of St. Patrick's history which, under the circumstances,

[1] *Dublin University Magazine*, March, 1876.

is of peculiar importance. The Bards were a powerful body in the century which immediately followed the death of St. Patrick : so powerful, indeed, that they became intolerable to the civil power, and their order was only saved from extinction by the influence of St. Columba, at the celebrated Convention of Drumceat, A.D. 575.[1]

This was the period at which the acts of St. Patrick were collected and made public. They appeared, therefore, under the eyes of a number of critics, who, as we shall see, had every inclination to act the part of *advocati diaboli*. The Bards, amongst their other avocations, were educated as professors of irony, and the ancient records of Ireland tell of many cases in which even kings had to give way before the withering onslaught of their sarcasms. When, therefore, we find that, instead of disputing the facts of St. Patrick's history, or the reality of his conquests, they are driven to fall back on lamentations and vituperation, we come to the conclusion that they had nothing better to say.

We must not suppose that Christianity all at once dethroned the ancient literature of Ireland. Indeed, we have direct evidence to the contrary, which proves that national traditions, enshrined in the writings of the Bards, became the stronghold of

---

[1] Lanigan, *Eccl. Hist.*, ii., p. 236 ; *Chronicon Hyense*, A.D. 575 ; *Life of St. Columba* (ed. Reeves), p. 334.

a long and jealous resistance. There were many
reasons for this. When the Christian religion sup-
planted paganism, it gave men something better in
its place. As far as their religious needs were concerned, it was all they wanted; but it made no
amends to them for the humiliation and reproof
which it gave to that ancestral worship which was
identified with the ancient glories of Ireland. With
his usual felicity, De Vere gives expression to the
national mind in his " Contention of Saint Patrick
with Oisìn ":

> "'One question, O Patrick ! I ask of thee,
>   Thou king of the saved and shriven :
>   My sire and his chiefs, have they their place
>   In thy city, star-built, of heaven ?'
>
> "'Oisìn, old chief of the shining sword,
>   That questionest of the soul,
>   That city they tread not who loved but war,
>   Their realm is a realm of dole.'
>
> "'By this head thou liest, thou son of Calphurn.
>   In heaven I would scorn to bide
>   If my father and Oscar were exiled men,
>   And no friend at my side.'"[1]

In the Ossianic poems, portions of which De Vere
has popularised, St. Patrick, with poetic licence, is introduced as contending with Ossian, who flourished
nearly two hundred years before the Saint. The
translation of the originals fills several volumes of

---

[1] *Legends of St. Patrick,* p. 107.

the *Transactions of the Ossianic Society*, and is probably as graphic and interesting an account of the struggles of expiring paganism as any country can produce. In Greece and Rome the gods were well-nigh worn out when Christianity made its appearance. In Ireland paganism was strangled by a giant, in the fulness of its life and vigour. The editor of the Ossianic transactions tells us that " there is reason to suppose that these compositions, in their original form, were coeval with St. Patrick's arrival, or immediately after ".[1] They are the work of many authors of very different merits, and one and all they need a poet like De Vere to give them the life of days long past. A few extracts will reveal the spirit which pervades them.

Ossian is represented alternately lamenting the old pagan glories of the past, or pouring forth invectives on their destroyer :

> " Sorrowful for me that the Tulach of the Fenians
> Is now under the bondage of clerics ".

Then having lamented the desolation of an ancient palace, over the site of which the chase now passes, he breaks out thus :

> " Thou man of the golden vestments,
> Who assumest the prosperous position,
> Happy for thee that Conan does not live,
> Lest his clenched hand might touch thee ".

[1] Vol. vi., p. 121 (n.).

Again, Ossian asks St. Patrick whether the heroes of his race had inherited heaven; and, on receiving an unfavourable answer, at first he mourns over them, then indignation masters him, and he tells the Saint:

> " Had Conan survived to my time,
> The foul-mouthed man of the Fenians,
> He would break thy neck
> For thy contention, O cleric ".

In another passage, on receiving a similar answer, Ossian replies—

> " Now on the virtue of thy white book,
> And the crozier which lies at its side,
> Under the chiming of thy high-sounding bells,
> Dost thou lie in what thou sayest ".[1]

These passages have no particular charm in themselves; even the poet cannot make vituperation attractive. They are very valuable, however, as a revelation of the nature of that intellectual resistance which was made to Christianity in Ireland, which was all the more prolonged in consequence of its peaceful character.

There is another characteristic of society in Ireland at this time which should be borne in mind when we come to consider the bloodless apostolic triumphs of St. Patrick in that country. Amongst her people, intellectual gifts appear to have been

[1] *Transactions of the Ossianic Society*, vol. i., pp. 69, 71, 99 ; vol. v., p. 121.

regarded with a religious reverence which it would
be unfair to call superstitious, seeing that it was the
simple-hearted worship of God's image dimly seen
in man. Cæsar, who got at the truth of things
more than most men, observed something very
similar in his time in Gaul,[1] and the conformity of
popular ideas in these countries is probably one
explanation of the striking resemblance between
the missionary career of St. Patrick, and that of
St. Martin, the apostle of the Gauls. In Ireland,
however, the honours which in Gaul were paid to
the Druids were extended to sages or philosophers
of every class. " The Ollamh, or philosopher,"
writes Mr. O'Curry, " when *ordained* by the king or
chief—for this is the expression used on the occasion
—was entitled to rank next to the monarch himself at table. . . . He was, besides, entitled to
a singular privilege within his territory, that of
conferring a temporary sanctuary from injury or
arrest, by carrying his wand, or having it carried,
around or over the person or place to be protected.
His wife also enjoyed certain other valuable privi-
leges. . . . Similar rank and emoluments were
awarded to the *Seanchaidhe*, or historian." And
he adds: " There is abundant evidence in the
MS. relating to this period (the authority and
credibility of which will be fully proved to you)

---

[1] *Commentaries*, bk. vi., c. xiii., &c.

to show that St. Patrick found on his coming to
Erin a regularly defined system of law and policy,
and a fixed classification of the people according to
various grades and ranks, under the sway of a
single monarch, presiding over certain subordinate
kings ".[1]

Those objectors are indeed frivolous who, in the
face of such evidence as this, fling the dust of Irish
battles in our eyes, and argue that because the
nation was warlike it must of necessity have been
uncouth and savage.   The history of the world is
against them.   King David was at once warrior
and poet ; and Socrates and Xenophon fought side
by side at Delium.   Whenever arms are a profession, then military discipline becomes one of the
most powerful factors in civilisation.   Moreover, no
men love their country so passionately as they who
are ready to bleed for her, and love of country is
love of the sanctuary of home and its treasures.
The soldier, with all his faults, is the representative
in the natural order of that sacrifice of self which
only needs a spark from the high altar of heaven
to become the heroism of the saint.   True courage
is always chivalry in one shape or another, and
ever does homage to weakness as to a sovereign.
Woman has ever been the representative of the
hardest battle of the weak against the strong, and

[1] *MS. Materials*, pp. 2-4.

she owes more to the sword than to the pen, the pencil, or the chisel. In every nation the heroic age of men has also been the heroic age of women. In the famous expedition already mentioned, which inspired the greatest of the Ossianic poems, Queen Meave is the central figure, and she is only one amongst many éxalted queens and heroines who brighten the pages of the romantic literature of pagan Ireland. That "Irish legend, with its morality ever so exalted and so pure,"[1] still flourished in all its original simplicity in St. Patrick's time, and a singularly chivalrous constitution of society in Ireland contributed to preserve that primeval chastity which Tacitus tells us was the glory of the barbaric races of Europe. Her insular position also protected her from the contagion which exhaled from the body of the dying Roman empire. Her sons were therefore strangers to the spectacle of those imperial and patrician orgies which defiled the cities of Gaul and Britain, and emasculated their inhabitants. Cloistered by the Atlantic, Ireland had produced generations of men of the stamp of Vercingetorix, Caractacus, and Clovis, and such men have always had mothers, wives, and sisters of the same stamp.

Of all providential preparations for the Gospel of

---

[1] "La legende Irlandaise, d'une moralité toujours si haute et si pure."—Montalembert, *Moines d'Occident*, iii., p. 109.

Christ, the social elevation of woman must be regarded as the most important.   It is from the altar
of home that the fire of heaven spreads over a
Christian land.   When St. Patrick had converted
those Irish women, whose number, he tells us, he
could not count,[1] he won auxiliaries who were
already conscious of their dignity and strength, and
prepared to assume the majesty and authority of the
Christian mother, wife, and sister ; and so the next
generation saw the sons of warriors elevated into
messengers of the Gospel of peace and love.

If the chain is a long one which binds Ireland to
St. Patrick, it is unbroken ; and thus the present is
the witness of the past.   Her title of "Virgin
Ireland, Island of Saints,"[2] is a summary of her
history for fourteen centuries.   Like the lily
amongst thorns, she has preserved her fair name
in morals as well as in doctrine, and purity has
multiplied the children of faith.   In our own time,
a renewal of that wonder which excited the admiration of St. Bernard has aroused the attention of the
world.   Millions have gone forth from Ireland to
plant the faith in the new world, or to revive it in
the old.   We may estimate the Episcopal Sees,
Vicariates, Apostolic Delegations, and Prefectures of
the Catholic Church at something over a thousand,

---

[1] "Nescimus numerum earum."—*Conf.*, iv., § 18.
[2] "Eiré óg inis na naomh."—O'Curry, *MS. M.*, p. 163.

and at least two hundred of these are found in
nations using the English language.   No hierarchy
of any race or language is so numerous, and no
other increases with such prodigious rapidity.
Pius IX. created thirty new bishoprics in the United
States of America alone ; and when we count the
number of prelates in that country, and in others
as well, who have received their faith itself, or their
flocks, from St. Patrick, we realise the place held by
the Apostle of Ireland in the Church of the nineteenth century.   " In the Vatican Council," writes
Cardinal Manning, " no Saint had so many mitred
sons as St. Patrick."   The vitality of nations, and
their promise of an imperial future, is an interesting
field of speculation, and they who forecast the
future by the help of the past will confess that,
amongst the conditions for national endurance,
there are none which carry with them such promise
as does fidelity to those moral laws which St.
Patrick so marvellously inculcated and established.

CHAPTER IV.

"PATRICK, A SINNER AND UNLEARNED, APPOINTED
BISHOP IN IRELAND"—LANDS IN WICKLOW—VOCA-
TION OF ST. BENIGNUS—ST. PATRICK REVISITS THE
SCENE OF HIS CAPTIVITY—THE DEATH OF MILCHO
—TARA—ST. BENIGNUS AND THE FIERY ORDEAL
—THE SHAMROCK.

WITH the year 432 begins the Christian history of
Ireland. St. Prosper, in describing the mission of
St. Palladius, tells us that "Palladius was consecrated by Pope Celestine, and sent as the first
bishop to the Scots believing in Christ".[1] Who
these Christians were it is impossible to determine.
No mention is made of them in the narrative of
St. Patrick's apostolate; and from the language of
all early Irish historians, as well as from the
incidental evidence in the Saint's own writings, it
is plain that before St. Patrick's advent Ireland
was a pagan nation from shore to shore. That
there were many foreign Christians in captivity in
Ireland is very probable, and it is not unlikely that
they had made some converts.

The return of St. Patrick to Ireland is one of

[1] *Chronica* (Migne, *Patrol.*, t. li., p. 595).

those events in the world's history, the full significance of which it has taken fourteen centuries to
develop. His history is an ever-increasing manifestation of prophecies fulfilled and divine promises
performed, when it is read in the light of his own
marvellous revelations. He came to Ireland with
a double commission; one direct from God, the
other from his Vicar on earth; and during the long
years of his probation the divinely-appointed
balance of these two ordinances had never been dis-
turbed. Obedience to the visible Church has ever
been the test of union with that which is invisible,
and the long-enduring patience of St. Patrick,
under the apparent opposition of a divine impulse,
and the restraints of authority, is one of the most
beautiful and instructive mysteries of his life up to
this point.

From this time forward, however, we shall meet
with very little evidence that St. Patrick had need to
look for advice or assistance from anyone save God.
We have indeed that remarkable entry, already
quoted from the *Annals of Ulster*, to the effect
that in the ninth year of his apostolate, on the
accession of St. Leo the Great, "Patrick, the
bishop, was approved in the Catholic faith".
Then, after an interval of nineteen years, in 460,
still in the reign of St. Leo, we find St. Mochta of
Louth, a disciple of St. Patrick, at Rome, where he

presented a profession of faith to the Pope,[1] which
was unquestionably an embodiment of the
" approved faith" of St. Patrick. This is, I
believe, all that has been told us regarding the
official relations of the Apostle of Ireland with the
Vicar of Christ. It is needless to say that the
silence of ancient records is no proof that other
messages from headquarters were not received in
Ireland in St. Patrick's time. It is incredible that
the young Church in Ireland, already known in
St. Patrick's time as the " Island of Saints," should
have escaped the vigilance of the five Pontiffs[2] in
whose reigns St. Patrick did his work. For twenty
years, from 440 to 460, in his own words, "Patrick,
a sinner and unlearned, appointed bishop in
Ireland,"[3] served under St. Leo. His " Catholic
faith " was " approved," and St. Leo's approval was
the first and last sentence which Rome has found it
necessary to pronounce in the matter of the orthodoxy of the Irish Church.

The hills of Wicklow were the first objects which
saluted the eyes of St. Patrick on his return to
Ireland, and authorities are pretty well agreed

[1] The MS. was discovered by Muratori amongst the treasures of
the Monastery of Bobbio, in Piedmont, the chief foundation of St.
Columbanus in Italy, and he agrees with Montfaucon in attributing
the MS. itself to the eighth century.—Card. Moran, *Essays on Ancient
Irish Church,* pp. 94, 296.

[2] Sixtus III., St. Leo, St. Hilary, St. Simplicius, St. Felix III.

[3] *Epistola S^{ti} Patricii,* § i.

that *Inbher Dea*, the mouth of the modern river Vartry,[1] in Wicklow, was the spot at which he landed. Wicklow had been the scene of the unsuccessful enterprise of St. Palladius in the preceding year, and at first it seemed as if a similar fate was about to involve the mission of St. Patrick. To Nathi, the son of Garchon, the territorial chieftain, belongs an unenviable distinction. He had driven St. Palladius from the shores of Ireland, and, in the first instance, St. Patrick was compelled to retreat before this ferocious enemy of the Christian name ; this being the only occasion mentioned in the life of the Saint in which he was ever known to give way to any force, material or moral.

It was to be expected that St. Patrick should follow in the track of St. Palladius. It was his duty to come to the assistance of those who had been converted to Christianity, if any such existed ; but as no allusion is made to them, either at this time or subsequently, by the Saint or his biographers, it is plain that the work of St. Palladius had come to naught. Hence, as Jocelyn tells us, it was a proverb amongst the Irish that, "Not to Palladius but to Patrick the Lord vouchsafed the conversion of Ireland ".[2] The account of the mission of St. Pal-

---

[1] It is remarkable how many local traditions about St. Patrick are identified with rivers and mountains, those natural monuments which time cannot efface.

[2] *Acta SS. Mart.*, xvii., cap. xxv.

ladius, already quoted from the *Book of Armagh*, is
written in the same strain : he is supposed to have
received nothing from heaven, and so he soon
departed from " the land that was not his own ".   St.
Patrick's proceedings, on the other hand, reveal that
there was no change in his determination.   Indeed,
it is not unlikely that his descent on Wicklow was
merely for the purpose of reconnoitring, and that
it had always been his intention to push on northwards, so as to commence operations in that part
of the country which had been the scene of his
captivity.

Leaving Wicklow, he set sail for the North, and
touching at Malahide and Holme Patrick,[1] he landed
in Meath, at *Inbher-Nainge*, the mouth of the
modern river Nanny.   It was here that, amongst
the first-fruits of his apostolate, if not actually the
first, God gave him his beloved disciple Benignus,
whose name will often meet us in the course of
this narrative.   The account of his vocation is
substantially the same in ancient records.[2]   The
Saint had lain down to rest by the river-side, and
as he slept, Benignus, who is described as a youth
of tender years, drew near, and collecting all the
fragrant flowers he could find, he placed them in
the old man's bosom.   Those who stood by forbade

---

[1] O'Curry, *MS. Materials*, p. 485.
[2] *Tripartite, Book of Armagh*, and Jocelyn.

him, lest he should awake the Saint; but he, rising up, and filled with the spirit of prophecy, foretold the boy's future greatness, and said : " He will be the heir of my kingdom ". Another writer, completing the touching record, relates how, when Patrick passed the night in the house of the parents of Benignus, the child would rest nowhere but at his feet, which he tenderly kissed ; and how, when the morning came, and the Saint rose to depart, Benignus again embraced his feet, and with many tears implored permission to follow him ; and that the Saint, blessing him, lifted him up, and from that hour he became the companion of the apostle in his labours and triumphs. It was because of his gentle and affectionate disposition that the other disciples [1] gave him the name of Benignus, or the " Benign ". He became the beloved disciple of the Saint, and was his successor in the See of Armagh.

From Meath St. Patrick proceeded on his way to the North, until he reached Strangford Lough, in Down, where he again landed. Here he was met by Dichu, prince of that province. According to

---

[1] *Tripartite*, p. 381; *Acta SS. Mart.*, xvii., p. 549. The *Tripartite* (p. 378) gives the names of Auxilius and Iserninus as ordained on the day of the Saint's consecration. The *Annals of Ulster*, under the year 439, states: "Secundinus, Auxilius, and Iserninus, being bishops, were sent into Ireland to the assistance of Patrick ". It may be that the two latter were with the Saint on his arrival, and then returned to the Continent, where they were consecrated bishops.

Jocelyn, he had received information of the arrival
of the Saint from the court of the chief monarch
Laeghaire at Tara.   There is a tradition that, some
years before, the King's Druids had foretold the
Apostle's coming, describing even his vestments
and tonsure, declaring that he would destroy
idolatry, and that the religion which he should
introduce would live for ever in Erin ; and whatever may be thought of druidical prophecies, it is
not improbable that at this time the ministers of
paganism in Ireland may have anticipated the
advent of those Christian missioners whose influence had been so destructive to the power of
their order in neighbouring countries.   Laeghaire
had therefore given orders that when this intruder
landed, he should at once be driven from the shores
of Ireland.   Accordingly, when Dichu's servants
brought the tidings of the landing of one whose
appearance seemed to correspond with that of the
prophet anticipated by the Druids, the chief descended to the coast.   At first, either from superstitious dread of the strange visitor, or disdaining
to draw his sword on an old unarmed man, the chief
set his dog at him.   Whereupon the Saint repeated
the words of the Psalm, "Deliver not up to beasts
the souls that confess Thee," and the animal stood
still, rigid as stone.   Then Dichu raised his sword,
but found his hand held in the air by the same

strange power; and fear brought light and faith to
his soul, and he was the first in Ulster who received
baptism from Patrick.

The Saint does not appear at this time to have
made any stay in Down, but steadfastly to have
set his face to the North.   One thought seems to
have urged him on, and to have given him no rest,
and this was his desire to see Milcho, his old
master : it was the man who had most wronged
him whom he most desired to save.   St. Evin
writes that Patrick took gold with him, that by his
gifts he might first win the heart of this man, who
was a great miser, and thus induce him to listen
to the message from heaven.   When Milcho heard
of the return of Patrick to Antrim, he appears to
have regarded his arrival as the beginning of the
fulfilment of that strange dream which had so
troubled him.   He could not have forgotten the
signs of supernatural greatness which had shone
forth in the poor boy whom he had so cruelly
treated ; but it was rage, the repentance of the
proud, which filled his heart at the thought of
having to yield to one who had been his slave, and
in a fit of despair he gathered all his treasures into
his house, and setting it on fire, perished in the
flames.   " Then it was that Patrick proceeded past
the northern side of Sliabh-Mis (there is a cross in
that place), and he saw the fire afar off.   He

remained silent for the space of three or four hours, thinking what it could be, and then said, 'That is the fire of Milcho's house, after his burning himself in the middle of his house, that he might not believe in God in the end of his life'."[1]

It was in 433, the year following his arrival in Ireland, that the Apostle was first brought face to face with King Laeghaire and the chief ministers of the religion then established in Ireland. When Easter drew nigh, the Saint, who was then at Slane, resolved to make an attack upon the reigning idolatry by celebrating the great Christian feast in the chief stronghold of superstition, Magh-Bregh, in Meath, near the royal residence of Tara. This was the time of the year when the pagans kept their great festival called the "Fes of Tara," and the subordinate kings and chieftains, as well as the priests and Druids, met at the court of Laeghaire. We may suppose that St. Patrick foresaw what the result of a victory of the faith would be in such a place, and under such circumstances, and how he might here strike at once at the superstition of the whole nation through its spiritual and temporal chiefs. He knew the risk that he ran, but he had come with his life in his hand for the sake of the Irish nation, and he was one of those who did not know what fear meant.

[1] *Tripartite Life,* p. 383.

The accounts given of St. Patrick's contests with the ministers of paganism at Tara are substantially the same in all the old lives of the Saint, though all are not equally minute. We gather from these narratives that while his success must be chiefly attributed to those prodigious supernatural powers which were his credentials as the Ambassador of Christ, there was something in the character of the people which prepared them for the Gospel. The honour they paid to learning was a sort of worship given to that which, in their eyes, was divine in man. They had the simple hearts of children ready to believe, and in their irresolute resistance we seem to see signs of a real though vague impression that there was a religion purer and more exalted than their own. It may also be that the traditions by which the Irish bards and historians had led the minds of the people back into an interminable past, while they preserved faint recollections of original truth, helped to keep them at the threshold of the invisible world listening for the voice of that unknown God whom, like the Athenians, they worshipped ignorantly.

The events now to be related are very strange and unearthly, very far removed from the common course and order of grace as well as nature. They are a revelation of the contest between the powers of light and darkness on a scale so gigantic that patience under the recital can only be expected from those who, in the matter of miracles and super-natural events, accept our primary principle that it is only the first step that can be really said to cost us anything. All writers of St. Patrick's life, like St. Gregory of Nyassa in the case of St. Gregory Thaumaturgus, must take the humble position of apologists; they cannot pretend that the evidence produced is on a par with that of a modern process of canonisation. The facts shall be given in almost the precise words of the authentic lives of the Saint, reminding the reader that "the very same scoffing temper which rejects the teaching of the Church, primitive and modern, concerning Satan's power, as 'pagan,' 'Oriental,' and the like, does actually assail the inspired statements respecting it also. . . . I have no wish to trifle or argue with subtlety upon a very deep subject. This earth had become Satan's kingdom. Our Lord came to end his usurpation, but Satan retreated only inch by inch. The Church of Christ is hallowed ground, but external to it is the king-dom of darkness. Many serious persons think that the evil spirits have even now extraordinary powers in heathen lands, to say nothing of the remains of their ancient power in countries now Christian." [1]

[1] Cardinal Newman, *Hist. Sketches*, ii., p. 109.

It was in Holy Week that our Apostle, leaving Slane, set out for Tara, and, arriving at a plain in sight of the king's palace, lit the Easter fire. Now, it was one of the laws of the festival which the pagans were then celebrating that upon this night the fires should be extinguished on every hearth in Erin, and death was the penalty if anyone kindled his own before the first fire lit in Tara was seen shining in the darkness of the night. "Patrick knew not this," says St. Evin, "and if he knew it, it would not prevent him."[1] King Laeghaire saw the sacred fire, and asked who it was that had thus violated the law. Then the Druids told him that if this fire was not put out before morning, it would never be extinguished, and that the man who had lighted it would be exalted above kings and princes. The king, infuriated at these words, mounted his chariot as the day was breaking, and set out to meet the Saint, at the same time declaring his determination to put him to death. When Laeghaire came in sight of St. Patrick and his companions, he was warned by his priests not to go near the fire, but to send for the Saint, and orders were given that no one should rise up to meet him. The servant of God was not slow in answering the summons of the king, and as he drew near he sang the Psalm, "Some trust in

[1] *Tripartite Life*, p. 385.

chariots, and some in horses; but we will call on
the name of the Lord our God ". The royal party
had dismounted, and, in the words of St. Eviu,
" They were before him, and the rims of their
shields against their chins, and none of them rose up
before him, except one man alone, in whom was a
figure from God, *i.e.*, Erc, son of Dega. . . .
Patrick blessed him, and he believed in God."

In the contest which followed, the Saint's chief
antagonist was Luchru, one of the heathen priests,
who had so deluded the people by his magical arts[1]
that they gave him something like divine honours.
We are told how he boasted that he had power to
ascend to heaven, and how, in the sight of all, he
arose from the earth; how the man of God,

[1] It is remarkable that a strongly-supported tradition records that
the first Milesian colony which, passing through Spain, found its way
to Ireland, halted in its migration westward for some time in Egypt,
in the age of the Pharaohs ("Celtic Ethnology," *Home and Foreign
Review*, Jan., 1864). That country seems then to have been the hot-
bed of magic and the black art, and it is therefore conceivable that
the descendants of the colonists retained a knowledge of Egyptian
necromancy, and remained under its influence until the arrival of
St. Patrick. Mr. O'Curry complains of the way in which this part
of the ancient history of Ireland has been handled by writers who,
on this point, as well as on the Roman mission of St. Patrick, have
managed to infuse a sectarian spirit into a purely historical question,
to the destruction of fair discussion and candid examination ; and
he observes of the opponents of this tradition that "not one has ever
ventured upon assigning any other origin to the peculiarly-
constituted race of the Gaedhil, at least none founded on anything
more than mere conjecture, and that of the weakest kind."—*MS.
Materials*, p. 446.

Patrick, prayed, and how his prayer brought the impostor down, and stretched him lifeless on the earth ; how the king and his people, maddened at the sight, rose against the Saint and made an attempt on his life : how he drew the sword of the Word and intoned the Psalm, "Let God arise, and let His enemies be dispersed, and let them that hate Him fly before His face" ; and how God heard His servant by sending a terrific tempest, which swept the plain, and, in the darkness and panic which ensued, the swords of the pagans were turned against each other. The queen, who was present, was won to the faith, and thus ended the first day of Patrick's struggle at Tara. Laeghaire, amazed but unsubdued, dissimulated, and asked the Saint to come to see him at his palace on the next day. Doubtless he thought, like Simon Magus when witnessing the Apostle's powers, that St. Patrick was no more than a magician, and that in the end he might find some way to subdue him. In the first place, he determined to make another attempt on the Saint's life, so with this design he posted men on all the roads which led from Slane to Tara. The Saint, to whom God had revealed the king's intention, took eight of his clerics and the boy Benignus to bear him company, and having blessed them, set out on his way ; and the soldiers of the king saw nothing but eight deer followed by

a fawn[1] passing them along the mountain.   It was
on this journey from Slane to Tara that the Saint
composed and sang that beautiful hymn of invocation known as St. Patrick's "Lorica," or Breastplate,
portions of which are still used by the Irish
peasantry in their prayers.

THE BREASTPLATE OF ST. PATRICK.

I bind to myself this day
The strong virtue of the
Invocation of the Trinity,
The Faith of the Trinity in Unity,
The Creator of the Elements.
I bind to myself this day
The power of the Incarnation
of Christ and His Baptism,
The power of His Crucifixion
with His Burial,
The power of His Resurrection
with His Ascension,
In virtue of His coming to the
sentence of the Judgment.
I bind to myself this day
The power in the love of Seraphim,
In the obedience of Angels,
In the hope of Resurrection
unto reward.
In the prayers of the Patriarchs,
In the predictions of Prophets,
In the preaching of Apostles,
In the faith of Confessors,
In the purity of Virgins,
In the deeds of holy men.

---

[1] In the *Lebher Brecc* (Whitley Stokes, Trans., p. 25) the words
are "one fawn with a white bird on its shoulder—that is, Benen with
Patrick's book-satchel on his back ".   The Saint himself was totally
invisible.

I bind to myself this day
The strength of Heaven,
The light of the sun,
. The whiteness of snow,
The force of fire,
The flashing of lightning,
The swiftness of wind,
The depth of the sea,
The stability of the earth,
The hardness of rocks.

I bind to myself this day
The Power of God to guide me,
The Might of God to uphold me,
The Wisdom of God to teach me,
The Eye of God to watch over me,
The Ear of God to hear me,
The Word of God to give me speech,
The Hand of God to protect me,
The Way of God to lie before me,
The Shield of God to shelter me,
The Host of God to defend me
Against the snares of demons,
Against the temptation of vices,
Against the lusts of nature,
Against every man that meditates injury to me,
Whether far or near,
Whether alone, or with many.

I have invoked all these virtues
Against every hostile, savage power
Warring upon my body and my soul,
Against the enchantments of false Prophets,
Against the black laws of heathenism,
Against the false laws of heresy,
Against the deceits of idolatry,
Against the spells of women, magicians, and Druids,
Against all knowledge which blinds the soul of man.

Christ protect me this day
Against poison, against burning,

Against drowning, against wounding,
That I may receive abundant reward.
Christ be with me, Christ in the front,
Christ in the rear, Christ within me,
Christ below me, Christ above me,
Christ at my right hand, Christ at my left,
Christ in the fort,
Christ in the chariot seat,
Christ at the helm,
Christ in the heart of every man who thinks of me,
Christ in the mouth of every man who speaks to me,
Christ in every eye that sees me,
Christ in every ear that hears me.

I bind to myself this day
The strong faith of the Invocation of the Trinity,
The Faith of the Trinity in Unity,
The Creator of the Elements.

Salvation is the Lord's,
Salvation is the Lord's,
Salvation is from Christ,
Thy Salvation, O Lord, be with us for ever.[1]

[1] The following account of the hymn is found in Father Colgan's
Latin *Tripartite Life* of the Saint, p. 126: "Thus did this wonderful man, with his companions, reach Tara, passing safe and un-
harmed through the midst of their enemies, the blessed child,
Benignus, all the while bearing on his shoulders the Book of the
Holy Scriptures; for, like a sacred shield, above them hung the
saving power of the prayer of the man of God. It was then that the
holy man composed in the vernacular the hymn, which by some is
called *Feth-fida*, and by others 'The Breastplate of St. Patrick,'
since held in great honour by the Irish, owing to the belief, which
experience has verified, that threatening dangers of soul and body
are averted from those who recite it with devotion."

Some trifling variations are found in the various translations;
but in all, Latin as well as English, the living fire of the original breaks
forth. It bears a striking resemblance to the "Canticle of the Sun,"
by St. Francis of Assisi. In both we find the same triumphant
assertion of the dominion of faith over matter, as well as spirit, with

On Easter Sunday St. Patrick arrived at Tara,
and appeared before the astonished king. The
pagans had resumed their festivities; Laeghaire
with his court was at table, probably seeking to
drown the terrible recollections of the previous
day, when, the doors being closed,[1] the man of God
appeared amongst them. The scene of the day
before was repeated; the king remained seated,
and all the royal party followed his lead, except
two, who rose to honour the Saint; these were
Dubhtach, the royal poet, and a tender youth
named Fiacc: with the former we are already acquainted, and the name of the latter, as saint and
poet, has become familiar in the Irish Church.
The circumstance that they rose to meet St. Patrick
is specially recorded, as to remain seated seems to
have been, in the customs of the country, the form
of protest against an unwelcome guest.

Patrick was then invited to eat, and was offered
a goblet of poisoned ale. The Saint blessed the
goblet, and turning it over, the poison alone fell

this difference, that whereas, in the mind of St. Francis, sun, stars,
and fire are his "brothers and sisters," St. Patrick summons and
"binds them to himself," as servants and soldiers of the Great King,
whose commission he bears.

Ussher says that the MS. of the hymn belongs to the seventh
century, and Dr. Petrie styles it the "oldest undoubted monument
of the Irish language remaining" (*Essay on Tara*, p. 55).

[1] The words in the *Tripartite* are "*Januis clausis ut Christus in
cennaculum*" (*sic*), "because Patrick meditated" (p. 387).

out in the sight of all.   When the party had arisen
from table they adjourned to a plain outside Tara,
and a great multitude went with them.   Here the
Druid Luchat Mael challenged the Saint to work
wonders before the multitude.   In the contest which
followed, God allowed the magician to exercise
strange and preternatural powers, which turned in
the end to his own confusion.   By his spells and
incantations he brought snow upon the ground up
to the men's girdles, and involved the whole plain
in darkness, but he could neither remove the snow
nor dispel the darkness, both of which disappeared
at the prayer of Patrick.   The king proposed that
they should both throw their books into the water,
and that whosesoever books came out dry should be
declared worthy of adoration.   Patrick consented,
but the Druid refused, saying that the waters were
Patrick's god, for he had heard that it was through
water that the Saint baptised.   At this the king
urged them to try their books by fire, but the
magician again objected, and said that this
Christian, in alternate years, venerated either a
god of fire or one of water.   The Saint, who at
first had shown an unwillingness to seem to anticipate the designs of God by demanding miracles,
saying, "I do not wish to go against the will of
God," was now inspired to make a proposal which
reveals at the same time the boldness of his own

fearless faith, and the power which he had of imparting it to others. He told his opponents that he adored, not any of the elements, but the Maker of all; and as an evidence that his God was the ruler of these elements, he made a proposal which nothing but a special inspiration could justify. He challenged them to raise a temporary structure, of which one-half should be composed of dry faggots and the other of green wood. Amidst the dry wood the boy Benignus, whom he loved, wearing the Druid's tunic, would take his place, if the Druid, invested with the Saint's *casula* would consent to bury himself amongst the green wood; then the structure should be set on fire, leaving it to God to defend His own. The faith of Benignus was equal to the emergency, and the Druid at once accepted an ordeal in which all the chances were on his side; and when the pagan priest and the Christian boy had entered the house, the door was fastened on the outside, and fire applied. As Patrick prayed, he guided the fierce element, which consumed the Druid, and the wet green wood around him, leaving the *casula* of the Saint untouched, while it passed through the dry wood, and, surrounding Benignus, only burnt the Druid's tunic which he wore. When the Christian boy came forth unhurt from the fire, while the smoke of the

magician's torments ascended to heaven, it seemed
as if the cause was finished; but it was not so; for
Laeghaire, irritated rather than humbled, like a wild
beast, seems to have lost his reason in his rage.

The concluding scene of this memorable day is
thus given in the Bollandists from Jocelyn:
"The heart of King Laeghaire was hardened
against the commands of God after the manner
of Pharaoh in the presence of Moses, for in spite
of all these miracles he did not fear to arouse the
wrath of the Most High God, or to irritate His
servant Patrick"; and again, with his followers, he
prepared to make attack on the life of the Saint.
"But the Omnipotent God, the supreme protector
and defender of His own, armed the zeal of the
creature against these senseless idolaters. For, in
obedience to its avenging Lord, the earth opened
and engulfed them, with many of their supporters,
from amongst the people of Teamhrach; as it is
written, 'Hell opened its mouth, and they were
taken down, as it were, in life'. The survivors,
and all that dwelt in that land, beholding and
understanding these things, being aghast and
stricken with a great fear, believed in Christ, and
came without delay to receive baptism, fearing
that a like punishment should fall upon themselves.
The terrified king, falling at the feet of St. Patrick,
implored mercy, and promised obedience for the

future to all his commands. The compassionate father mercifully forgave all the wrongs done to himself; but although he spent a long time in teaching him the faith of the Lord Jesus, he never could bring him to baptism. So the Saint dismissed him, that, using his own free will, he might go according to the inventions of his own heart, lest he should seem to compel him to receive the faith. Nevertheless, by an interior revelation he openly declared to him the things which were coming upon himself and his descendants. 'Because,' said he, 'you have ever resisted my teaching, continuing to cause me sorrow beyond all measure, scorning the faith of the Creator of all things, thou art a son of death, and with, yea, more than your adherents, you deserve even now to begin your eternal punishment; but as you have come to me humbly asking forgiveness, and since, like the King Achab, you have humbled yourself before my God, the Lord will not bring upon you at once the evil things you have merited, but none of your seed after you shall ascend your throne; your younger brother shall believe in my God, and his seed shall rule for ages.' The queen believed in Christ, and, receiving baptism and the blessing of Patrick, made a holy death in the Lord. Then Patrick with his followers passed through the whole country, baptising the believers in the name of the Holy Trinity, and God was his helper, and confirmed the word by the signs which followed."[1]

This is a rude picture, which at first sight seems to be very much out of proportion with the revelation which the Saint makes of himself. But after all it is true to nature. Heaven is often open over men's heads when the frenzy of their passions is wildest, like Raphael's picture of the Transfiguration, with Christ and the Prophets above in light, the Apostles overpowered by its brightness, and at the foot of the mountain the demoniac and the excited multitude. St. Patrick's Hymn is the best commentary on what we have just read. It rises even to a higher supernatural level, although, in condescension to the infirmities of his converts, the Apostle prays with them against such weak antagonists as the incantations of the pagan : the man who composed that Hymn was united to God, *consors divinæ naturæ*, in a way which no thoughts of ours can ever even approach.

Again, we recall his own amazement at the gifts of God, as the best proof of their immensity. " Who am I, or what is my prayer, O Lord, who hast thus laid bare to me such a plenitude of Thy divinity " *(tantam divinitatem)*. He is as familiar with the terrors of the Invisible as with the tenderness of the Incarnation, with the " Creator of the

[1] *Acta SS. Mart.*, xvii., p. 550.

Elements" as with "Christ in the heart"; and, without effort or violent transition, he reveals and reconciles the justice and mercy of God. It is from the Hymn that we learn how St. Patrick preached at Tara, and what it was that he preached on that memorable occasion, which may well be styled the birthday of Christian Ireland. As was natural, his awe-struck converts reported the signs and wonders, which to St. Patrick himself were matters of little importance when compared with those eternal truths on which they attended as witnesses. So we are not surprised at finding that the reporters of that eventful day, at least as far as we know, should have omitted to mention the part that the lowly shamrock was made to play in the great contest of Tara. If we had no image of St. Patrick other than that which is presented for our contemplation in the pages of the *Tripartite* and Jocelyn, we should find it hard to introduce the tradition that on this occasion St. Patrick taught men to read the mystery of the Holy Trinity in the simple form in which it is written on the triple leaf of the shamrock.[1] It is evident,

---

[1] St. Patrick's consecration of the shamrock has had its gainsayers. "This story," says Dr. Joyce, "must be an invention of recent times, for we find no mention of it in any of the old lives of the Saints."—*Irish Names of Places*, p. 54. The obvious answer is that there were very many things said and done by St. Patrick which were not written down. The tradition exists at Tara, and it is easy

however, from the Saint's writings, and from incidental allusions in his ancient biographers, that the doctrine of the Trinity was the one which he pressed with special force upon his converts, and in the account in the *Tripartite* of the discussion at Tara it is the only doctrinal question which is mentioned.

The following extract from the *Confession* tells us how St. Patrick taught men to believe in the Trinity, and how from that primal mystery he led them on to faith in the Incarnate Word:

"There is no other God, and never has there been, or will be, save the Lord, the unbegotten Father, without Beginning, from whom is all Beginning: for by Him have been made all things, visible and invisible [who has begotten a Son consubstantial with Himself], made man, drawn back to heaven to the Father when death was overcome. And to Him He gave all power over every name in heaven and earth and hell, so that every tongue should confess that the Lord Jesus Christ is in the glory of God the Father: Him we believe, and we

to conceive that it continued to be a local one until some unrecorded circumstance raised the shamrock to its present dignity as the national emblem. It is worthy of notice that in the modern Church of the Braid, at the foot of Slemish, we find an ancient stone font in the form of a shamrock, which is said to have come down from St. Patrick's time. It has been built into the wall to save it from marauding antiquaries.

expect His speedy coming as judge of the living and the dead, who will repay to each one according to his works : and He has poured into us, in its fulness, the gift of the Holy Spirit and the pledge of immortality. Who makes believers and subjects to be the sons of God the Father, whom we confess and adore, one God in the Trinity of the most holy name. . . . Without any doubt, in that day we shall arise in the brightness of the Son, that is, in the glory of Jesus Christ, and, all redeemed, we shall be, as it were, the sons of God and co-heirs of Christ, and made like to His image in the future. For from Him, and by Him, and in Him, are all things : to Him be glory for ever. Amen.

" Verily, in Him we are to reign ; for that sun which we look upon, at His command rises daily for our sakes ; but it will never reign, neither will its splendour last. Moreover, all those unhappy ones who adore it shall end miserably in tortures. But we believe and adore the true Sun, Jesus Christ, who will never fail, neither shall he who does His will, but for ever he shall stand, as Christ stands for ever, who, with God the Father Omnipotent and the Holy Spirit, reigns before all time, and now and for ever. Amen."

It is very remarkable that from this time forward the *Ard Righ* Laeghaire is almost entirely

ignored by the Saint's biographers. His reign was
prolonged until the year 458 — that is, during
twenty-six years of the most eventful period of
St. Patrick's apostolate. He makes his appearance
once more in 438, when he assisted with the Saint at
the great council of the nation, already described,
in which *Senchus Mor*, or great book of the Irish
laws, was purified and elevated to a Christian level
by St. Patrick. In the *Book of Armagh*, however,
there is an allusion to another attempt on the part
of our Saint to convert the king. " Laeghaire, the
son of Nial," says the writer, " had made a treaty
with him that he should not be killed in his
dominions, but he would not believe, saying : ' For
Nial, my father, did not allow me to believe, but
rather that I should be buried on the heights of
Tara, as it is with men who stand up in battle ' ;
for the pagans are wont to be buried in their
sepulchres with arms ready, face to face (with the
foe), until the day *erdathe* of the Magi, that is, the
Day of the Judgment of the Lord." [1] His wishes
were scrupulously carried out, and another ancient
writer tells us how " The body of Laeghaire was
afterwards brought from the south, and interred,
with his arms of valour, in the south-east of the
external rampart of the royal Rath-Laeghaire at
Temar (Tara), with his face turned southward upon

[1] *Lib. Armach.*, Fr. Hogan, p. 63.

the Lagenians—as it were, fighting with them ; for he was the enemy of the Lagenians (men of Leinster) in his lifetime ".[1]

This concordat, and the homage paid to St. Patrick's authority by this fierce king, is a remarkable disclosure of the Saint's success. It is clear that even at that time Laeghaire was convinced that Christianity was already in the ascendant, so, like many a sovereign in subsequent ages, the *Ard-Righ* of Ireland made peace with the spiritual power from motives of political expediency.

[1] *Leabhar na Huidre,* ap. Petrie, *Antiq. Tara,* p. 170.

CHAPTER V.

ST. PATRICK's success at Tara laid the country at
his feet. By attacking paganism in its secular and
religious stronghold, and thus breaking its power,
he won for himself a sort of sovereignty over Ireland, and from this time he met with little or no
resistance. It is no exaggeration to say that the
picture given of him in all the ancient records is
that of a conqueror subduing a nation in one battle.
When we remember his prodigious supernatural
powers, and that he came to a people to whom
everything about him was new and strange, we are
not surprised at the impersonal style of the old
lives of the Saint. It seems as if the profusion of
his miracles concealed the personal character of the
Saint from his contemporaries. If his life had been
more like that of other men, checkered by reverses
and disappointments, and if the proportions of his

supernatural character had been less colossal, we should probably know more about him; but, evidently, in the eyes of his followers he was more like some being from another world mingling in human affairs than a mortal man subject to the vicissitudes of life; so they chronicled his deeds without attempting to measure the man, looking at him in some such way as we may fancy men will regard Elias, the precursor of the second Advent, when he visits the earth again.

We shall follow the chronological division of the Saint's life given in the *Tripartite.* The first of the three parts into which this life is divided contains all the events already recorded; the second describes his journey into Connaught, and his work in that province, embracing a period of seven years; and the third gives us his return by Ulster, north and east, and his mission in Leinster and Munster, terminating with his journey back to Ulster, and his death at Saul, in the county of Down.

From Tara St. Patrick went to Telltown, in Meath, where he found Cairbre and Conall, two of the sons of Nial of the Nine Hostages, and brothers of the reigning King Laeghaire. Conall, receiving the Saint joyfully, was baptised, and at his desire St. Patrick founded the Church at Donagh-Patrick; but Cairbre, like the king, his brother, remained obstinate in his unbelief.

Passing through the western part of the territory of Meath, and preaching as he went, the Saint
arrived at "Magh-Slecht" (the plain of adoration,
or genuflections), in the modern county of Cavan,
which appears to have been the chief seat of
idolatry,[1] properly so called. O'Curry thus trans-
lates the account of St. Patrick's visit given in the
Tripartite Life :—" Patrick after that went over
the water to Magh-Slecht, where stood the chief
idol of Erin—*i.e.*, 'Cenn Cruaich'—ornamented
with gold and with silver, and twelve other idols,
ornamented with brass, around him. When Patrick
saw the idol from the water, which is named Guth-
ard—[loud voice]—(*i.e.*, he elevated his voice);
and when he approached near the idol, he raised
his arm to lay the staff of Jesus on him, and it did
not reach him, he bent back from the attempt
upon his right side, for it was to the south his face
was, and the mark of the staff lives in his left side
still, although the staff did not leave Patrick's
hand; and the earth swallowed the other twelve
idols to their heads; and they are in that condition
in commemoration of the miracle; and he called

[1] It is hard to determine the extent of the worship of idols in
Ireland at this time, but it does not appear to have been the prevalent superstition : no mention is made of it in the contest with
the Druids at Tara. St. Patrick alludes to idolatry once in the Confession, but, as we have seen, it is the worship of the sun which he
specially attacks.

upon all the people, ' Cum rege, Laeghaire '—they it was that adored the idol; and all the people saw him (*i.e.*, the demon), and they dreaded their dying if Patrick had not sent him to hell."[1]

It is very interesting to follow the great Irish scholar and critic just mentioned, as he identifies the very spot where the miracle took place, having found in the *Annals of Loch Cé* an account of the battle of Magh-Slecht, which took place A.D. 1256. He says: "Magh-Slecht (that is, the plain of adoration or genuflections), the situation and bearing of which are so minutely laid down here, was no other than the same plain of ' Magh-Slecht,' in which stood Crom Cruach [called ' Cean Cruach ' in the *Tripartite Life*], the great idol of Milesian pagan worship, the Delphos of our Gadelian ancestors from the time of their coming into Erin, until the destruction of the idol by St. Patrick, in the early part of his apostleship among them. The precise situation of this historical locality has not been hitherto authoritatively ascertained by any of our antiquarian investigators; but it. is pretty clear that if any man fairly acquainted with our ancient native documents, and practised in the examination of the ruined monuments of antiquity so thickly scattered over the face of our country—if, I say, such a man, with this article in his hand and an

[1] *MS. Materials*, Appendix, p. 539.

extract from the life of St. Patrick, should go to
any of the points here described in·the route of the
belligerent forces, he will have but little difficulty
in reaching the actual scene of the battle, and
will then stand, with certainty, in the veritable
Magh-Slecht; nay, even may, perhaps, discover
the identical Crom Cruach himself, with his
twelve buried satellites, where they fell, and were
interred when struck down by St. Patrick with
his crozier, the Bachall Josa, or Sacred Staff of
Jesus."[1]

Before leaving Cavan, St. Patrick founded a
church on the spot where he had overthrown the
idols; then, turning his face westward, he passed
over the Shannon into Connaught, near the present
Clonmacnoise. Here we find him again in relations
with members of the reigning royal family. Ethna
and Fidelm, the two daughters of King Laeghaire,
were living at Cruachan, the residence of the
kings of Connaught. This palace lay near the

---

[1] *MS. Materials,* p. 103. This crozier, or "baculus" as it was
called in the ecclesiastical language of the time, was said to have
been given to the Saint by our Lord Himself. It is mentioned by
St. Bernard, in his *Life of St. Malachy,* Archbishop of Armagh, as
being, in his time, one of the chief insignia of that See. It was plated
with gold, and adorned with precious stones, on account of the
tradition that the Lord Himself had fashioned it, and held it in His
own hands. So great was the veneration in which it was held, says
St. Bernard, that whoever possessed it was regarded by the simple
and foolish populace as the true Bishop.—*Vita S. Malachiæ,* c. xxi.

place now occupied by the village of Tulsk, in Roscommon, and two of the king's Druids, Mael and
Caplait, were appointed to guard and educate the
royal maidens.

The account of their interview with St. Patrick
supplies us with a specimen of his style of preaching
that is more in accordance with the spirit of the
Confession than any other of his recorded utter-
ances. The Saint's sermon, or rather catechetical
instruction, is given in almost identically the same
form in the *Book of Armagh*, the *Tripartite Life*,
and in an ancient Life of SS. Ethna and Fidelm,
in Father Colgan's Collection;[1] and as the latter
account is specially praised by this great authority
for its copiousness and exactitude, it is the one that
has been followed. , This writer tells us that St.
Patrick, on his journey westward, arrived with a
numerous attendance of clerics at a fountain called
Clibech, near Cruachan, where he halted, and with
his followers began to sing the praises of God.
From the narrative it would seem that they had
spent the night in prayer, for it goes on to say that,
as the morning dawned, Ethna and Fidelm, the
daughters of the king, arrived at the fountain.
They were filled with astonishment, supposing the
strangers to be beings of another world; but,
that there was nothing in their appearance or voices

---

[1] *Acta Sanctorum Hiberniæ*, Die xi. Januarii.

calculated to inspire terror is evident from the fearless bearing of the royal maidens. At once they began to interrogate the white-robed band, and asked them from whence they came, and whither they were going: whether they came from the spirits who dwell beneath the earth, or from those who lived in the heavens. Then says the ancient writer:

"Patrick, the glorious herald of Christ, answered: 'You have no need to be solicitous about our origin or the place of our abode. Better for you to inquire concerning our true and only God, the Maker of all creatures in heaven and on earth.' Then the elder sister said: 'Who is this God of yours, and where does He dwell? Lives He above the skies, or beneath them, or upon the earth?. In mountains or in valleys, or perhaps His dwelling is in the sea, or in the rivers? Has He daughters and sons whose forms are beautiful, is He rich in silver and gold, and does His kingdom overflow with all treasures? In what manner is He to be worshipped; as one in the flower of life, or as one laden with years? Has His life a fixed limit, or is it interminable?' Then the man in whom was the plenitude of God replied: 'Our God is the God of all things; the God of heaven and earth; the God of the sea, and of the rivers; the God of the sun, the moon, and the stars; the God of high mountains and of lowly valleys; the God who is above the heavens, in the heavens, and beneath the heavens. He has many mansions in heaven, on the earth, in the sea, and in all things that exist within their compass. From Him are the sun and moon, the luminaries of the world, and by Him is their light infused. His hand has brought forth the rivers and fountains from the earth, and the islands from the sea. He has a Son coeval with . the Father; for the Father is not prior to the Son, neither is the Son subsequent to the Father. Also, there is the Holy Spirit who proceeds from the Father and the Son, in the same eternity and equality, and these three are one, and inseparable. Wherefore, as you are daughters of an earthly king, it is fitting that you should lift your eyes from things that perish to those that are eternal, and that you should aspire to those espousals which last for ever in endless joys, rather than wait for an ignoble union with husbands from whom you must soon separate, or be separated.'

"Pierced by these words as if by arrows, the virgins, as it were with one heart and one voice, replied: 'In your compassion, teach us how we may obtain the favour of so great a King, and do His will, or see Him face to face, and whatsoever commands you impose upon us we will gladly obey '.

" ' Do you believe,' said the holy man, ' that by the power of so great a King all your sins and offences can be remitted by the pouring of water; or that if sins are committed after this outpouring, they can be blotted out, and atoned for by penance ?' And when the Virgins, anointed with the preventing grace of the Holy Spirit, replied that they were prepared to believe these, and the other mysteries of the faith which was preached to them, not only were they baptised by the holy man, but likewise, by the reception of the sacred veil from the hand of St. Patrick, they were still more closely united to the Heavenly Spouse.

"Then, as more and more ardently they desired to see the Spouse face to face, the holy man said : ' As long as you are clothed in this mortal flesh you cannot see the Son of God : before you can see Him in the brightness of His majesty, the vesture of this corruptible body must be laid aside. More-over, His Body and Blood, hidden and invisible under the visible form and appearance of bread and wine, must be first received.' At these words the virgins, burning with a still more ardent fire of love, earnestly asked that they might receive the Sacrament of the Body and Blood of Christ, and that, laying aside the burthen of the flesh, they might be transported into that Presence which, above all things, they longed to behold. The holy man, to whom the divine decrees were revealed, assented, and the virgins having received the saving Viaticum, lay down on the same couch, and, as if resting and sweetly reposing in the Lord, passed to that marriage feast of the Heavenly Spouse so ardently desired."

This narrative deserves special attention. It is the only complete specimen of the Saint's manner of dealing with gentle opponents which is found in his ancient acts. And yet such must have been the ordinary work of his ministry in an apostolic career which was bloodless. Like every event in St. Patrick's life which rises above the dead level of the natural order, doubt has been thrown on the authenticity of the story,[1] and we need not complain of this if objections lead to a more careful study and appreciation of its beauty. If we look upon the episode as altogether supernatural, then nothing more need be said on the subject; but this we have no right to suppose. It was a conversion which, in all essentials, was brought about according to the usual rules; and when the narrative is read with light borrowed from St. Patrick's writings and the

---

[1] Dr. Todd gives this "curious anecdote" from the *Book of Armagh*, with the cautious proviso "whether true or false," although he acknowledges that it "bears internal evidence of high antiquity; it was evidently written when paganism was not yet extinct in the country".—*Apostle of Ireland*, pp. 451, 455.

history of the period, the poetical form which it assumes becomes an additional argument in favour of its authenticity. We know enough now of St. Patrick to understand that his words and actions were heroic in the highest sense of the word, and such characters have always power to lift others to the same level. Sudden conversions, with the unhesitating acceptation of all the consequences of faith, have been phenomena of conquering grace in all ages. Such were those Saints without a name, the *Adaucti*, with whose commemorations the Martyrology is studded, who were converted at the mere sight of Martyrs on their way to victory, and by the baptism of blood became their companions. If even now the written words of St. Patrick are like a torrent of living fire in the heart, what limits can we place to the power that went with them, as they fell from the lips of one who seemed to his auditors to be " one of those spirits who inhabit the heavens "? When we compare St. Patrick's language on this occasion with his " Breastplate " and many parts of the Confession, we observe the same irresistible flood of exalted doctrinal ideas, which are so identified with his own thoughts, that they advance with a sort of rhythm and melody, like the *Charitas patiens est,* or the *Quis ergo nos separabit,* of St. Paul. St. Patrick's style is inimitable. As Tillemont observes, it is its own evidence ; and

we have here got a priceless revelation of the spirit
of our Saint.

At all times the effects produced by his words
depended in great measure on the preparation of
the minds of the recipients, and there can be little
doubt that the daughters of the king had quite
singular advantages in this respect. The interview
took place some time after the contest at Tara. St.
Patrick's fame must have been spread far and wide;
and although the royal maidens were at first in
doubt as to the identity of the mysterious strangers,
there can be no doubt that they soon realized
who St. Patrick was. We observe that when the
first impressions of superstitious dread had passed
away, the princesses begin the conversation with a
certain imperiousness of manner which was natural
in persons of their condition. It is evident also that
they were very ardent in their religious inquiries,
and that they were prepared for the discussion into
which St. Patrick led them. At their father's
court, and in the society of bards and Druids, they
had been accustomed to religious discussions, wild,
indeed, and fantastic, but for all that impregnated
with the pure and exalted morality of that *Legende
Irlandaise* which won the admiration of Montalembert. We have no more striking example than
this of the effect produced by Irish romantic and
heroic literature, on the minds of the women of

Ireland, and the conversion of Ethna and Fidelm was the type of myriads of similar victories of grace, which were sudden and perfect because God had already prepared the heart for the heavenly messenger.

All the ancient narratives tell us that the instructors of the princesses, Mael and Caplait, soon appeared on the scene, and the account given of their conduct is a remarkable illustration of the way in which, at this time, St. Patrick's supernatural authority seems to have quelled every idea of violent resistance in the minds of his opponents. These Druids were brothers, and Caplait, who was the first to arrive, wept bitterly, while he complained that St. Patrick, not satisfied with separating the king's children from the gods of their nation, should have also taken them away from the world. Before long, however, he and his brother were subdued by the Saint's words, and became converts to Christianity.

Leaving Roscommon, St. Patrick went up northwards to Sligo, baptising many on his way, and founding churches for his converts; then descending, he passed to the West, through Mayo, until he reached that high mountain, now bearing his name, which looks to the North on Clew Bay, and to the West over the Atlantic.

Amongst the many monuments built by Go

which St. Patrick has appropriated to himself, and on which he has set his seal, *Cruachan Aigle*, now Croagh Patrick, is the most eloquent in its abiding recollections. There we read his history in the pathways worn on its rugged sides by those pilgrims who, for fourteen centuries, have kept alive the memory of its consecration by the presence and the prayers of the Father of their faith. This mountain was the scene of that memorable prayer and fast of forty days, which has ever been regarded by St. Patrick's biographers as the occasion on which the Apostle obtained for Ireland the gift of perseverance in the faith. The appearance of Croagh Patrick, as we approach it from the east, reminds us of that other mountain in Antrim where first the Saint had learned the power of austerities and prayer. There is something characteristic of our Saint in the choice of such a place as Croagh Patrick from whence to lay siege to heaven; for from his youth he had learned to ascend to God on the wings of the elements. At Slemish, Tara, and Croagh Patrick we find the same revelation of the conscious and triumphant supremacy of his soul over the forces of the visible world. It is hard to tell how much of the details of what passed between God and His servant on this occasion are authentic history, for no one supposes that there was any human witness present at the time. It is

14

certain that for forty days and nights he was alone
upon the mountain wrestling in prayer with God,
who has made His omnipotence the servant of
prayer. No food or drink passed his lips, and his
heart was wrung out before the throne of God
while he prayed for the salvation of his people, and
the living fire of his words, now so familiar to us,
tell us what was the character of that prayer. It
is said that, while an angel acted as his messenger,
St. Patrick prayed and wept until his tears
drenched his monastic cowl, and that amongst
other petitions he prayed that the barbarian,[1] by
which is understood the unbeliever, should never, by
consent or force, hold Erin while he was in heaven.
Also, it is said that he made a demand, which faith
alone can appreciate, to the effect that seven years
before the day of doom the waters should cover
the island that he loved; and our Lord's words

---

[1] *Tripartite,* p. 415. In Mr. Hennessey's translation the term
used is "Saxon": Father Colgan makes St. Patrick pray against the
"barbarian". The Saxons had probably appeared off the coast of
Ireland before St. Patrick's time. The *Annals of Ulster* record their
first incursion in the year following St. Patrick's mission to Connaught (A.D. 434, Prima preda Saxonum in Hibernia). We may
suppose, therefore, that the words "Saxon" and "barbarian" or
"heathen" were used indiscriminately. Father Colgan, in a note
(*Trias Thaumat.,* p. 179), appears to interpret the words in a spiritual
sense, to which the more generic term "barbarian," as opposed to
Christian, is better suited, and adds: "Hitherto we have witnessed
their fulfilment, and so, we may piously believe, they will be for
ever".

explain the meaning of this prayer when He tells us that, *Unless these days had been shortened, no flesh should be saved : but for the sake of the elect those days shall be shortened* (St. Matt. xxiv. 22). Then, says the writer of the *Tripartite*, he claimed from God that on the day that " the twelve royal seats shall be on the Mount, and when the four rivers of fire shall be about the Mount, and when the three peoples shall be there —viz., the people of heaven, the people of earth, and the people of hell—I myself shall be judge over the men of Erin on that day". The angel said this thing could not be obtained from the Lord ; then Patrick said : " Unless this is obtained from Him, I will not consent to leave this Cruachan from this day for ever ; and even after my death there shall be a caretaker for me there". The angel went to heaven ; Patrick went to his offering. The angel came in the evening. " How now ? " asked Patrick. " Thus," answered the angel, " all creatures, visible and invisible, including the twelve Apostles, entreated, and they have obtained. . . ." " Strike thy bell," said the angel ; " thou art commanded from heaven to fall on thy knees, that it may be a blessing to the people of all Erin, both living and dead." "A blessing on the bountiful King that gave," said Patrick ; " the Cruachan shall be left." It was on Holy Thursday, according to

Jocelyn, that the Saint came forth from his solitude and returned to his people.[1]

> [1] "'That thou sought'st
> Shall lack not consummation. Many a race,
> Shrivelling in sunshine of its prosperous years,
> Shall cease from faith, and, shamed though shameless, sink
> Back to its native clay ; but over thine
> God shall the shadow of His hand extend,
> And through the night of centuries teach to her
> In woe that song which, when the nations wake,
> Shall sound their glad deliverance : nor alone
> This nation, from the blind dividual dust
> Of instincts brute, thoughts driftless, warring wills
> By thee evoked, and shapen by thy hands
> To God's fair image, which confers alone
> Manhood on nations, shall to God stand true ;
> But nations far in undiscovered seas,
> Her stately progeny, while ages waste,
> The kingly ermine of her faith shall wear.'
> . . . Then Patrick knelt, and blessed the land, and said :
> 'Praise be to God who hears the sinner's prayer'."
> —De Vere's *St. Patrick*, p. 49.

CHAPTER VI.

THE *Tripartite Life* tells us that St. Patrick went
three times across the Shannon into the land of
Connaught, and that he spent seven years preaching in that province, at the end of which time he
gave its people his blessing, and bade them farewell.[1] As those years were not consecutive, it may
be that, in the intervals, the Saint returned to
watch over his first converts in Ulster and Leinster.
The record of our Saint's labours in Connaught
occupies twenty-five quarto pages of Mr. Hennessey's translation of the above-mentioned life.
It gives us an account of his journeys, and the
churches he founded in Roscommon, Connemara,
Mayo, Sligo, and Leitrim, and this so minutely,
that the reader is perplexed, and finds it hard to

Tripartite, p. 432.

get a clear sight of the Saint himself amidst a maze of local references.[1] In like manner we can trace the Saint's course when, leaving Connaught, he went up to the North into Tyrone and Donegal; then, retracing his steps to Antrim, he descended to the South, passing through Louth, Kildare, Queen's County, and Ossory, until he arrived at Cashel in Munster. The writer does not mention the length of time devoted by St. Patrick to evangelising these counties, but as the life in this part is little more than a diary of the Saint's actions, if we measure the time by the number of events recorded, taking the seven years in Connaught as the basis of our calculation, we must conclude that several years elapsed before he reached Munster. The singular accuracy of the writer in naming places and persons, although wearisome, is valuable, as bearing witness to the veracity of the life. A great part of the record of our Saint's apostolate reads like an account of an ordinary bishop's visitation of his diocese. It is because he met with so little opposition that we miss in his life those struggles and alternations of fortune which make up the lives of other missionaries, and enable writers to give a distinct

---

[1] In the notes appended to the translation more than two hundred of the places consecrated by St. Patrick's presence in the course of his apostolate in Ireland are identified.

picture of their labours. St. Patrick in his work, as we have before observed of his personal character, is well-nigh lost in the blaze of his own glory. With the exception of the stern and obdurate Laeghaire, who so soon disappears from the scene, there is no formidable opponent to bring out the Saint's greatness, no background to the picture, which is consequently indistinct from its very brightness. For the same reason, there is little to say about the conversion of Ireland—less, perhaps, than of that of any other country. It was a campaign where all the victories were on one side.

In Munster, miraculous signs and wonders had prepared the minds of the people for the coming of the man of God. In the south of Ireland, the provincial king resided at " Cashel of the Kings," as it was then called, and thither St. Patrick directed his steps ; for it seems to have been his custom to seek out the rulers of the provinces which he entered, knowing that if he could win them over the people would more easily follow. Ængus, the prince whom the Saint found there, appears at this time to have been acting for his father, whom he ultimately succeeded on the throne. It is related that when the prince arose on the morning of the day of the Saint's arrival at Cashel, he found all the idols in the fort prostrate on the ground, and that, influenced, doubtless, by this sign from heaven, he received Patrick and his followers joyfully. While the Saint preached and prepared the people for baptism, Ængus stood beside him, and the sharp point of the sacred crozier, or "staff of Jesus," upon which the Saint supported himself, resting on the prince's foot, pierced it; but Ængus neither moved nor gave any sign of pain. When the blood flowing on the ground revealed the torture endured by the patient and heroic listener, St. Patrick asked him why he had been silent, to which the prince replied that he had supposed he was only submitting to one of the ordinances of the faith.

When we compare the account given by St. Evin of the Apostle's work in Munster with the earlier parts of the life, we are struck by the signs of that rapidly-increasing power which was so soon to make St. Patrick master of the country. We are told how the men of North Munster, to the north of Limerick, came in their boats, "a very fleet," as St. Evin describes them, and that finding the Saint at Terry-Glass, in Ormond, on the shores of Lough Derg, they were there baptised. Then St. Patrick ascended a hill at Finnine, north-west of Domnach-Mor, which commanded the view to the north of Limerick, and gave his blessing to the men of North Munster, and also to the islands, and the country north and west. From St. Evin's account, our Saint does not appear at this time to have entered Clare or Kerry,[1] but before he retraced his steps he prophesied of the saints who were to follow him, and carry on his work : of St. Senanus, " the green island in the West," said Patrick, " in the mouth of the sea ; the lamp of the people of God shall come unto it, who will be the head of counsel to this district—*i.e.*, Senan of Innis-Cathaigh[2]—six score years from this ". He also foretold the birth of St. Brendan, of the race of Hua-Alta, one of the greatest of the Irish monastic founders, in the century after St. Patrick.

St. Evin gives a graphic account of the enthusiastic devotion manifested towards our Saint by

[1] The writer is indebted to Mr. Hennessey for the following facts in support of St. Evin's statement :—" The tradition so widely known and so carefully handed down, that the churches founded by St. Patrick in the course of his itineraries were afterwards distinguished by the name Domnach-Mor (*Dominica magna*), receives some confirmation from the fact that, whereas there are churches called Donaghmore in the neighbouring counties of Cork, Limerick, and Tipperary, there is no place bearing the name in Clare or Kerry. Even at the present day, Irish-speaking people are often heard to say to persons situated to the west of them, ' *Bennaigim uaim siar sibh mar adubairt Naem Patraic las na Ciarraidib*' ('I bless you all to the West, as St. Patrick said to the Kerrymen ')." It is not improbable, however, that the tradition, that St. Patrick was content to give Kerry his blessing from the hill of Finnine, having its origin in St. Evin's words, refers only to St. Patrick's *first* journey to the south. Clare and Kerry may have been converted, and their churches founded by St. Patrick's deputies, and visited later by the Saint, during the long period which elapsed before his death.

[2] Scattery Island, at the mouth of the Shannon.

the people of Munster. "After that Patrick had founded cells and churches in Munster, and had ordained persons of every grade, and healed all sick persons, and resuscitated the dead, he bade them farewell, and left his blessing with them." When the people heard that the Saint had left them, they rose up like one man and followed him, overtaking him at Brosna,[1] in King's County, and filling the air with shouts of joy at seeing him again. St. Patrick blessed them once more, and continued his journey.

It is at this time, as the Saint passed through Leinster on his way to the north, that we find the record of the martyrdom of St. Odran, the only martyr of the Irish Church in St. Patrick's time. An obstinate pagan, named Foilge Berrad, had long nourished murderous designs against St. Patrick, the destruction of the chief idol of Erin, Crom Cruach, in the Plain of Adoration, having robbed him of his favourite deity : "for it was this," says St. Evin, "that was a god to Foilge".[2] He had declared his intention of assassinating St. Patrick, but St. Evin adds that, for some reason or other, St. Patrick's people said nothing to him concerning

---

[1] *Tripartite*, p. 476. St. Evin tells us that the name Brosnacha, now Brosna—from the Irish word *brosnugad*, excitement—was given to this place in memory of the event.

[2] *Ibid.*, p. 477.

the designs of the conspirator; perhaps experience had taught them that it was vain, or unnecessary, to warn their master against such dangers. We gather from St. Evin's narrative that St. Patrick sometimes travelled alone with Odran, passing swiftly through the country in one of the light chariots then used in Ireland, and that one day, when the faithful servant knew that they were likely to fall in with Foilge Berrad, he asked St. Patrick to change places with him, and take the reins; the Saint consented, and, by his stratagem, Odran won the crown of martyrdom, falling beneath the blow intended for St. Patrick.[1]

The foundation of the Church and See of Armagh is the next great event commemorated in St. Patrick's life, and in the course of St. Evin's narrative it comes almost immediately after St. Patrick's return from Munster. The territory of Macha, or Armagh, which was held at this time by a certain man named Daire, whom St. Evin styles a " prosperous and venerable person," seems to have been but a small one; at one time, however, it had been a place of great importance, owing to the neigh-

---

[1] Father Colgan (*Trias Thaumat.*, Notes to Fourth Life), following Ferrar's *Catalogue*, fixes the Feast of St. Odran, martyr, and disciple of St. Patrick, on the 26th of October. It is remarkable that the Protomartyrs of Ireland and England, SS. Odran and Alban, both met death in the same way, each offering his own life to save that of a priest.

bourhood of the fortress of Emania, the residence
of the kings of Ulster. The immense rath, or
mound, with its deep circular entrenchments, is
still to be seen, and in the middle of the seventeenth
century Colgan describes Emania,[1] " with its broad
trenches, and the rugged and towering ruins of its
walls," as still retaining signs of its former splendour. At first Daire refused to give the Saint the
land he had chosen, which was on a hill to the
north of the city, but he allowed him to build a
church lower down, where, according to St. Evin,
the Saint remained a long time. Daire had soon
reason to regret his refusal; he was seized with
sickness, which seemed unto death ; Patrick blessed
water, and sent it to him, and by its miraculous
power the sickness departed. Daire then sent the
Saint a thank-offering, in the shape of a brazen
cauldron, on receiving which he merely said, " Deo
gratias ". On the return of the messengers, Daire
asked them what St. Patrick had said; and, in
their ignorance of the language, they replied that
he had only said one word, *gratzicum.* Daire was
indignant at the Saint's indifference to his gift, and
ordered his servants to bring it back; upon which
Patrick again repeated, " Deo gratias ". When
Daire heard this he wondered much, and said,
" This is a good word with them; *gratzicum*

---

[1] *Trias Thaumat.,* p. 6.

when giving it to him, and *gratzicum* when taking it away from him ";[1] and he and his wife, touched by the Saint's patience, went to him and gave him back their gift, adding the grant of the hill which before they had refused. The *Book of Armagh* thus completes the narrative : " And they went forth together, both St. Patrick and Daire, to view the admirable and well-pleasing gift ; and they ascended the height, and found a roe, and a little fawn with her, lying on the spot where the altar of the northern church in Ardmacha now stands. And St. Patrick's companions wanted to catch the fawn and kill it, but the Saint objected, and would not permit them ; nay, he even took up the fawn himself, and carried it on his shoulders, and the roe followed him like a pet lamb until he laid down the fawn on another eminence at the north side of Armagh, where, according to the statements of those who are familiar with the ground, miraculous attestations are to be witnessed to this day."[2] It is the opinion of those learned in the topography of Armagh, that the hill on which the new Cathedral of Armagh is now built is the identical spot to which, like the Good Shepherd, St. Patrick carried the fawn—a touching image of that Church

[1] *Tripartite*, p. 484.

[2] *Book of Armagh.* Reeves, *Ancient Churches of Armagh*, p. 7.

of Ireland which for ages he has loved so tenderly,
and borne faithfully in his paternal arms.

The foundation of the Church and See of Armagh
was evidently regarded by St. Evin as the crowning
event in the missionary career of the Apostle of
Ireland.   At this point, therefore, we are obliged, in
imitation of this writer, to bring the chronological
part of our narrative to a close, devoting the
remainder of the book to the consideration of
separate incidents in the life of our Saint.

We observe that, although there is some discrepancy in the Chief Irish Annals as regards the
date of this event,[1] their silence about St. Patrick's
mission, from this period - until his death, is in
accordance with the style of the *Tripartite Life*.
All ancient Irish records point to the fact that the
spiritual conquest of Ireland was completed within a
comparatively short period of time, and that the

---

[1] The *Annals of Ulster* register the foundation under the year
444, and the *Annals of the Four Masters* in 457.   When we consider
how quietly institutions take root when there is no opposition, this
discrepancy will not surprise us.   Dr. Todd's suggestion (*Apostle of
Ireland*, p. 469), that we have here one of "the chronological difficulties created by the story of his Roman Mission," is a characteristic
specimen of his controversial insinuations.   The truth is, the supremacy of Armagh dates from the death of St. Patrick : the Apostle
himself was supreme, everywhere, and at all times.   The five
bishops who occupied the see in his lifetime were his subjects, and
there is nothing that is either suspicious or extraordinary in the fact
that the beginnings of Armagh should have left an uncertain mark
in history.

greater portion of St. Patrick's archiepiscopate was devoted to the consolidation of his work ; and if this was done rather by oral teaching and personal influence than by written laws, it only brings his government into a more striking conformity with that of Christ and His Apostles.

The event which drew from St. Patrick his celebrated *Letter to the Christian Subjects of the Tyrant Coroticus* now invites our attention. It merits careful study, for, like the *Confession*, in addition to its intrinsic interest, it contains many incidental allusions, which, when separated from passages which are devotional or hortatory, help us in our work of knitting together the fragments of St. Patrick's history.

Coroticus—or,. to give him his native name, Caradoc—was one of those marauding chieftains of the day who traded in human beings, after the manner of modern Arabs in Africa ; and at some period in St. Patrick's episcopate he made a descent on the Irish coast, and carried off a vast number of the Saint's flock. When and where he landed is unknown; all that seems certain is that he was a British chief, and that the incursion took place towards the termination of St. Patrick's apostolate. The narrative which is contained in the Saint's letter is merely incidental, as is natural when the facts themselves were before the eyes of the readers.   St. Patrick alludes to a previous letter, which, unfortunately, does not exist, which he says had been sent by a holy priest whom he had instructed from his infancy;[1] but the Saint's messengers had been treated with scorn.   No doubt the first letter was addressed to Caradoc himself, whereas the second, as Villanueva points out, repudiates all connection with the sacrilegious and excommunicated prince, and appeals to his followers.   The Saint first briefly states the case, in language which might be supposed to appeal to the consciences of Christians, as the mere fact of slave-capture would hardly shock people in those days.   He begins in a style which, with some variations, seems to have been his ordinary formula as an introduction to his ecclesiastical documents. "I, Patrick, an unlearned sinner, have been appointed bishop in Ireland, and most certainly I know that from God I have received that which I am.   Therefore, I dwell amongst foreign nations, as a pilgrim and wanderer, for the love of God. He is my witness that it is so.   Although I have no wish that anything rigorous or austere should fall from my lips, I am urged on by zeal for God and the truth of Christ, who has summoned me for the love of my neighbours, and of my children, for whom I have abandoned fatherland

[1] Quem ego ex infantia docui.

and kindred, and my own life I have consecrated
to God, even unto death, for the teaching of the
nations, if I am worthy, although now some despise
me.   And with my own hand I have written, and
confirmed these words to be written, sent, and
delivered to the soldiers of Caradoc; I say not to
my fellow-citizens, nor to the fellow-citizens of the
Roman saints, but to the fellow-citizens of demons,
who, because of their evil deeds, live in death,
making war after the manner of barbarians, the
companions of the Scots, and apostate Picts,
desiring, as it were, to fatten on the blood of
those innocent Christians, whom, in numbers beyond all counting, I have begotten in God, and
confirmed in Christ."

The Saint then draws a vivid picture of the out-
rage, which was perpetrated in the midst of some
religious ceremony—probably a confirmation, for he
describes the victims as anointed with chrism and
arrayed in white.   " Wherefore," he continues,
"let everyone who fears God know again that
they are separated from me, and from Christ my
God, for whom I am ambassador, as parricides and
fratricides, as ravening wolves, 'devouring the
people of the Lord as they eat bread'; as He has
said : 'The wicked have dissipated Thy law, O
Lord,' wherein, in these latter days, Ireland has
been most perfectly and mercifully planted and

instructed." Again, in the same strain: "Not
from myself, but God Himself has put this desire in
my heart, that I should be one of those hunters, or
fishers, whom of old the Lord foretold in these
latter days. He envies me, O Lord! what shall I
do? I am grievously despised. Behold, Thy sheep
around me are torn to pieces, and carried off
by the robbers already named, by the command
of Caradoc, Thine enemy: this betrayer of Christians into the hands of the Scots and Picts is
far indeed removed from the charity of God.
Ravening wolves have devoured the flock of the
Lord, which truly was increasing in Ireland with
the greatest rapidity and perfection; and I cannot
number the sons of the Scots, and the daughters of
princes who have become monks and virgins of
Christ. . . . It is customary with the Christians of
Rome and Gaul to send priests, who are holy and
fit for the office, to the Franks, and other foreign
nations, with many thousands of gold pieces for the
redemption of baptised captives. You slay them
without pity, or sell them to a foreign nation which
knows not God: you, as it were, deliver up the
members of Christ into a den of ill-fame. What
hope, therefore, have you in God?

" Whosoever agrees with you, or makes common
cause with you, by arguments adverse to mine, or
flattery, him God will judge. I know not what I can

add, or what more I can say concerning the departed children of God, who have been struck by that sword that was cruel beyond all measure. For it is written, 'Weep with those that weep'; and again, ' If one member suffer anything, all the members suffer with it'. Therefore the Church weeps, and bewails her sons and daughters, whom as yet the sword of the enemy has spared, and who have been transported to distant lands, where sin is open and shameless : there the lawless one dwells, and is filled : there free-born Christians are sold and reduced to slavery, especially amongst the most unworthy, the most infamous and apostate Picts.

"Therefore, I cry out in grief and sorrow : O most beautiful and most loving brethren and children, whom, in Christ, I have begotten in such multitudes that I cannot number you, what shall I do for you ? "

These extracts demand some commentary. In the first place, we see that St. Patrick was himself conscious of a divine power that went out from him, in addition to his purely ecclesiastical authority. It is the very obscurity and incoherence of his style which impress us with conviction that his language is the voice of prophecy and inspiration, and that his soul was the dwelling-place of some power which overflowed and broke down all the barriers of human language ; while complaints of outrages done to God, and wrongs to himself, are mingled together with that inimitable simplicity which reveals that, like St. Paul, he no longer lived, but Christ lived in him. The historical revelations of this letter are also most interesting. The allusion to the Franks as heathens reminds us that Ireland was already a Christian nation at a time when the ancestors of Charlemagne were still pagans.[1]

The appearance on the scene of the Scots of Caledonia, and the Picts as enemies of the Irish Scots, reveals the complete separation which Christianity had wrought between the Scots abroad and their parent country, which continued until Ireland sent St. Columba in search of her lost children. The abhorrence manifested by St. Patrick for the Picts is also very remarkable. The mere fact that they were heathens could not possibly excite such feelings in the mind of an apostle, although it is clear from the *Life of St. Columba* that they were an inferior race as compared with the Scots. St. Patrick's horror of the nation must, therefore, be attributed to their apostasy; and, as Dr. Lanigan remarks, this stain rested only on the Southern Picts, who, in St. Patrick's own lifetime, had been

---

[1] The conversion of the Franks dates from the year 496, when, four years after the death of St. Patrick, Clovis was baptised by St. Remigius.

converted to Christianity by St. Ninian, and subsequently relapsed into idolatry. At this time the Picts, united with the pagan Scots from Argyleshire, were ravaging Britain, and so Caradoc had a market close at hand for the sale of his captives.

We have no record of the effect of St. Patrick's appeal, further than the statement which is found in three of the ancient lives in Father Colgan, to the effect that God punished Caradoc after the manner of the malediction which fell upon the proud king of Babylon. On a certain day, we are told, as he stood in the midst of his attendants, suddenly, in the sight of all, he was seen to take the shape of a wolf, and in this guise he fled from the face of men. Villanueva has a long disputation on the credibility of the miracle. Some writers are very much shocked at the idea, as if it were St. Patrick's own act, which it certainly was not; but Jocelyn is satisfied with remarking that "this fact no one can lawfully discredit who will read the narrative of the wife of Lot, turned into a rock, and that of king Nabuchodonozor".

CHAPTER VII.

OF ST. PATRICK'S FAITH AND HOW HE IMPARTED IT TO OTHER MEN.

THE reader must have already observed that it is easier to get an idea of what St. Patrick was than of what he did. Statistics without dates are always unsatisfactory, and they are peculiarly so in a missionary career which embraced the lifetime of well-nigh three generations. It is possible that records will yet be brought to light which will enable the historian to complete the picture of the conversion of Ireland, but in the present state of our knowledge the writer feels that he is inadequate to the task. As it is, he is conscious that he has again and again tried the reader's patience by repetitions, especially in cases where some sentence in St. Patrick's writings has been made to do duty in commenting on different events in the Saint's life. He hopes, however, that this literary imperfection will be condoned by those who, like himself, in the study of St. Patrick's life, are looking, not for pleasure, but for light. In obedience to this principle, he will devote the remainder of the work to a commentary on St. Patrick's virtues, with illustrations given, as far as possible, in the antique style of his ancient biographers.

Our Lord's promise that "All things whatsoever you ask when you pray, believe that you shall re- ceive, and it shall come unto you," was wonderfully fulfilled in the Blessed Patrick. If we may estimate his faith by his works, we shall be inclined to consider it to have been his predominant virtue. Faith belongs to this world : it has no place in heaven. Consequently, it seems to have a special reward and glory in time ; for it appears to be almost an unvarying law in God's government of the world that spiritual power on earth is attributed to faith. We have seen the Saint's enduring faith in his prayer on Croagh Patrick, in that trial of strength with God which has been called "the striving of St. Patrick," for, like Jacob, he wrestled with God, and in the end obtained what he desired. It is this spirit of superhuman faith revealed in his writings which has led so cautious a writer as Tillemont to compare him with the inspired Prophets and Apostles, and especially with St. Paul. The extracts from the Saint's *Confession*, in the beginning of this life, give us a picture of enduring faith in the soul of a boy, more wonderful than miracles. He tells us how, alone upon the moun-

tain-side, in the silence of the night, the faith, and
the fear of God grew within him, and how, without priest or sacrament, during those six years of
slavery, his soul remained in constant union with
God. His faith was tried, and its enduring patience
manifested in a probation of more than thirty years,
during which he awaited that mission to Ireland
which he so ardently desired. A vision from
heaven, in his youth, brought to him from afar
"the voice of the Irish," but he was an old man
before God allowed him to begin his work. In his
humility he styled himself "an ignorant sinner,"
"a fool," "the rudest and least of the faithful";
but, when he spoke in the name of God, faith gave
him majesty and authority, and he became in very
truth that which he announced himself to be, "the
Ambassador of Christ". There was a vehemence,
a sacred intolerance in his faith, which swept away
all obstacles; it made him a stranger to respect of
persons; he spoke as one conscious that he came
with a message direct from God, and faith made all
men equal in his eyes. It was this sense of his
mission, and the conviction that "he could do all
things in Him who strengthened him," which gave
his apostolate its peculiar character. He seems to
have seldom sought to persuade—he subdued men
by the intensity of his own faith.

We have a striking instance of the way in which

he infused this faith, and took instantaneous possession of souls, in the conversion and penance of the robber chief MacKyle, afterwards a Saint and bishop. This man and his band were the scourge of Ulster, and when he heard of the arrival of the Saint in the neighbourhood, his first thought was to make away with the priest whose teaching brought such shame on his own unholy trade ; but, bad and bloodthirsty as he was, some sort of wild chivalry in his heart restrained him. He therefore determined to make sport of the Saint, and thus bring discredit upon him and his mission, and, with this design, arranged that one of his band, named Garban, should simulate death. Accordingly, Garban laid himself upon a bier, and his companions, having covered him with a pall, entreated the Saint to bring the dead man to life. St. Patrick, who knew by divine revelation all that had occurred, prayed over the man, and then went on his way. When his associates approached, and drew the pall from the face of Garban, they found that the jest had become earnest, and that the man was really dead. In fear and trembling, the whole band followed the Saint, and, falling at his feet, implored his pardon for their own sins, and life for their friend. St. Patrick took pity on them, and at his prayer the dead man arose ; and he, with his companions, believed in Christ, and was baptised. Then their leader MacKyle came forward, and confessed how it had entered into his mind to take away St. Patrick's life, and then, in the simplicity and energy of his repentance, he asked how he could atone for the crime which he had meditated. The Saint must have seen that he had to deal with one already transformed by grace, and equal to any sacrifice, for the penance imposed and accepted could only have been justified by a divine revelation. At the command of St. Patrick, MacKyle went down to the sea-shore, and having bound and locked his feet together with an iron chain, he flung the key into the sea, and in a light coracle, or boat made of a single skin, committed himself to the waves, with God alone as his pilot. And the Lord, mindful of the faith of His servant Patrick, and of the sublime sacrifice of the penitent, guided the boat until it was cast on the shore of the Isle of Man. Living there at this time were two Christians, Conindrus and Romulus, who are said to have been sent by St. Patrick to preach in that island. These men received and entertained the mysterious penitent, and instructed him in the Catholic faith; and in time he became bishop of the island, and his name was held in great veneration both in the early Irish and British Churches.

Another famous penitent was St. Assicus, whom

St. Patrick had consecrated, and appointed Bishop
of Elphin : he was also the founder of a monastery
in his diocese, over which he presided. Now, it
happened that this servant of God once told a lie,
and then, entering into himself, was filled with
such bitter regret, and such a spirit of penance,
that he fled the face of men, and buried himself in
solitude, where for seven years he remained concealed, for he judged that he was unworthy any
more to be a pastor and guide of souls. During
these years his monks sought him sorrowing, and
at length discovered his hiding-place, which was a
cavern in a lonely valley. They besought him in
vain to return to that Church which was his spouse,
and expected him ; they even tried violence, but
failed, for the Bishop declared himself unworthy
ever again to exercise his pontifical office, since
from his lips had proceeded a wilful lie, which,
coming from a priest, the sacred canons declare to
be a sacrilege. Such are the words of the ancient
chronicler. Seeing that their beloved father and
founder was fixed in his resolution, the monks, who
could not bear to live away from him, turned the
cave into a monastery, and remained with St.
Assicus until his death, and then over his grave
they built a monastery, which was afterwards
rendered famous by the sanctity of its inmates.

The same intensity of faith which shrank from

no sacrifices was seen in the fervour of those religious vocations which, even' in the Apostle's own time, made Ireland the wonder of the Christian world. In the history of the Church there has been no other example of a heathen nation, in the lifetime of one man, springing up into the maturity of the Christian life, and becoming, in truth, what even from that time she was called, "The Island of Saints".

As we have seen from the Saint's letter to Coroticus, this passion for the religious life took hold of the Irish people almost as soon as the Gospel was preached to them; and when the great Patriarch at the close of his life looked back upon his work, and poured forth the fulness of his heart in his *Confession*, this was one of his consolations: "Wherefore now in Ireland, they who never had the knowledge of God, and hitherto only worshipped idols, and unclean things, in these latter times have been made the people of the Lord, and are called the sons of God. The sons of the Scoti and the daughters of princes have become monks and virgins of Christ." They did not fly from persecution, unless so far as the sight and the presence of men are a torture to those who seek to be alone with God. St. Patrick brought with him to Ireland those traditions of the religious life which, beginning in Palestine and Egypt, had been imported into the West by St. Martin and St. Ambrose ; and the sacred cóntagion spread, so that the whole nation presented a sight similar to that seen at Milan when St. Ambrose preached his famous sermons on virginity, and mothers feared to let their daughters listen to him, and shut them up at home, because the Divine Bridegroom threatened to bear them all away. When we find how marvellous were the signs and favours by which God encouraged His chosen servants at this time, and attracted them to Himself, we are prepared for the statement that, before he died, the Saint had consecrated every tenth man and woman in Ireland to God.[1]

In the biographies of the early Irish saints we

---

[1] *Acta SS. Mart.*, xvii., p. 475. As it was after St. Patrick's death that the great Monasteries of Clonard, Bangor, Clonfert, &c., were founded, we may suppose that the majority of the men and women whom St. Patrick consecrated to God lived in the world like members of those Third Orders, now so common in the Church, and that, in process of time, the spirit infused by St. Patrick gathered them into communities. Many of these, like that of Bangor, in Down, counted their members by thousands. St. Bernard, in his *Life of St. Malachy*, tells us that one monk from Bangor is said to have founded as many as a hundred monasteries ; and the glory of this great sanctuary reached its climax when, about the year 823, being attacked by the Danes, it gave in one day nine hundred martyrs to Christ. It appears also that the number of anchorites dwelling in complete solitude and silence was very great ; and Mr. Haverty (*Hist. Ireland,* p. 92) tells us of some who, in their passion for solitude, spent their days at sea, where, alone in their light coracles, they sought and found a *desert* on the ocean.

find all that freshness and simple beauty which are
the special grace of those souls who are led by God,
with little interference on the part of man.   There
was the blessed child, St. Treha, whose holiness
was foretold by St. Patrick before her birth.   She
was the daughter of a powerful chief named
Cartheud, who was converted to the faith; and
when he and his wife were receiving baptism, the
Saint told the mother that the unborn child whom
she bore was one, whom, in the fulness of time,
he should veil, and consecrate for a heavenly Lover.
When the child had reached her tenth year, she set
out in search of the Saint to obtain the fulfilment
of his promise.   On her way she arrived at the
shores of a lake, from whence she saw the Saint in
the distance, on the other side of the water.
Wearied with the journey, she sat down on the
bank, and, with an anxious heart and longing eyes,
followed the distant form of the man of God.   Then
St. Patrick, understanding and compassionating her
trouble, prayed, and, the waters receding, made
way for the child to pass.   When the Saint had
received her vows, and consecrated this spouse of
Christ, there is a tradition that an angel of the
Lord laid a veil upon her head, which, covering
her eyes, extended to the nostrils.   The Saint was
about to lift the veil, but the maiden objected, and
earnestly besought him, saying, "I implore thee,

O my lord, to allow this veil to remain as it is, so
that never again mine eyes may see the vain things
of this world, and that thus, with pure interior
vision, I may be able to contemplate the bright
beauty of my Spouse". The Saint, filled with
consolation, assented; "and thus," continues the
narrator, "this veil, descending from heaven, remained all the days of her life, covering those
cheeks and eyes, which were like those of the
turtle-dove; keeping out all visions of evil, lest
death should by any chance enter in at the
windows ".[1]

St. Cinne, another soul consecrated by St. Patrick to God, was the only child of a prince named
Eochaidh, and her parents had promised her in
marriage to Cormac, son of Cairbre M'Neill. At
the exhortation of Patrick, the virgin declined this
alliance with one who appears to have belonged to
the reigning royal family, and consecrated herself
to Christ. When her father found that his daughter's determination was immovable, he sent for the
Saint and made a strange proposal. He told him
how he had expected to find in his grandchildren
his own consolation and the strength of his house,
but that, in thus influencing his daughter, St.
Patrick had cut off his succession, and frustrated
all his hopes: if, however, in return for this loss,

---

[1] *Acta SS. Mart.*, xvii., p. 558; *Tripartite Life*, p. 445.

the Saint would promise him the kingdom of
heaven, and at the same time not compel him
unwillingly to receive baptism, he would allow his
daughter to go her way.   St. Patrick, trusting in
the mercy of God, made the strange agreement
demanded, seeing, we may suppose, something in
the man's simplicity which made both his sacrifice
and his demand acceptable in the sight of God.
The maiden received the veil, and was consecrated
to Christ ; and, serving God in virginity and great
holiness, she led many people to follow her example,
and was glorified by miracles in her life and after
her death.   At length the time came when the old
man, her father, was struck down by sickness, and
knowing that he must die, he sent a messenger to
summon the Blessed Patrick, for he now desired to
receive that baptism which in health he had refused ; at the same time, he gave strict orders that,
in the event of his death, his body should remain
unburied until the arrival of the man of God.
Patrick, who at this time was at Saul, in Ulster,
having had a revelation of the chieftain's death, set
out on his journey before the arrival of the messenger ; but Eochaidh had been dead twenty-four
hours before the Saint reached his house.   Kneeling
down beside the corpse, St. Patrick prayed over it
and forthwith Eochaidh was restored to life, and,
having received baptism, he related to the awe-

struck bystanders all that he had learned concerning the joys of heaven and the tortures of the damned, and declared that he had seen the place in heaven which Patrick had promised him; but, because he was unbaptised, he had not been able to enter. The Saint asked him whether he would now rather remain in this world, or go at once to the reward prepared for him? And Eochaidh answered that he counted the dominion of the whole world, with all its riches and pleasures, as an empty shadow, compared to those joys of heaven which with his own eyes he had witnessed. So, when he had received the Viaticum, he lay down again and died.[1]

Like St. Francis Xavier, who was wont to send children to work miracles for him, our Saint sometimes appointed deputies to do these wonderful works. There was a chief named Elelius, who obstinately shut his ears to the teaching of St. Patrick, until at length sorrow and tribulation changed his heart. He had one child, a son, whom he loved tenderly, who was attacked by a herd of swine, and torn limb from limb. The wretched father came to the Saint, and declared that he would believe in his God, and obey Him, if in His name he would restore his son to life. Whereupon St. Patrick turned to one of his disciples, named Malachy, and

---

[1] *Tripartite Life,* p. 453; *Acta SS. Mart.,* xvii., p. 557.

told him to go and do as the sorrowing father wished; but Malachy's faith was weak, and he refused, saying that it would be tempting God were he to attempt such a thing.   Then the Saint asked him if he had not read the promise of the Lord beginning, " Whatsoever thou shalt ask the Father in My name "; and again : " If you have faith as a grain of mustard-seed, you shall say to this mountain, remove from hence thither, and it shall remove "? and he foretold that, for the future, Malachy should be empty-handed in the Church. Then St. Patrick chose two other disciples, who, with great faith, accepted his commission, and while the Saint remained in prayer, they restored the child not only to life, but to all his former strength and beauty.   It is needless to add that the father believed and was baptised with all his house.[1]

[1] *Acta SS. Mart.*, xvii., p. 558 ; *Tripartite Life*, p. 467.

CHAPTER VIII.

OF ST. PATRICK'S TENDERNESS OF HEART, AND HOW HE TAUGHT HIS DISCIPLES CHARITY.

THE reader will recall St. Patrick's language in his letter to Coroticus, wherein we find such eloquent revelations of our Saint's passionate love for those whom he had begotten in Christ, and of that sympathy which made their sufferings his own. "We have become outcasts," he cries, "in our sadness and mourning"; and again : "Not from myself, but God Himself has put this desire into my heart. . ... He (Coroticus) is envious of me. What shall I do, Lord? I am grievously despised. Lo, Thy sheep on every side are torn to pieces and made the prey of these robbers."

As it has been with all the saints, St. Patrick manifested not merely compassion, but reverence for the outcast and the afflicted. Especially was this seen in his loving service of those who were · stricken by the loathsome malady of leprosy. In this, if our Saint had need of an instructor, he had found one in his glorious master, St. Martin, of

whom we are told, that on a certain occasion, when
he came to one of the gates of Paris, and its
inhabitants went forth to meet him, his eyes were
drawn away from the triumphant multitude by
the sight of a deformed and hideous leper who
was near.   Approaching the poor man, he put his
arms round his neck and kissed him, and at his
touch the leper was healed.   In St. Patrick's time,
the victims of this terrible malady were the object
of a superstitious horror and fear, which must have
greatly aggravated their miseries.   The Jewish law
had forbidden anyone to touch a leper, ordaining
that, "All the time that he is a leper and unclean,
he shall dwell alone, without the camp,"[1] and
during the reign of paganism lepers were considered as accursed by the gods.   The example of
our Lord, in the tenderness which He showed to
this afflicted class, was enough for the saints, but it
was a long time before the popular feeling gave
way to the divine charity of the Gospel.   St.
Patrick had great tenderness for these unhappy
beings, for he saw in them the image of Him of
whom the Prophet has written, "And we have
thought Him as it were a leper, and as one struck
by God and afflicted".[2]   It is recorded how the
man of God retained several lepers near him, and
ministered to them in all things for Christ's sake;

Levit. xiii. 46.   [2] *Is.* liii. 4.

and of one especially we are told how, with his own hands, the Saint washed the ulcers which devoured his flesh, and gave him the food suited to his state. This poor man, destitute of all bodily gifts, grew wonderfully in those of the Spirit, so that he spent all his time in prayer and giving thanks to God. At length, that he might spare his companions, and free them from the sight of his horrible malady, in his humility, of his own accord, he withdrew from their company, and made a dwelling for himself in a hollow tree, where he lived alone with God. The extraordinary sanctity to which this man attained by his sufferings was probably the reason that St. Patrick did not exert his miraculous powers on his behalf. At length the time came for this great lover of the Cross to receive his reward. On the day of his death, which had been revealed to him, looking out from his hiding-place, he saw a man passing by, and, calling him, he inquired what religion he professed. When the other replied that he was a Christian, he begged him, for the love of Him in whom he believed, to go to a wood close by and pluck one of the saplings from the earth, and bring it to him : the man did as he was asked, and forthwith a bright fountain burst forth on the spot. He returned to the solitary and told him what had happened, whereupon the dying man gave thanks to God, and said : "Be it known to thee, dearest brother, that our Lord Jesus Christ has brought thee hither that thou mayest wash my body in the water of that fountain, and bury it in the same place". Saying this, and lifting his eyes and hands to heaven, he expired. When the man had washed the leper's body in the fountain, every trace of leprosy disappeared, while the air was filled with the fragrance which exhaled from those sacred remains ; and, having buried the body, the traveller went on his way. Some time after, one of the disciples of St. Patrick, being on a journey, halted at this spot, and, in the silence of the night, he heard angelic choirs singing, while a great light surrounded the grave of the leper. He related this to St. Patrick, and expressed a wish to remove the body of this Saint from so unhonoured a place ; but St. Patrick forbade him, predicting that there, in time to come, should dwell Ciaran, "a son of life yet unborn," who should people it with an army of saints, and give great glory to these relics.[1]

We find mention of St. Patrick's charity towards lepers at other times in his life ; as when at Armagh he cured at one time sixteen, who had

---

[1] St. Ciaran, born in 516, was the founder of Clonmacnois, which continued to be the seat of learning and sanctity, the retreat of devotion and solitude, and the favourite place of interment for the kings, chiefs, and nobles of both sides of the Shannon, for a thousand years after the founder's time.—O'Curry, *MS. Materials,* pp. 58-60.

come together from various quarters, attracted by the fame of his mercy and power, and were all restored to health in the act of receiving baptism from the Saint's hands. Again, when St. Mochta had retired to his hermitage, we are told that St. Patrick often visited his disciple to hold communion with him on divine things, and that he gave over to him, as a precious inheritance, twelve lepers whom, hitherto, the Apostle had served and tended himself.

The Saint's supernatural knowledge ministered to his gift of sympathy. On one occasion, when engaged in instructing and baptising, he remained so long in the same place, that the ardent Benignus grew impatient at the delay, and complained with all the freedom of a beloved disciple. The Saint then declared that he could not bring himself to leave the neighbourhood before the arrival of some of his followers, who were on the sea, coming from a distance. On the following day the sky was darkened, and so violent a tempest arose that those who watched the waves said the boat must certainly perish. The Saint's face became very sorrowful, and he told his companions that his children in the boat were in sore distress, and that he compassioned one in particular, a boy named McErc, who was quite beside himself with terror, whereupon the Saint betook himself earnestly to prayer. After a

short interval, in the hearing of all present he commanded the winds and the waves, in the name of
God, to cease their fury and be still, and forthwith
the sky cleared, and the sea became quiet. On the
same day the travellers arrived, and it was found
that they had been delivered from their danger
at the very hour that the man of God had seen
them in spirit, and prayed for their deliver-
ance.

The holy master Patrick was one who taught
clearly that charity was not a mere matter of
feeling, but a duty, as we see from the punishments
he inflicted on those who sinned against this virtue.
An instance of this is recorded in the case of the
cure of a blind man, who, hearing that the Saint
was passing, ran to meet him in the hope of receiving his sight; and as he hurried on, staggering
and falling, as he had no one to guide him, one of
the clerics in the Saint's company burst out laugh-
ing, and made sport of the poor man. St. Patrick
was filled with indignation, and as a warning to
those around him, when he had rebuked the scoffer,
and chastised him with his own hand, he said, "Amen:
I say to you that, in the name of my God, the eyes
of this man, now shrouded in darkness, shall see
the light, while your own, that are open to evil,
and provoke others to mockery, shall be closed".
When he had made the sign of the Cross on the

eyes of the blind man, his sight was restored, and the jester became blind.[1]

A still more terrible judgment fell upon a chief named Trian. Patrick, being on a journey, passed through a wood in which he found some men cutting trees, and saw that their hands were bleeding. To the questions of the Saint they replied that they were the slaves of a hard master named Trian, who condemned them to work in this way, and that, to make their work intolerable, he would not even allow them to sharpen their axes. Patrick blessed the axes, and the men were able to use them without difficulty. He then visited the chief, and tried to soften the obduracy of his heart. Finding, however, that words failed, the Saint sat down at Trian's gate, and "fasted upon him," remaining there for a long time without food, for Patrick was his creditor in the name of the charity of Christ; but all was in vain, and the Saint departed, declaring that the hard-hearted man would come to an evil end. Trian was only exasperated by the Saint's remonstrances, and in revenge he bound and grievously tortured the poor slaves who had informed Patrick of his cruelty, until at length, as the Saint had foretold, the wrath of God fell upon him. Driving one day on the shores of Lake Trena, his horses ran away, and carried chariot and driver into the lake.

[1] *Acta SS. Mart.*, xvii., p. 566.

St. Evin adds : " Loch Trena is its name. This was his last fall. He will not arise out of that lake till the Vespers of Judgment, and it will not be in happiness even then." [1]

St. Patrick once gave two brothers a lesson in fraternal charity in the following manner. Their father had lately died, and a dispute arose between them about the inheritance ; and passing from words to blows, they drew their swords, and attacked each other in the presence of the Saint. Filled with horror and fear of the threatened fratricide, he betook himself to prayer. Then, raising his hand, he blessed them, whereupon the arms of the combatants became immovable, and remained uplifted and rigidly fixed in the air. The Saint again gave them his benediction and made peace between them ; whereupon they surrendered the disputed land to St. Patrick for the repose of their father's soul, and he built a church on the spot.

[1] *Tripartite Life*, p. 479.

CHAPTER IX.

THE man of God, Patrick, was marvellously favoured with heavenly visions and revelations in prayer. "When," says his biographer, "he every day in the Mass sacrificed the Son to the Father, or devoutly recited the Apocalypse of St. John, it was granted to him to see the heavens opened, and Jesus standing surrounded by a multiude of angels; and whilst he meditated on these great visions his soul was altogether lost in God." Three times in the week the angel Victor visited and conversed with him, filling his soul with celestial consolations. The labours of the day amongst men seem to have been less arduous than those of the night with God. He divided his time, so that in the first part of the night he recited a hundred Psalms, making at the same time two hundred genuflections;[1] the second part he spent immersed in the water of some cold spring,[2] keeping heart, eyes, and hands lifted up to heaven until he had finished the other fifty Psalms. After this he gave the short time that remained to sleep, lying on a rock, with a stone for a pillow, while the rough haircloth which he wore macerated his body even in his sleep.

This is really the prodigious part of St. Patrick's life. We are not surprised that God should give power over nature to a man who had such power over himself, and we are therefore prepared for the statement that the working of miracles was of almost daily occurrence with him, that he gave sight to the blind and speech to the dumb, cured all manner of diseases, and raised thirty-three

[1] Repeated prostrations and genuflections seem to have been common even in the most sublime contemplations of the saints of this period. It is related of St. Simeon Stylites, a contemporary of St. Patrick—"He had adopted the habit of expressing his worship at times by deep reverences, bowing so low that his forehead nearly touched his feet. One of Theodoret's companions once counted twelve hundred and forty-four of these adorations, one after another, and then grew weary of counting" (*Fathers of the Desert*, Hahn Hahn, p. 334). The practice of frequent genuflections in prayer is recommended by the Council of Clovesho in England, A.D. 747 (Haddan and Stubbs, vol. iii., p. 372).

[2] In subsequent ages, St. Patrick had many imitators of this austerity. The practice passed over into England with the Irish missioners. St. Wilfrid of York probably learned it in his novitiate under the Irish monks at Lindisfarne, for in the latter years of his life we find the Pope forbidding him to continue this penance, in consideration of his age and infirmities.

persons from the dead in the name of the Holy Trinity.[1]

It will be worth our while here to pause, and look back over that life into the abysses of which we have been reverently gazing. This is all that we have been able to do in a biography like the present, in which the mysteries of the ascetical, mystical, and apostolic life are all so immeasurable. On the other hand, the bare statement of these wonders does not satisfy us: they have even a tendency to weary the mind unless we can trace them to their source. Now, if we would discover the fount and origin of St. Patrick's strength, the explanation of all the prodigies of his life, we must try to get some idea of the nature of his intercourse and union with God in prayer. If we say that the comparative greatness of saints and their super-natural powers are always in proportion to the perfection of their spirit of prayer, we shall have Holy Scripture and all sacred authority on our side. At first it seems as if it were an intrusion into the secrets of God to attempt to sound such mysteries, and that we can get no farther than the thought that St. Patrick's prayer was like that of Moses and

[1] *Acta SS.*, pp. 576, 578. St. Francis Xavier appears to have approached nearest to St. Patrick in this greatest exercise of miraculous power. Twenty-four resurrections were juridically proved to have been worked by St. Francis in his lifetime.—Giry, *Vie des Saints,* 3rd Dec. (n.).

St. Paul : that inspired prayer, which is more like prophecy than supplication. But this comparison is after all incomplete, although in so many ways St. Patrick resembled those saints who belonged to the invisible rather than to the visible world. The prayer that is a perpetual fiery sacrifice of self; . that sacred recklessness which sees nothing, and fears nothing, while it looks only to God—all these characteristics of the prayer of the Prophet and the Apostle are found in St. Patrick; but here our comparison must stop. In St. Patrick's prayer we find nothing of that inimitable and unapproachable majesty, that conscious power which belongs to inspiration alone. St. Patrick's use of the word "imitate,"[1] on more than one occasion, in referring to the gifts and graces of God, reveals how abiding was his sense that he was always and ever a scholar, and not a master in the school of Christ. The vehemence of his spirit of self-abasement before God is hardly equalled, certainly not exceeded, by anything in the language of the most lowly and penitent saints. He who could use such language, and at the same time convince us that it was the language of the heart, must indeed have been great before God,

---

[1] "Imitarer illos quos Dominus jam prædixerat." . . . "Si aliquid boni imitatus sum, propter Deum meum quem diligo " (*Conf.*, c. iii., § 14 ; v., § 23).

whose grace descends in proportion to the depths of the creature's lowliness.

There is no point clearer in St. Patrick's life than the fact that it was on prayer that he relied for success. His own writings, and the evidence of his biographers tell the same tale in different ways : one supplements the other. The elevations of his soul to God in his youth on Slemish were not less wonderful than his prayer on Cruachan, and those vigils at Saul and Armagh, when he was about to bid farewell to earth and take his flight to heaven. If we had faith in prayer like that of St. Patrick, there would be no mysteries in his life. It was by prayer that he converted the Irish nation ; by prayer he legislated, and obtained obedience to his laws ; and by prayer he organised the work of God, and built up His spiritual and enduring empire. He had many holy and zealous auxiliaries in his work, but we may safely assert that his prayer flowed into all their operations, like that of Moses on the mountain, while his followers were fighting in the field.[1]

His union with God in prayer infused such beauty and power into his preaching that on one occasion, when a great multitude had come together

---

[1] "Moses plus profecit in monte adorando, quam multitudo magna bellantium " (*Walter Hilton*, Pref., p. xl. ; ed. Guy).

to hear the word, and the Saint interpreted the four
Evangelists, for three days and nights the people
were so entranced and spellbound by his inspired
eloquence, that the time seemed to them but as the
space of one day.

Not only was the conversion of the Irish people
to Christianity effected with extraordinary rapidity,
but to this first grace God added another almost as
great, in the abiding presence of the great Patriarch
with his children. Other Apostles have had to
leave their work to be finished by inferior men, but
for fifty-nine years after the power of paganism
had been broken at Tara, St. Patrick held undisputed sway as Pontiff and Teacher of the Church in
Ireland. He lived long enough to see the grey
hairs on the heads of those whom he had baptised
as children, so that he had time to organise and
consolidate the infant Church, and to create a
native clergy : works, under the circumstances,
quite as superhuman as the conversion of the
nation.

The evidence on this point in St. Patrick must,
as usual, be extracted from detached sentences.
He alludes to the thousands of men (*tot millia homi-
num*) whom he had baptised. "Greatly am I in
debt to God, who has given me such grace that
great multitudes are, by my ministry, born to God,
and then confirmed. And that for this people

whom the Lord hath taken, coming to the faith in those latter days, clerics should everywhere be ordained." [1]   Again, in the following sentence he plainly refers to the first year of his apostolate, before Christianity had become identified with the laws, as the constituted religion of Ireland : " Wherefore in Ireland they who, hitherto, had no knowledge of God, and up to this time only worshipped impure idols, have lately become the people of the Lord, and are styled the sons of God.   The sons of the Scots and the daughters of princes are seen as monks and virgins of Christ.   Even as it was with that Scottish lady in the prime of life, blessed, noble, and beautiful, whom I baptised ; and after a few days, in the same spirit, she came to us, and disclosed how she had had a revelation from a messenger of God,[2] telling her to continue a virgin of Christ, and that thus she should come nigh to God.   Thanks be to God, six days later, in all perfection and ardently, she took hold of it, in like manner as do all the virgins of God, and this against the will of their parents : nay, under the pressure of persecutions and unjust reproaches on the part of their relations.   Nevertheless, their number increases the more, and we know not the

---

[1] *Conf.*, c. iv., § 16.

[2] *Responsum accepisse nuntio Dei:* the style of St. Patrick's usual form of expression for special divine inspirations addressed to himself.

17

number of those of our own race who are born there [to Christ] besides widows and the uncorrupt. But they (the virgins) who are slaves endure the most grievous trial, and they endure in spite of terror and threats. Truly the Lord has given grace to many of His daughters ; for although they are forbidden, for all that they courageously follow His example." [1]

There seems to be no doubt that St. Patrick retired from the government of the See of Armagh many years before his death, probably in 455, and during the long interval between that period and his own death he saw four bishops successively fill that see. It was Cormac,[2] the fifth successor of the Saint, who outlived him. Sixty years of ecclesiastical rule in Ireland gave St. Patrick time, not only to teach the faith, but to establish traditions. The rulers of the Church during this long period were his own spiritual children, so while one generation passed away, and another succeeded, there was no change or disturbance in the life of that Church, which had all its organisation and discipline, as well as its doctrines, from one man. The same prodigious power, which in the beginning had broken all opposition, preserved unity and peace when the struggle was over, and made the ·

---

[1] *Conf.*, c. iv., § 18.
[2] Colgan, *Acta SS. Hiberniæ*, p. 358.

fold of St. Patrick like the infant Church in Judæa, when " the multitude of believers were of one heart and one mind ". As we have seen, it was St. Patrick who imprinted on the Church in Ireland that monastic character which was her strength and glory for centuries ; and so great and universal was the enthusiasm of the people, that he devoted a tenth of the people, as well as of their herds and the produce of the land, to the service of the Church and the monasteries.[1]

St. Patrick's example in retiring from his bishopric, and that of St. Assicus in resigning the See of Elphin, suggest an explanation of a statement in the Saint's life which has been too much for many modern writers—viz., that he consecrated over three hundred bishops with his own hand. Grave authors have held it to be probable that St. Patrick introduced the order of Chorepiscopi into Ireland ;[2] and if we accept the view that these prelates were often nothing more than simple priests, and that they have been included in the total number of those styled bishops, there is no difficulty in the numbers. But even if we take the statement in its ordinary sense, as meaning bishops with or without

[1] *Acta SS. Mart.*, xvii., p. 575.

[2] In our Saint's time the great number of Chorepiscopi had in some countries grown into a serious abuse. See St. Leo's letter to the Bishops of Gaul and Germany (*Bullarii Rom.*, Appendix, p. 193 ; Taurin., 1867).

sees, there is no extravagance in the conjecture
that many may have resigned their sees, induced
either by their master's example, or by love of solitude and the contemplative life, which had such
attractions for fervent Christians in those ages of
faith ; while St. Patrick could not fairly refuse them
the consolation which he had chosen for himself in
his solitude at Saul. It was truly an age of wonders in Ireland, when grace was given without
measure, and the records of that time cannot be
tried by ordinary standards. Jocelyn tells us that
in those days no one was chosen for the episcopal
office, or the government of souls, unless he was
declared worthy by divine revelation, or some
evident sign.

"Before long," says this ancient writer, "there
was no desert, no spot, or hiding-place in the island,
however remote, which was not peopled with perfect monks or nuns ; so that, throughout the world,
Ireland was justly distinguished by the extraordinary
title of the Island of Saints : for they lived according to the rule imposed upon them by St. Patrick ;
in contempt of the world and desire of heaven ; in
holy mortification of the flesh and renouncement
of self-will, rivalling the monks of Egypt in merits
and in numbers, and by word and example they
were a light to foreign and distant lands. In
St. Patrick's time, and long after under his suc-

cessors, none were elevated to the episcopate, or the care of souls, except those who were proved to be worthy by divine revelation or some manifest sign." [1]

The latter years of the Saint's life were spent for the most part at Saul or Armagh, where in retirement he held communion with God, and again tasted the ineffable joys of his youth, when his soul was espoused to God in solitude on Slemish. The Last Day alone will reveal the lights then given to him, and the graces which he obtained for his children. Once the Saint had a great vision, in which the actual state, and the future of the Church in Ireland were revealed to him. In the first place, he saw the whole land, as it were, like a great furnace whose flames reached to the sky, and he clearly heard the voice of an angel saying, " Such is now the state of Ireland in the sight of the Lord ". After a little time, instead of this far-spreading universal fire, he saw flaming mountains here and there over the land, then torches shining, succeeded by glimmering lights amidst an ever-increasing darkness ; and last of all, a few live coals buried, and burning deep in the earth. And an angelic voice was heard, saying, that such, in times that were coming, should be the successive states of the Irish people. Then, with

[1] *Acta SS. Mart.*, xvii.

tears rolling down his cheeks, the Saint repeated many times those words of the Psalmist, " Will God then cast off for ever ? Or will He never more be favourable again ? Or will He cut off His mercy for ever from generation to generation ? Or will God forget to show mercy ? Or will He in anger shut up His mercies ? " And the angel answered and told him to look to the north of the land, and that there he should see the change of the hand of the Most High. The Saint lifted up his eyes, and, behold, a little light arose in Uladh (Ulster), which struggled long with the darkness, until at length the whole island was filled with the brightness of its glory, and Ireland returned to its first state of all-pervading fire.[1] At the time when Jocelyn wrote, in the twelfth century, conflicting interpretations of this vision were prevalent. The days of darkness were taken to be the terrible time of the Danish persecution in the ninth century. The light that began in Uladh was thought by some to be a figure of the great St. Malachy, first Bishop of Down in Ulster, then of Armagh, and Legate of the Holy See under Innocent II., whose life and labours have been recorded by his friend St. Bernard ; while the English invaders boldly asserted that the light was a figure of the state of things which they had introduced. Jocelyn

[1] *Acta SS.*, p. 575.

himself abstains from giving any opinion on the subject.[1]

The time at length came when St. Patrick understood by divine revelation that his end was near. He was then in Uladh; and as he desired to be buried near his children at Armagh, for whom he seems to have had a special love, he turned his steps towards that city; but on the way the angel Victor met him, and told him that it was the will of God that he should die in Uladh, which was the province he had first converted, and that the city of Down was to be the place of his resurrection; at the same time reminding the Saint of his prediction and promise to the sons of Dichu, his first converts, that he should die in their land. The Saint for a moment was troubled by this message; then recovering himself, he accepted the obedience, and returned to Uladh.

A few days after this, the holy old man Patrick sat down, surrounded by a number of his followers, in a certain place not far from the city of Down, and began to treat of the glory of the saints and of the mansions of the blessed. While he spoke, a bright light was seen shining over one particular

---

[1] Although Jocelyn had come to Ireland in the train of the invaders, he had nothing in common with the very unworthy clerical associates of Henry Plantagenet, and the fact that he was a foreigner gives additional force to his evidence: no Irish writer goes further in admiration for St. Patrick and the Irish Church.

spot in a neighbouring cemetery, and when the
lookers-on asked the Saint to tell them the meaning
of this light, he turned to St. Brigid,[1] and ordered
her to explain the mystery, upon which the holy
virgin declared it to be a sign that in this place
would soon be laid the body of some great servant
of God.   St. Ethembria, described by Jocelyn as
the first of the virgins of Ireland consecrated to
Christ by Patrick, was present, and secretly asked
St. Brigid to tell her the name of the Saint.   She
replied that it was the Father and Apostle of
Ireland himself, and at the same time revealed to
her friend her desire to have the privilege of invest-
ing his sacred remains in a shroud which she had
herself woven for his burial.   St. Patrick, who
knew in spirit what was passing in his daughter's
mind, turned to her and bade her go back to her
convent and bring this shroud which she had prepared.   The Saint himself then set out for his
monastery at Saul, and upon his arrival took to his
bed, knowing now that the end of his life was come.
When St. Brigid had reached her convent on the
Curragh, she took the shroud, and with four of her
daughters to bear her company, with all speed re-

---

[1] St. Brigid died A.D. 525.   A poem attributed to St. Berchan,
about A.D. 690, says that St. Brigid came to Downpatrick at this time
to procure that St. Patrick might be buried at Kildare (O'Curry,
MS. Materials, p. 415).

traced her steps to Saul; but, worn out with fasting and the length of the journey, she and her companions grew so faint that they could proceed no farther. Their distress was revealed to the dying Saint, and in the same hour he sent five of the light chariots of the country to meet them, so that they arrived in time to present their offering ; and having kissed his feet and hands, they received his benediction.[1]

St. Patrick died March 17, 492. The conclusion of his life shall be given in the words of St. Evin : " A just man, indeed, was this man ; with purity of nature like the patriarchs ; a true pilgrim, like Abraham ; gentle and forgiving, like Moses ; a praiseworthy psalmist, like David ; an emulator of wisdom, like Solomon ; a chosen vessel for proclaiming the truth, like the Apostle Paul ; a man full of grace and the knowledge of the Holy Ghost, like the beloved John ; a fair flower-garden to children of grace ; a fruitful vine-branch ; a sparkling fire, with force and warmth of heat to the sons of life, for instituting and illustrating charity ; a lion in strength and power, a dove in gentleness and humility ; a serpent in wisdom, and cunning to do good; gentle, humble, merciful to the sons of life, —dark, ungentle towards the sons of death ; a servant of labour and service of Christ ; a king in

[1] *Acta SS.*, p. 579.

dignity and power, for binding and loosening, for liberating and convicting, for killing and giving life.

" After these great miracles, therefore—*i.e.*, after resuscitating the dead ; after healing lepers, and the blind, and the deaf, and the lame, and all diseases ; after ordaining bishops, and priests, and deacons, and people of all orders in the Church ; after teaching the sons of Erin, and after baptising them ; after founding churches and monasteries ; after destroying idols, and images, and druidical arts—the hour of death of St. Patrick approached. He received the Body of Christ from Bishop Tassach, according to the advice of the angel Victor.   He resigned his spirit afterwards to heaven, in the one hundred and twentieth year of his age.   His body is here still in the earth, with honour and reverence.   Though great his honour here, greater honour will be to him in the Day of Judgment, when judgment will be given on the fruits of his teaching, like every great Apostle ; in the union of the Apostles and disciples of Jesus ; in the union of the nine orders of angels, which cannot be surpassed ; in the union of the divinity and humanity of the Son of God ; in the union of the Holy Trinity, Father, Son, and Holy Ghost."[1]

A little before his death the Saint had composed what may be fittingly called his last will and testa-

---

[1] *Tripartite Life,* p. 500.

ment; and his language, in spite of his humility,
reveals how he was conscious that he was restoring
to God a nation which he had held in trust for his
Master. " Behold," he writes at the termination of
his *Confession,* " I now commend my soul to my
most faithful God, for whom in my lowliness I
am ambassador; and, therefore, He who makes no
account of persons has chosen me for this office, so
that, from amongst the least of His creatures, I
should be His minister. ' What shall I render to
Him for all the things that He hath rendered to me?'
Or what can I say, or what can I promise to my
Lord ? For of myself I am worth nothing, unless He
Himself shall give ; but He who is ' the searcher of
the heart and reins ' knows how I desire, in measure,
and beyond all measure, and how I was prepared
that He should give me to drink of His chalice, as
He has lovingly granted to others, who have loved
Him. Wherefore may my Lord avert that it should
ever come to pass that I should lose His people,
whom He has gained at the ends of the earth. I
pray, therefore, that God may give me perseverance,
and that He may deign to make me a faithful witness until the hour of my departure, for the sake of
my God. And if for the sake of my God, whom
I love, I have ever imitated anything that is good,
I beseech Him to grant that, in the likeness of
those who were converts, or captives for His Name,

I may also pour out my blood, and even have no place of burial, and that my miserable body may be cut into pieces, and cast out to be the food of birds and dogs and wild beasts. For of a certainty I know that, if this service is paid to me, I shall gain my soul with the price of my body; for without doubt in that day we shall rise in the brightness of the sun, that is, in the glory of Jesus Christ."

The body of the Saint was wrapped in the shroud woven by St. Brigid, and the prodigies attendant on his death were in keeping with those of his life. A sweet fragrance exhaled from his sacred flesh, and during the twelve days that his body lay unburied, a bright light was seen in that part of the country, and it is said that the voices of angels were heard singing, night and day, the praises of the servant of Christ. At the end of this time a dispute arose between the people of Armagh and the Ulidians, as to who should possess the relics of the Apostle, and a miracle decided the contest; for when the body was laid upon a funeral car, drawn by two oxen, the men of Armagh, as it seemed to them, followed it, going towards their own city, until they found that they had been led astray, and pursued what was only a phantom; while the Ulidians carried away the body of the Saint, and buried it, as he predicted it should be, amidst the sons of Dichu in Downpatrick.

APPENDIX.

APPENDIX.

LES FLEURS DE ST. PATRICE.

THE traditions and monuments which are bound up with the beautiful legend of *Les Fleurs de St. Patrice,* are, historically, as important as they are poetical. The subjoined account is from the pen of Mgr. Chevallier, President of the Archæological Society of Touraine, and it was sent to the writer by his lamented friend, M. Fleurat, Curé de St. Patrice.

We have already observed how, in Ireland, natural monuments are a distinguishing feature of St. Patrick's history, and it is certainly very remarkable that the same characteristic should attach to the record of his life in France, where, year after year, thousands come to gather those winter flowers which are believed to be an undying witness of St. Patrick's connection with St. Martin of Tours.

It seems as if nature would fain repay St. Patrick for the way in which he had honoured the inanimate creation when he made high mountains his altars, and " bound to himself" the elements as attendants in the service of his Lord.

(Extrait des Annales de la Société d'Agriculture, Science, &c., du Départment d'Indre et Loire, t. xxx., année 1850, f. 70.)

A quelques lieues de Tours, sur les bords de la Loire, il se produit chaque année, de temps immémorial, un phénomène fort remarquable, dont la science n'a point encore donné d'explication satisfaisante. Ce phénomène trop peu connu, c'est celui de la floraison, au milieu même des rigueurs de l'hiver, de l'épine noire, *prunus spinosa*, connue vulgairement sous le nom de prunellier.

Ce phénomène, nous venons de le constater nous-mêmes de nos propres yeux, et nous pouvons l'affirmer hautement sans crainte d'être démenti. Nous avons cueilli ces fleurs merveilleuses et nous pouvons appeler à notre aide les témoignages des milliers de personnes qui chaque année à la fin de décembre les voient se renouveler sous leurs yeux. C'est donc un fait incontestable. C'est à S. Patrice, non loin du château de Rochecotte, que se trouve ce curieux arbuste, sur le penchant du coteau. Le mouvement de la sève, qui devrait être stationnaire à cette époque de l'année, se manifeste d'une manière sensible. L'écorce, toute humide de cette sève d'hiver, se sépare sans peine du bois qu'elle recouvre ; les boutons se gonflent, les fleurs s'épanouissent comme au mois d'Avril et chargent les branches d'une neige odorante ; quelques feuilles essaient plus timidement d'exposer leur verdure délicate à la bise glacée. Le dirai-je ? Aux fleurs succèdent les fruits, et dès les premiers jours de janvier, on voit apparaitre au sein des pétales, flétris et décolorés, à l'extrémité d'un long pédoncule, une petite baie qui bientôt se ride et se dessèche.

Cette floraison si curieuse est presque inconnue, et cependant elle se produit chaque année de temps immémorial. Les vieillards les plus âgés de S. Patrice l'ont toujours vue s'accomplir à une époque précise quelle que fût la rigueur de la saison. C'etait aussi l'antique tradition de leurs pères; et la légende que nous racontons plus bas semble attribuer à ce fait une origine très reculée.

L'arbuste dont nous parlons semble cependant être encore fort jeune ; mais il est probable qu'il se renouvelle par les racines. Du reste le phénomène est circonscrit à la localité et à l'arbuste en question. Les branches que l'on a voulu transplanter ailleurs n'ont offert que la floraison du printemps, et les aubépines qui croissent au milieu des prunelliers ne manifestent aucun mouvement de sève.

Mais, nous diront les incrédules, après tout, ce phénomène n'est pas plus merveilleux que celui de la floraison des lilas dans le mois de novembre, lorsque les bourgeons, par une méprise imprudente, croient trouver dans une température encore tiède les douces haleines du printemps. Que nos lecteurs se détrompent : l'épine noire de S. Patrice croit, se développe et fructifie au milieu des rigueurs de l'hiver, par la température la plus froide. Cette année, les fleurs se sont épanouies depuis Noël jusqu'au 1er janvier, c'est à dire à une époque où le thermomètre a été presque constamment au dessous de glace Quoique sur le penchant du coteau, l'arbuste n'est point abrité des vents du nord, le givre en couvre les branches, une bise glaciale y souffle avec violence, et il arrive souvent que l'arbuste est chargé tout à la fois et des neiges de l'hiver, et des neiges de ses fleurs.

(L'auteur réfute l'hypothèse d'une source thermale qui serait à une faible profondeur : le sol, dit-il, reste couvert de neige—les autres arbustes ne fleurissent pas.)

Les habitants de S. Patrice se racontent une vieille tradition qui, dans sa naïvete, est pleine de fraîcheur et de poésie. Un jour, disent-ils, S. Patrice vint d'Irlande dans les Gaules. Il se rendit auprès de S. Martin, attiré par la réputation de sa sainteté et de ses miracles. Arrivé sur les bords de la Loire, non loin du lieu où depuis fut bâtie l'église qui porte aujourd'hui, son nom, il se reposa sous un arbuste. C'était au milieu d'un hiver rigoureux, à l'époque des fêtes de Noël. L'arbuste par respect pour le Saint, étendit ses branches, secoua la neige qui le recouvrait, et, par un prodige inouï, se couvrit d'une neige de fleurs. S. Patrice traversa la Loire sur son manteau, et arrivé sur le bord opposé, se reposa sous une autre épine noire, qui fleurit aussitôt. Depuis lors, dit la chronique, les deux arbustes n'ont cessé de fleurir chaque année, à Noël, en témoignage de S. Patrice.

[*Translation.*]

"On the banks of the Loire, a few leagues from Tours, a very remarkable phenomenon is repeated year by year, and from time immemorial, one concerning which science as yet has given no satisfactory explanation. This phenomenon, too little known, consists in the blossoming, in the midst of the rigours of winter, of the blackthorn, *prunus spinosa*, commonly called the sloe. We have lately verified this circumstance with our own eyes, and can vouch for its truth without fear of contradiction. We can appeal to the testimony of thousands who at the end of December in each year are eyewitnesses to its repetition, and we have ourselves gathered these extraordinary flowers. This remarkable shrub is to be found at *St. Patrice,* upon the slope of a hill not far from the Chateau de Rochecotte. The circulation of the sap, which should be suspended in winter, is plainly revealed by the moist state of the bark, which easily separates from the wood which it covers. The buds swell, the flowers expand as in the month of April, and cover the boughs with odorous and snowlike flowers, while a few leaves more timidly venture to expose their delicate verdure to the icy north wind. Shall I venture to add? to the flowers succeed the fruit, and at the beginning of January a small berry appears attached to a long peduncle in the midst of the withered and discoloured petals, which soon shrivels and dries up.

"This singular growth of flowers is almost unknown, although it has been repeated every year from time immemorial. The oldest inhabitants of *St. Patrice* have always seen it take place at a fixed period of the year, no matter how severe the season may be, and such has also been the ancient tradition of their forefathers, while the legend we are about to relate appears to attribute a very remote origin to the fact; but, as the shrub itself appears quite young, it is probable that it is renewed from the roots. However, this phenomenon is limited to the locality and to the shrub in question. Cuttings transplanted elsewhere have only blossomed in the spring, and the hawthorns which grow amidst the sloes do not manifest any circulation of sap.

"The incredulous will object that, after all, this circumstance is not more extraordinary than the flowering of the lilac in November, when the buds by an unwary mistake suppose that, in the still mild temperature, they have found the soft breath of spring. Our readers must not be deceived; the blackthorn of St. Patrick grows, develops, and bears fruit in the midst of the rigours of winter in the most icy temperature. This year the flowers were in bloom from Christmas until the first of January, that is, at a time when the thermometer was almost always below freezing point. Although growing on the slope of a hill, this shrub is in no way sheltered from the north wind, its branches are encrusted with hoar-frost; the icy north-east wind blows violently amongst them, and it often happens that the shrub is loaded at one and the same time with the snow of winter, and the snow of its own flowers."

(The author refutes the hypothesis of the proximity of a thermal spring; the ground, he observes, remains covered with snow, and the other shrubs do not blossom.)

" The inhabitants of *St. Patrice* record an ancient tradition, which in its simplicity is full of freshness and poetry. St. Patrick, it is said, being on his way from Ireland to join St. Martin in Gaul, attracted by the fame of that Saint's sanctity and miracles, and having arrived at the bank of the Loire, near the spot where the church now bearing his name has been built, rested under a shrub. It was Christmas time, when the cold was intense. In honour of the Saint, the shrub expanded its branches, and shaking off the snow which rested on them, by an unheard-of prodigy arrayed itself in flowers white as the snow itself. St. Patrick crossed the Loire on his cloak, and on reaching the opposite bank, another blackthorn under which he rested at once burst out into flowers. Since that time, says the chronicle, the two shrubs have never ceased to blossom at Christmas, in honour of St. Patrick."

When the present writer visited *St. Patrice* in August, 1881, he was struck by the extraordinary beauty and luxuriance of the foliage on the tree: it was so dense from the ground upwards that it was impossible to distinguish the stem, and he could understand how, when it flowers at Christmas, it supplies the country round with trophies of St. Patrick. It also appears that they are objects of religious veneration, as we learn that M. Dupont always kept a branch of the *Fleurs de St. Patrice,* hung up in his room. The whole neighbourhood is redolent of St. Patrick. The railway stops at the *Station St. Patrice,* the *Commune* is also named after the Saint, while at about thirty yards from the tree stands the ancient parish church dedicated to the Apostle of Ireland. From the style of its architecture it is clear that this church dates from the tenth or eleventh century, and in the *Cartulaire de l'Abbaye de Noyers,* beginning with the year 1035, we find no less than thirty charters relating to this church, and the parish and cemetery attached to it.

FATHER COLGAN.

(Account of his Life and Labours, extracted from the Report of the Historical MS. Commission. Appendix to Fourth Report, p. 599. London, 1874.)

Among the institutions which, after the Reformation, were established for Irish Roman Catholics on the Continent, the College of the Irish Franciscans, or Minor Friars, at Louvain, acquired the highest national literary reputation, as the centre, in the seventeenth century, of an organisation for the preservation and publication of the early history and hagiography of Ireland. . . . The project of editing the Acts of the Irish Saints and other ancient monuments of Ireland was first conceived by Friar Hugh Ward, professor and subsequently guardian of the Franciscan College of Louvain. Ward,

or Mac and Bhaird, a graduate of Salamanca, was of an
ancient Donegal family, which from remote times pro-
fessionally cultivated literature.   His proposed work
was no doubt promoted by the literary controversy
which sprang out of the attempt made by some inju-
dicious Scotch writers to appropriate to their country
the renown for religion and learning which Ireland had
acquired in the ages during which she was styled
" Scotia Major ".   The design of Ward having received
the sanction of the heads of his Order, was entered
upon with zeal by Friars Patrick Fleming and Brendan,
O'Connor, who commenced researches for him in foreign
libraries.   The learned Irish Jesuit Stephen White,
professor at Dilengen, also co-operated, and supplied
transcripts made by himself of documents at Biburg,
Ratisbon, and Reichenau.

The task of collecting all Gaelic materials to be
obtained in Ireland was committed to the lay brother
Friar Michael O'Clery, who belonged to a family of
native hereditary Irish chroniclers, and was himself
considered one of the most learned in that line.   Aided
by some support from native Irish proprietors, to whose
religion and pride of ancestry he appealed, and supplied occasionally with food and shelter in the places
of refuge of the proscribed Franciscans in Ireland,
Michael O'Clery indefatigably laboured, with some of
his kinsmen and other Irish Antiquaries, to collect,
transcribe, and methodise all available native materials.
Among the works in the Irish language thus executed
and transmitted to Louvain were the *Leabhar Gabhala,
or Chronicle of the Conquests of Erin ; the Calendars of the
Irish Saints; the Successions and Pedigrees of the Irish
Kings and Saints*, in the present collection ; the *Annals
of Ireland by the Four Masters*, styled also the *Annals*

of Donegal, from having been compiled in a hut built
amid the ruins of the then lately dismantled Franciscan
Convent of Donegal. Fleming made considerable collections from libraries in Italy for the history of St.
Columbanus, but before they reached the press he was
sent to take charge of the Irish Franciscan house at
Prague, and was murdered amid the commotions inci-
dent to the siege of that town in 1632. Ward died in
1635, without having completed any of the works which
he had projected. The materials then came to the
hands of John Colgan, also a native of Donegal, professor of theology in the same college. In 1643
Michael O'Clery's vocabulary or glossary of difficult
Gaelic words was printed in Irish type at Louvain.

Colgan, though suffering severely from bodily infirmities, applied with energy to the task of preparing
some of the hagiographical manuscripts for the press,
and received much encouragement from Hugh O'Reilly,
the Roman Catholic Primate of all Ireland, who de-
frayed the cost of printing a collection of the Acts of
the Irish Saints for January, February, and March.
This, which Colgan intended to form the third volume
of the *Ecclesiastical Antiquities and History of Ireland*,
was published at Louvain, with the following title, in
1645, a few months after the death of Michael
O'Clery :—

"Acta Sanctorum veteris et. maioris Scotiæ, sev
Hiberniæ sanctorvm insvlæ, partim ex variis per Euro-
pam MS. codd. exscripta, partim ex antiquis monu-
mentis et probatis authoribus eruta et congesta ; omnia
notis et appendicibus illustrata per R. P. F. Joannem
Colganvm, in conventu FF. Minor. Hibern. Strictioris
obseru. Louanij S. Theologiæ Lectoris Jvbilatum.
Nunc primum de eisdem actis juxta-ordinem mensium

et dierum prodit tomvs primvs, qui de Sacris Hiberniæ
antiquitatibus est tertius, Januarium, Februarium, et
Martium complectens."

Another volume, containing ancient Lives of SS.
Patrick, Brigid, and Columba, was, mainly at the expense of Lord Slane's son, Friar Thomas Fleming,
Archbishop of Dublin, published two years subsequently
at Louvain, under the following title :—

"Triadis Thavmaturgæ sev divorvm Patricii Columbæ et Brigidæ, trivm veteris et maioris Scotiæ, sev
Hiberniæ, sanctorvm insvlæ, commvnivm patronorum
acta, à varijs, ijsque pervetustis, et sanctis authoribus
scripta, ac studio R. P. F. Ioannis Colgani in conventu
FF. Minor. Hibernor." &c., &c.

The following additional particulars appear in a
unique and torn copy of a printed obituary memorial
ssued by the Order at the time :—

"Anno Domini 1658, 15 Januarii, Lovanii in Col-
legio S. Antonii de Padua, Fratrum Hibernorum,
strictioris observantiæ, omnibus ecclesiæ sacramentis
præmunitus, migravit ad Dominum anno suæ ætatis 66,
sacerdotii 40, professionis 38, R[everendus] A[dmodum]
P[ater] Frater Joannes Colganus, S. theologiæ lector
jubilatus, et collegiorum suæ provinciæ aliquamdiu
commissarius. Vir erat ab eruditione, pietate et animi
candore valde commendabilis, et præclare meritus de
suo instituto, patria [ejusque] sanctis, quorum actis, in
publicam notitiam proferendis [triginta sex] et amplius
annis pertinaci labore, indefessoque ad mortem usque
sedulus incubuit patrocinium prome . . . humana
fragilitate aliquid adhuc luendum . . . vestris precibus
enixe commendamus. Requiescat in pace."

A catalogue of the MSS. in Colgan's cell at the time
of his death is extant in this collection. Some of these

are now in the library of the Dukes of Burgundy at Brussels, and others, as will be seen, in the present collection. Among the unpublished compilations of Colgan and his fellow-workers were some of great interest on the labours of, and establishments by, Irish missionaries in England, Belgium, Bretagne, Alsace, Lorraine, Burgundy, Germany, and Italy.

THE BOOK OF ARMAGH.

(Extracted from Sixth Report of the Deputy-Keeper of the Public Records in Ireland, p. 105.)

The *Book of Armagh* is now defective at the commencement. Its first portion is occupied with notes in Latin and Irish on St. Patrick's Acts; a collection styled "Liber Angueli," relating to the rights and prerogatives of the See of Armagh, and the Confession of St. Patrick, ending, "hucusque volumen quod Patricius manu conscripsit sua". These are followed by St. Jerome's Preface to the New Testament; Gospels of Matthew, Mark, Luke, and John; Epistles of St. Paul, including that to the Laodiceans, with prefaces, chiefly by Pelagius; Epistles of James, Peter, John, and Jude; Apocalypse; Acts of Apostles, and Life of St. Martin of Tours by Sulpicius Severus. It also contains coloured drawings of the evangelistic symbols, and of these, one page, in four compartments, is reproduced on Plate XXVIII.

The name of the scribe of the *Book of Armagh* was ascertained in recent times by the Rev. Charles Graves, now Bishop of Limerick. Having noticed ancient and elaborate erasures on some of its pages, he conceived that matter connected with the history of the book might be recovered through a careful examination of them. Under these erasures vestiges were found of entries in which Ferdomnach, in the customary manner of ancient Irish transcribers, entered his name, and requested a prayer from the reader. The only scribes named Ferdomnach mentioned in Irish records are two who died at Armagh in A.D. 790 and A.D. 844 respectively. The latter was characterised as a wise man and a distinguished scribe. That he wrote the first part of the *Book of Armagh* in A.D. 807 is assumed mainly on the following grounds :—

At the end of the Gospel of St. Matthew, the scribe records, in semi-Greek characters, that he finished the writing of this Gospel on the festival of that Apostle. That this was during the single year A.D. 807, in which Torbach held the bishopric of Armagh, is inferred from a fragment—*bach*—of the name of "the successor of Patrick" brought to light from under another ancient erasure. Torbach was the only bishop of the see whose name terminates with those letters during the time of any known scribe styled Ferdomnach.

The collections concerning St. Patrick in the first part of the *Book of Armagh* constitute the oldest writings now extant in connection with him, and are also the most ancient specimens known of narrative composition in Irish and Hiberno-Latin. They purport to have been originally taken down by Bishop Tirechan from Ultan, who was Bishop of Ardbraccan towards A.D. 650, and by Muirchu Maccu Machteni, at the request of his preceptor, Aed, Bishop of Sletty, in the same century. . . . It would seem that the *Book of Armagh* was supposed to have been written by St. Patrick's own hand from the following passage on page 21, at the end of the copy of his Confession : *Hucusque volumen quod Patricius manu conscripsit sua.* (See text p. 46.)

THE DOMHNACH AIRGID.

The Domhnach Airgid (the Silver Shrine):—

Among ancient manuscripts preserved in, or connected with, Ireland, which have survived to the present time, the first place in point of age is assigned to that contained in the antique metal case styled in Irish, *DOMHNACH AIRGID* (the silver shrine).

This reliquary would appear to be that mentioned as follows in an old *Life of St. Patrick*, to have been given by him to his disciple and companion, St. MacCarthen, when he placed the latter over the See of Clogher in the fifth century :—

"Aliquantis ergo euolutis diebus MacCœrtennum sive Cærthennum Episcopum præfecit sedi episcopali Clocherensi ab Ardmacha regni Metropoli haud multum distante : et apud eum reliquit argenteum quoddum reliquiarium *Domnach Airgidh* vulgò nuncupatum, quod viro Dei, in Hiberniam venienti cœlitùs missus erat ".
—*Vita Sancti Patricii*, by St. Evin.

The Domhnach Airgid was preserved as a reliquary in the neighbourhood of Clones, in the county of Monaghan, till deposited in the Museum of the Royal Irish Academy, about the year 1832.

The manuscript in the reliquary was then in four portions, the membranes of each of which had become tenaciously incorporated into an opaque solid mass. Some of the external leaves, successfully detached and expanded, were found to contain part of the first chapter of a Latin version of the Gospel according to St. Matthew, in uncial character not inconsistent with the age to which, on examination, the manuscript was assigned by the eminent archæologist, George Petrie, LL.D., author of a treatise on *The Ecclesiastical Architecture of Ireland anterior to the Anglo-Norman Invasion.*

The view of Dr. Petrie, communicated by him to the
Royal Irish Academy in 1838, was that "we might with
tolerable certainty conclude that the Domhnach is the
identical reliquary given by St. Patrick to St. MacCarthen"; and that "as a manuscript copy of the Gospels,
apparently of that early age, is found with it,·there is
every reason to believe it [the manuscript] to be that
identical one for which the box was originally made".
—*Ibid.*, pp. 90, 91.

THE ANCESTORS OF ST. PATRICK.

A critic has dealt rather severely with my views
(p. 58) regarding the uncertainty of the text of the
Confession in the matter of St. Patrick's ancestors,
which he characterises as an instance of "the hopeless bondage in which an Orthodox Roman Catholic
historian lies," and he paraphrases my line of reason-
ing as follows: "In other words rather than admit
the obvious and common-sense meaning, which might,
though supported by innumerable other historical
proofs, run counter to an opinion of our own, let us
either put a perfectly gratuitous gloss on the text, or
shipwreck its authority by suggesting that the copyist
has made a mistake".

I reply, that, as to the "hopeless bondage" of the
Catholic historian, which excites the commiseration of
my reviewer, we need not quarrel with the expression:
the service of truth is more akin to bondage, than to that
domination to which some historians aspire. In the
particular instance quoted against me, I have to choose
between the bondage of the spirit, and that of the letter.
I do not think that the suggestion of an error in
any manuscript is equivalent to "the shipwreck of its

authority ". If this be so, then indeed we may bid farewell to the writings of St. Patrick, seeing that the learned Villanueva has noted 311 variations in the different manuscripts of St. Patrick's *Confession* and *Epistle.* The most prodigious feature of these writings is the fact that the spirit survives, and preserves its living identity in spite of the errors of copyists.

When I say that the spirit of St. Patrick's writings is opposed to the idea that his immediate ancestors were in Holy Orders, I am bound to state my reasons. I have given some already (p. 58), and I am now glad of an opportunity of re-opening the question, and still further developing my argument. In the first place, as I have remarked, St. Patrick speaks of his father, Calphurnius, alternately as a *Decurio* and a *Deacon,* and this discrepancy in itself is enough to throw doubt on the accuracy of one at least of the statements. He gives no explanation of what would be an anomaly, whether we interpret *Decurio* in the military or civic sense of the word. When, however, we find that St. Patrick, according to his own *Confession,* was, at the age of sixteen, ignorant of the existence of the true God,[1] it certainly seems incredible that his father and grandfather could have been Christian ecclesiastics. Again, as I observe (p. 57), St. Patrick, who is so eloquent in his humility in all that concerns himself personally, seems, for some reason unknown to us, to attach extraordinary importance to the nobility of his ancestry; and it is inconceivable that a Bishop could have grounded such a claim on the fact that his father was a Deacon. On the other hand, the theory that his father, Calphurnius, was an officer in the Roman army

---

[1] Deum enim verum ignorabam. . . . Deum unum non credebam.—*Confessio Sti. Patricii,* i., § 1; iii., § 12.

fits in with both statements of the Saint; for the life of the soldier is as unfavourable to the religious instruction of his children as it is noble and exalted in the estimation of men of the world. By his mother's side, St. Patrick belonged to a distinguished military family. His kinsman, St. Martin, who was the son of a tribune in the Imperial army, had served under the Emperor Julian in Gaul,[1] and a common profession would very naturally bring St. Patrick's father, Calphurnius, and St. Martin's relations together at some of the world-wide stations of the Imperial army : the whole spirit, therefore, of St. Patrick's writings is in accordance with the opinion that he was the son of a Roman officer.

Besides the strange discrepancy between *Decurio* and *Deacon*, there is another fact which tends to throw suspicion on the accuracy of this part of the text of the *Confession*. At this point in the manuscript in the Book of Armagh, the scribe has made an addition to the pedigree of St. Patrick, and the words "son of Odissus" are found written on the margin. These words Dr. Whitley Stokes has introduced into the text of his recent edition of the *Confession*,[2] and he has done so without any note or comment. This bold treatment of the text by an editor in the nineteenth century reminds us that such manipulations of manuscripts have only been too common in all ages. Ancient scribes, like modern editors, are often afflicted with

---

[1] Sulpicius Severus, *Vita Sti. Martini*, cap. ii. & iv.

[2] *The Tripartite Life of St. Patrick, with other Documents relating to the Saint.* Edited, with translations and index, by Whitley Stokes, D.C.L., &c. Published by the authority of the Lords' Commissioners of Her Majesty's Treasury, &c. Vol. ii., p. 357. London, 1887.

the malady of desire to do more than their duty, and to ancient Celtic scribes, with that rage for genealogies which they inherited from the bards, the subject of pedigree would easily become a fatal temptation.

The wild language of my reviewer about "obvious and common-sense meaning" and "innumerable historical proofs" is only a too common specimen of that partisan credulity which has so dishonoured Patrician literature. It is impossible to preserve our gravity when we find learned critics and archæologists gravely discussing the pedigree of one whose birthplace is unknown, and raising critical structures on the text of a document which, in its career of fourteen centuries, has been so maltreated by copyists. The Rev. J. F. Shearman is as credulous as Archbishop Ussher. In *Loca Patriciana* (p. 437, n.²), the mystery of "Odissus" is thus solemnly discussed.

"In the *Nacmsenchus Lebhar Breac*," says this learned author, "the pedigree of St. Patrick, son of Calphurn, son of Potitus, a presbyter, son of Odissus, &c.; is carried down in sixteen generations to Britain Moel, grandson of Nemidh, and from him to Lamech, son of Noe. Ussher (vol. iv., p. 378) gives only fourteen generations; some of the names appear to have got Latin terminations. In their present form they are not Celtic. This pedigree gives a common, though remote, ancestor to both Patricks. The *Confession* gives only the names of the father and grandfather of the writer. It is probable that subsequent biographers used sources of information long lost or unknown. Calphurn, or Alphurn, is styled a deacon in the *Confessio*, which, as Mr. Nicholson remarks (p. 7), was a guess on the part of the transcribers of the

Book of Armagh, for he writes at this word 'incertus liber hic '."

It is to be hoped that the publication of so many original Patrician documents by Dr. Whitley Stokes will put a stop to such wild speculations as are found in the above extract. The simple fact that the most important of the ancient *Acta* of St. Patrick are now conveniently collected together will probably save us from that piecemeal treatment of his history, under cover of which so many absurdities have grown and flourished. It needs but a novice in criticism to observe that writers like Archbishop Ussher and Dr. Todd, who in other departments of literature are both learned and careful, evidently treat St. Patrick's history as a mere peg on which to hang their own fantastic religious and archæological theories.

THE ROMAN MISSION.

Although the "Introduction" and "Notes" of Dr. Whitley Stokes' *Tripartite* are evidently the work of one in whose philosophy supernatural heroes have no part, it would be very ungracious on the part of Catholics if they did not acknowledge the great services which his work has done to ancient truth, and the ancient faith. It is true that to those acquainted with the writings of our great Catholic authorities, O'Curry and Hennessy, there is little that is new in Dr. Stokes's imposing volumes. Their chief interest arises from the fact that they bring what will be regarded as inde-pendent testimony to the support of truths which have always been familiar to the Irish inheritors of the ancient Faith. In the present position of the Church in these countries, it would be foolish affectation on our part to pretend to make light of the testimony of our adversaries. However unimportant it may be in itself, we must remember that, both by numbers and position, they are dominant and established. They rule in our seats of learning, and their literature is to a great extent the pasture on which the minds of Catholics feed, so "in the fatness of these pursy times" truth must submit to be patronised for the sake of her unprotected offspring. When, therefore, " By the authority of the Lords' Commissioners of Her Majesty's Treasury, under the direction of the Master of the Rolls," Dr. Whitley Stokes comes forward as the champion of the Roman Mission of St. Patrick, we have good reason to lift up our heads. The Roman St. Patrick may be regarded as " by law established " when a Government editor writes as follows : *"He (St. Patrick) had a reverent affection for the Church of Rome, and there is no ground for disbelieving his desire to obtain Roman authority for his mission, or for questioning the authenticity of his decrees, that difficult cases arising in Ireland should ultimately be referred to the Apostolic See"*.[1]

No doubt Ireland has to thank Germany for the final collapse of the Protestant "Apostle of Ireland" of Ussher and Todd. It was an auspicious day when German scholars took up the study of ancient Irish literature. While at home its genuine voice was stifled under the influence of party spirit, in Germany it was allowed to speak for itself. At length Ireland has obtained her place in the great republic of letters : her history has passed out of the hands of a clique, and no British historical writer endowed with the most

---

[1] *The Tripartite Life of St. Patrick,* vol. ii., pp. 356, 506.

moderate sense of the ludicrous will now venture to brave the ridicule of his foreign associates by asserting that St. Patrick was the founder of the Protestant Church in Ireland.

POSTSCRIPTUM.

The writer is sorry to find that, in his second chapter, he has omitted to notice the statement of the Scholiast on St. Fiacc (*Trias Thaumaturga*, p. 5), to the effect that, in 429, St. Patrick came to Britain in the train of the Papal Legate, St. Germanus of Auxerre. The Bollandists (*Acta SS. Mart.*, xvii., p. 529) tell us that they can not bring themselves to believe this; but their arguments against the Scholiast are very weak. The fact is accepted by Cardinal Moran (*Essays on Irish Church*, p. 17) and by Dr. Lanigan (*Eccl. Hist.*, p. 180). The remarks of the latter writer are very much to the point, when he observes that in the Lives which are silent about the fact there is no circumstance to be met with which might tend to invalidate the record. "The Bollandists," he continues, "do not admit it, as it would not accord with their calculations, and their presupposing that our Saint was at that time still in Lerins."

INDEX.

INDEX.